Poetic Violence

John Collins

LET'S RETHINK THAT
ATLANTA, GA
www.letsrethinkthat.com

You may contact John Collins at:
johncollinspresents@gmail.com
Twitter: authorjohncollins Instagram: princeofpages
Poetic Violence Copyright © 2015

Dedication

This novel is dedicated to anyone who's ever loved deep enough to live in that moment. However, sometimes the reciprocity and expression we wish to receive won't be heard from whom we wish to obtain it from. And though you cleave to the hope of knowing the right one will actually give a damn about your heart, I pray their genuine sentiments won't fall upon deaf ears...

Table of Contents

Hearing People, Places, and Things 1

Gary and the Baby Boy 9

Open My Eyes 19

Dreams vs. Reality 39

Follow My Directions 59

Down Low Darius 71

Family Reunion 91

Paint by Numbers 113

Gary and Darius Cross Paths 133

Soiled Linen Sheets 143

Seven-Year-Old Tears 159

A Matter of Time...173

Masculine 185

Little Him the King Bee..203

Poets and Brushstrokes 215

Knitting My Thoughts..231

One Man's Trash One Man's Treasure 243

She Just Clung to Me...259

So Ya'll Go Together..271

To the Color Orange 283

Everything's Crossing My Mind......................................295

Hearing People, Places, and Things

What the hell is this tree doing in my car? I asked myself this question while studying this solid thick wooden pole that looked as if it was a hitchhiker I unwontedly picked up. My eyes, which were wide open to the point of being dislodged from the socket, took in the depth of its dark splintered surface as pain raced its way back and forth through my leg and up my entire spine until I couldn't take it anymore. My nerve endings burned and pulsed with consistent agony. I clinched my teeth paralyzed by the constant sting that urgently ripped its way down the left side of my body like angry storm water paying no regard to the duties of a taxed dam.

I had been in a car accident. This wasn't good. I had to get to my best friend Michael. *He tried to kill himself! I need to rescue my friend! I screamed.* I didn't care about my own pain because my friend, I couldn't let my closest friend die. Life isn't pain, but pain is life. If no Michael, who else was left to assist my vulnerable side? I tried putting the car in gear fighting the pain I was feeling with every attempt to depress the clutch pedal. I let out a yelp just before I looked at the cracked face of the watch I was wearing. I revved the engine trying again to drive off. The six cylinders screamed in unison with my inner voice. I gotta move! I screamed out Michaels name hoping maybe the phone was still connected. And somehow, I was calmed by His voice telling me to "*Hold on, son.*"

Suddenly, I was unaware of my surroundings. It felt as if time were standing still yet progressing forward in muted haste. Nothing looked familiar, but the chaos from the sounds had a familiarity all their own as I struggled hard to comprehend their role. Strategic movement took place all around me pushing its way forcefully into position to salvage and sustain what seemed to be left of my human experience. I could hear voices. I could hear machines. I could hear metal upon metal. Crunching, grinding, pulling, and creaking. I could vaguely make out a siren and the muffled drone of a diesel engine at full throttle. I imagined lights but could not see them. I heard an array of noises all jumbled together in what felt like a muted chamber. I could only feel temperature changes shifting from warm to cold quickly and purposely while my imagination quickly processed what the feelings might look like. I didn't have an understanding of what I was experiencing. I could only hear its slight toned out presence. I was trying my best to wake up. It was as if the pilot light to my furnace had been extinguished. I could literally hear the tick, tick, tick the dial on a gas stove would emit when turned to light. But I couldn't find a way to reignite it.

I imagined the long match that Grandma used to light her stove with so that she could get an awesome breakfast ready before church. I kept trying to listen to what was going on outside of me. The feeling in my body slowly started to come back. I tried to wake up and join the voices conversing within close proximity to me. One of the voices belonged to my mother, Janice Ann, while the other was my on again ex- boyfriend Gary's mother, Mrs. Audrey Larrieux. They were having a heart to heart from the sounds of it. I could hear the tension in my mother's voice. She sounded... on edge, like she was covering her concern. An image of shattered glass crossed my mind. I felt the laws of physics pulling and tugging at my body. I saw lights, a flash of white bulbous material enveloping me, a cloud of smoke, screeching tires, a loud boom, a halting jerk, my head hitting what looked like satin curtains, all mixed with pain and the heat of a fire, followed by the two mothers engaged in conversation...

"Ooooh, Audrey, I would have whooped Jason's lil' narrow behind if I caught him in my bed like that," Mama chuckled. I hadn't heard her laugh like that in a long time.

"Janice, I was so mad, I had just bought that camera. I can't imagine what the people developing that film was thinking. Lordy Lord," she said in her Caribbean accent before letting out a laugh. "And had the nerve to say it wasn't him. I say, boy, look at the face in half these pictures rea'guud! Yah gon' sit dere, lie, tell me it's not you dere boy?" she said as Mama laughed.

"Mmm-HMPH!" Mama mused. "But it's harder with boys. I can't relate to them and why they do what they do. Girls I can handle. But he's my favorite. And that makes me think about Jason and his daddy. Now,

3

neither one of us can relate to our son. I felt sorry for Jason sometimes because I could see it in him, and I felt powerless to stop it. Because you know it's happening. When we sent him off into the world, I cried, I cried, I cried. Because I knew he was going to... be this... thing you fear. Now here I am... praying for him to wake up out of this coma and call me Ma again." There was a long pause, followed by, "What did your husband say?" Mama asked in a hesitant tired voice. I'm sure she must have had a flashback from when she told my dad my "horrible" secret.

"Oh no. I couldn't tell Waddie. I didn't know how to tell him until one day he woke me up outta me sleep sayin' we needed to talk about the possibility. I was shocked at him because I was in denial about it. You know we mothers do that because we succumb to that, *not my child syndrome that's not how I raised mine.*" She took a brief pause and continued. I could hear someone shift in a seat. "Oh no, not the men. They either face it, or ignore it, you know? Waddie says he knew when Gary was seven years old. He thought it best we wait until he came to us. He said we should reserve some restraint in how we felt about it," she took a moment to cackle and sigh. "Lordy Lord! My little Gary would bring these little tacky girls to my house pretendin' dey goin' steady, you know? Waddie would laugh and would say, *he be picking sum STUPEED wuns!*" The two women took a moment to giggle before Mrs. Larrieux continued. "We love him so much. My first-born son, Lord. What was your clue?"

"I can't decide when. I only know that I had to love him differently for some reason. I couldn't give him the type of love I felt in my heart to give," Mama said. There was tightness in her tone, as if she couldn't believe she was saying it in front of me.

"I understand that. You just wanna shield them from this ol' evil world we taken space in, ya know?" Mrs. Larrieux said pausing. "But then one day you give a good look and realize dey are still men... dey just like men, ya know." The two women let out a hearty chuckle.

After a few moments of silence, I could feel someone manipulating my hand. I thought maybe I was awake, but I wasn't. I couldn't see the outside world. I felt trapped hearing everything around me contradict everything I was imagining in my head to see. I guess I had too much time to dream. This coma is unleashing some stuff in my mind that I thought I was over. I thought I got over the fact that I wasn't happy with Gary cheating but held on to that relationship because it was all I knew besides the one I had with Darius.

Darius is a very close friend and one of my shipmates from my Navy days, who I loved from day one. This sounds stupid to me too, now that I have no choice to think about it, but I was waiting on him to say it first. To me it's only fair because... it just is. I've been waiting on him. Because whenever I was awake during idle time, I was daydreaming about something. And that something usually involved him. I would imagine being with the love of my life on a beach some place half way around the world.

I got caught up in the mystique of Gary and I don't know maybe thought because he was from the islands, that his love would be the paradise I had always daydreamed about. I'm actually throwing up in my coma right now, but how can I give myself to someone who didn't respect me enough to put on a condom with his cheating ass! And that's why if Darius said those words...

No, he can't say that to me because if he did, yo! I can't... no I gotta think of something else. Okay, yeah like how I am running out of excuses as to why I won't let Gary touch me. He doesn't feel the same between my thighs the way he once did. He's starting to get a little more aggressive with me trying to reclaim his role as the Alpha male in my life. I'm trying to get onboard because that's the choice I made, and I feel like I need to remain loyal to my decision and him because he's all I know. The more I run, the more he'll give chase, since he's supposedly all in this time. I need to be having this conversation with wait... MICHAEL!

Oh my God I gotta get to him I hope he didn't die on me. God! Please help me get up from here! Please let my best friend be all right! Why can't I get up? I felt trapped in my own mind; it was like everything was on continuous news feed taking me on a quality check of all my relationships. I think this fresh start with my mom is going to work out this time. I think. I hope. I remember our conversation. I remember her saying something about accepting me, but never accepting this. I think there is a difference. I had a conversation with... MICHAEL! God, please let him be alive. I don't know what I'd do without my big bro.

I need to wake up from this, but I can't move... it's too much going on right now and I need to fix It. It's like a game of Russian roulette with whom I can and cannot trust. I've quickly learned to love all, trust few, and more recently, guard my heart. I hope Gary was able to get Mike some help. I just know I'm going to wake up and he'll be standing there. I believe that. I finally stopped thinking as if I felt Gary next to me somehow...

Gary and the Baby Boy

I waited until Jason's mom and my mom and his two giggly friends left so that I could love on my babes. It's a damn shame it takes something like this to appreciate the person that has your heart. That's my fucking babes, and his knucklehead ass friends always keep him and his mind into some shit. I need him to be all right. I keep praying that over and over. I know he's going to be fine, God... you can't take him like this. I don't wanna lose the man I just got back. I was in bed next to him and rubbed his face. He was warm but the life in his face was gone. I got out of the bed and adjusted his pillow before taking a seat in the chair. If I see his stupid ass friend Michael, I'm kicking his ass. I already got in the doctor's ass, but if I see Michael! Got my baby in here all beat up.

I'm sure he probably the reason Jason won't give me no ass. I know he said something to him. Jason looks up to that fool for some odd reason or another. I know, I know, I know. I can't really blame him because I did cheat on him and damn, gave him a STD. But I had my reasons and we should be past all that. I mean, I am and if he forgave me, then why punish me by not giving me that beautiful ass I miss so fucking much. Let me chill 'cause ain't no need in getting hard. I'm beating that dude ass if I see him though. Now I really ain't gon' get none with Jason all taped up. Dude better not come up in this hospital.

Gary and the Baby Boy

I stared at Jason in the hospital bed in a coma. He has the little oxygen thing in his nose, tubes all in his fucking arm, bruises and shit. I promise I won't mess around on him no more if he'll just come back. I started thinking about what it was like without Jason when we broke up. Damn, I don't know why I did what I did, but Jason I'm sorry man. From the most tender place in my soul, babes, I'm fucking sorry. God, please wake this man up from this remembering what we had. This wasn't right! Look at what we did. If I'da been there, he would have been boo'ed up on the couch with me pretending to enjoy the game with me. Ignoring his phone. Damn, maybe I'm being selfish.

I just kept looking at him lying there like this was one of his great ideas to get me to think about what it would mean to lose him. Guess what babes, it's workin' that's for damn sure. The sad part is, I think I'm the only one who had those ideas, and me being me, felt like I always had something to prove. This thing we had, and the way he just stepped up to the plate in my life as the lead came so natural to him. I'm sitting here thinking what is it about this man who got all types of niggas getting' at him that makes him want to deal with my grumpy ass? I don't know but I'm glad he does. I love this man. He motivates me to want to get up.

I kissed his hand and closed my eyes. I felt my dick get hard as I thought about the first time I gave it to him. I think I was more scared than he was. I wanted to mold that shit to my dick and make sure he knew that it was only mine. He was the first virgin I ever had, even the females I used to try to bang had been around a time or two but not Jason. It was new for the both of us because it was the first time I had to make love to somebody. I looked in this man eyes and felt the depth of who he was and it...messed me up. I can't even explain it, but I damaged that bond because I couldn't handle the man I had to be for him. And maybe that's why he... But never mind that. I know he's the best thing for me. I hope he wakes up out of this coma and remembers that first time and touches me like he used to because I miss that shit.

This mug had the gall to tell me a couple weeks ago he wanted to jump out of a plane for fun. I told him hell no, what if the parachute don't open or sum'n jams. Hell, I wouldn't let him do that. And then this shit happens and hits home. Just the thought of losing him... scares... My thoughts were disturbed when I felt the touch of a hand on my shoulder. I opened my eyes and looked up. It was Jason's mother. I smiled and stood up to try and hug her.

"Hey, Mrs. Williams, how you doin'?" I asked as she half-heartedly hugged me back. I had been trying to avoid a moment alone with her for as long as I could, but I guess my luck ran out.

"How's he doing, Gary?" she asked. I thought to myself, Well hello to you too! Damn! I'm fine! I dug deep and took a breath.

"He's still out like a light. His vitals and everything have been steady according to the nurse," I said stepping out of her way. I pulled the chair back and she inspected his IV fluid, adjusted the monitor, and fluffed his pillow. She dropped the bed rail and sat alongside him. She took her hand and felt his forehead. She then took his pulse as she looked at her watch. I guess she said fuck what I'm sayin'. I only been by his side more than you, lady.

"Yes, he's still the same," she sighed. She pulled the bed rail back up and covered his chest with the blanket. I offered her the chair and she pulled her coat off and sat down. I pulled another chair up next to her.

"Mrs. Williams, I'm sorry about what happened. I wish I could have been there to…" I started before she stopped me.

"Gary, let's save all the shoulda, coulda, wouldas," she said flipping her hand. "What happened to my son that night?" She was staring at me searching for answers I didn't have.

"I don't know too much more than you to be honest, Mrs. Williams. I just know that he was supposed to take his friend Michael to the airport the following morning. I got a call from him telling me he left because they got into a fistfight, and next thing I knew, he was in a rush to get back to Mike 'cause the fool swallowed a bottle of pills. I was on the phone with him when he crashed. I went out looking for him and had to figure out what hospital they had him in." I took a deep breath and tried to relax some of the tension I was feeling. She pursed her lips and turned her head towards Jason. I kept staring at her, waiting for her to say something, smart.

"Hmph. Well, thank you for finally telling me what happened. Did you find out if his friend was okay at least because I ain't seen him here with the rest of ya'll," It was something about the way she said ya'll that really pissed me off all of a sudden. But I was determined to just let her speak her peace for the sake of Jason because this ain't about me.

"I just didn't know how to face you Mrs. Williams. Alone anyway, I didn't... I just felt like it was my fault he's in here. I don't know, and then I see you tonight and it's like, here goes nothin'," I said. I didn't mean to come across as a punk, but that's probably how it sounded. I thought to myself, *yeah, get ready 'cause she bought to grab you by the balls.*

"So, what do you want to say to me, Gary? Let's clear the air because this isn't the first time you haven't been man enough to say what you feel. This is the second time you and whoever else have my son. My child. In the hospital within just a few short years of knowing ya'll. I had him my whole life and the only time my baby boy has ever visited a doctor in my care was for routine check-ups," she said, with me sitting there in silence. I was getting more and more pissed as she kept goin'. "It wasn't until he started hanging around with ya'll and this *lifestyle* that he keeps ending up in here, and I can't help but wonder if this is a sign because Lord knows... " she said removing her glasses and dabbing her right eye on her sleeve. She reached in her purse and pulled out a small package of Kleenex. I thought to myself, she probably pasted that damn tear to her face before she came in this mug. Ain't this about a bitch!

"Mrs. Williams, I don't know what to say to you at this point," I lied. Because I couldn't unleash on this woman with her son, my babes, knocked out.

"So, was that you that called my phone that summer, Jason and I had that argument about him and this *lifestyle?*" she asked me, in a stankin' ass tone too. I thought back to the time I called her phone and was going to give her a piece of my mind. But I punked out and hung up the phone out of respect for her as his mom. It ain't my place to tell a grown woman to love her son the way my moms' loves me. The way a moms is supposed to.

"Yes, ma'am. That was me that called you that night," I said trying to call this woman at her bluff. I had to let her know me a rude boy, me no shaky warrior.

"So be man enough to tell me what you couldn't tell me then because when Jason wakes up, I hope he has nothing to do with any of ya'll. I'm playing nice right now because I'm in prayer for my son's life, but I don't want yall's lifestyle influencing him anymore. Look at what ya'll did to him," she said looking at him then me. It took everything I had to get a grip on my temper. And damn was it slippin'!

"I care about your son too, Mrs. Williams. And the crap you put him through hurts me. I love your son, that's my heart!" I said hitting my chest.

"*Your* heart. Let me tell you something, especially about love because you probably were going to tell me off about what it means to you and what I should be doing if you had the gall to open your mouth that day on the phone," she turned in her chair towards me and turned into Mother Love all of a sudden. "That is my little boy laying there. No matter how big he gets in this world, he is still and will forever be my little boy. And if I have to show him the toughest love possible to brake him from falling into the traps of life, then dammit, Gary, that's what I as a mother of a black son who wants to sleep with a man like he a woman will do. You don't have the right to tell me about love because a mother's love is much more complex than you think it is. I gave birth to that little boy over there. I knew this day was coming, and I will not rest until he is... fixed," she stated confidently.

"Why can't you just face the fact that this is him? Your baby boy is not going to change. A coma isn't going to make him wake up and be this straight nig... this straight boy that *you think* he should be. Just because you're his mudder, dat don't giv'ya the right to run his life. He a grown man not a little boy, ya know. You really need to have a seat with my moms because you and your ways ain't right." I said knowing that was the cure all to end all. I could tell I was pissed because my accent was starting to show. I caught my breath and listened to more of her bullshit.

"I don't need to talk to nobody but Jason. I need him to know that he'll end up just like his uncle and that man he was with if he keeps this lifestyle up," she said.

"So what was the point of you coming up here for

Thanksgiving, ay?" I asked confused as to her wish washy decisions involvin' Jason.

"I needed to get into his head and figure out his surroundings. It's my new plan to change him into a normal man," she said sounding serious. I must'a stared at her for a whole minute. It was so much I wanted to say, but she was stuck on being right. I shook my head and stopped looking at her. I heard my dad's voice in my head, *"Gary, a mon don't argue wit'ta wo'mun. A mon speak to her from his heart or mind an' he move on. A man plants the seed. A woman waters."* I stood up and walked over and kissed Jason dead on his sexy lips.

"You have a pleasant night, Mrs. Williams. Excuse me. Miss Mosley. That's your maiden name, right? I'm actually late for work. I'll be back to check on my man in the morning. That's what I had to say," I said turning to place the chair up against the wall. She rolled her eyes while I made my way out the door.

"When he wakes up, you limit your contact with my son. Hi and bye is all you'll need," she said making an extra attempt to get a rise out of me. I need to add her name to my list of ass kickee's. I need my moms to holler at her 'cause she is, crazy.

I couldn't wait to be there when Jason wakes up. I hope he can see through the bullshit mask his momma is putting on. He a smart man. It's something wrong with that lady for her to be this obsessed with changing something she has nothing to do with. I had to get up out of there. I wanted to stay until my shift started this evening, but she forced me to fold.

Hopefully, there will be a fire tonight so that I could take out some of my frustrations on the job. Especially, since I ain't getting no ass. Hosing down a fire would be the next best thing. The fuck am I thinking. I laughed and unlocked the truck. I got in and started the engine. I looked up at myself in the mirror and noticed how tired I looked. I couldn't tell if I was physically tired or not, but I know I wasn't sleeping much these days. It was a cycle of work, hospital, and work... repeat. I put the truck in gear and drove through the parking deck, prayin' I'd be the first one to see Jason when he woke up...

Open My Eyes

I woke up as the cool sensation of IV fluid made its way through my system. I thought to myself, *what am I doing in the hospital?* I looked around noticing that everything around me was blurry. But I knew I was in the hospital. I remembered putting my contacts in, but I didn't remember taking them out. I was trying to figure out why I was in the hospital though. I was just at home talking to Gary on the phone. At least that was the last thing that I remember doing except Gary wasn't there.

I reached up to rub my head and quickly put my arm back down when I noticed how sore I was. I tried to remember what happened. I then remember Mike and me fighting at his apartment, but I don't think it was enough to put me in the hospital. I was just about to panic, when I heard a female voice pipe in...

"Well, hello, Mr. Williams," I turned my head to the left to see a nurse with short hair smiling at me. She was a beautiful deep chocolate woman who looked to be around my age. I looked at her with confusion smeared on my face. My neck was stiff. I coughed and motioned to sit up. "Take it easy, sweetheart. You've been through a lot. Take it slow. Can you speak?"

"Yes," I said clearing my throat. I had to squint my eyes, to get a clearer image around and saw flowers, plants, balloons, and cards. It looked as if I were in a gift shop. "What the entire hell is going on?" I said trying to get my eyes to focus on everything commanding their attention. It was as if they were image starved or maybe it was because things weren't as visually sharp as they were before.

"You're in the hospital. You were in a car accident, and we are nursing you back to great health. I'm one of the nurses on duty tonight. My name is Aerie."

"A car accident? What... I'm not... what?" I said processing what was said. I tried to remember something about what she was telling me.

"Yes sir. You don't remember anything about it, do you?" She asked placing fresh tape on the IV tubing. She reached into her pocket and pulled out a pin light.

"Obviously," I said on impulse. "I'm sorry. I don't think... I don't know about any accident. When did that happen?" I was a bit confused and startled at the news she had just given me. How did I survive a car accident I know nothing about?

"Well let me ask you a couple of questions first, okay?" she said smiling sweetly.

"Sure," I said still trying to focus. Then I realized my contacts were missing so I stopped straining my eyes.

"What's your full name?"

"Jason Allen Williams," I said rubbing my eyes. Or JAWs, as my homeboy Darius has affectionately started calling me. I was trying to offer her a little of my charm to get her to see that I wasn't a complete grouch.

"I'm going to leave that one alone boo!" she quickly chuckled. "How old are you?" I smiled and rested my head on the pillow in an attempt to relax.

"Twenty-five. No... twenty-four! I'll be twenty-five soon," I said briefly picturing a birthday party.

"What city do you live in?" she asked. Looking at my eyes with her light.

"Chicago," I said really thinking about my answer. "What's 3 + 3?"

"It's... um... six," I said as she moved the cover back to expose my feet. She grabbed a tongue depressor.

"What's next in this sequence, H I J K...?" she said looking me in the eyes.

"L M N O P," I said shaking my head and chuckling.

"Good sir, can you feel this?" she asked.

"Yes. It tickles," I said, starting to get irritated with this game of Doctor.

"Wonderful! Okay, how are you feeling?" she asked with the sweetest smile.

"I'm a little confused..." I said pausing trying to open my mouth. "Wait! I can't move my jaw. Why can't I move my jaw?" I asked in a panic.

"We had to wire your jaw shut because your cheek bone was broken. You also have a fractured jaw. They did a simple surgery to fix your cheek. And your jaw should heal rather quickly. It was a slight fracture here," she said gently touching my face.

"Okay, well that explains my jaw," I said focusing on the small equality pendant on her lab coat. The uniform did all it could to contain her sizable breasts. "Why am I here? What day is it?"

Open My Eyes

"It's Wednesday afternoon. You've been unconscious since Sunday night. I was on duty the night they brought you in. I recognized you from Poetic Expressions," she winked.

"Cool. Well I'm glad I have one of the kids taking care of me," I winked and offered a friendly smile. I wanted to know where my people were. I felt a need to get up and just leave like there was someone I had to go and check on. But who?

"You are in good hands. You have a lot of people who love you and support you. There have been a slew of kind visitors here for you. Your mother is here and someone who I presume is your... boo?" she stated with obvious female intuition. Usually I don't fully let down my guard around the opposite sex, but there was something about her that relaxed me even in my uneasiness. I could sense a nurturing spirit in her. Or maybe it was just because I knew she was a lesbian.

"Was he a rugged looking black guy?" I was fishing to make sure she wasn't referring to Darius.

"Yes. A real cutie! Little Jamaican accent. You did good, Jason, because he is a few pounds of phyne. If only I didn't *lickety split*," she joked. Great lesbian jokes. I don't need this fish telling me about her surf and turf. And I hope she doesn't call that man Jamaican because he would have a fit. He was from the Bahamas. He says there are differences. Where the hell are my family and friends? I faked a laugh before noticing a throbbing feeling in the front of my head. My thoughts were everywhere. "His mother is here too; her

Jamaican accent is strong!" she smiled rubbing my knee. "Along with some friends of yours. Do you need anything?"

"They are Bahamian. And yes, drugs! Is it normal for my head to throb like this?" I asked, closing my eyes. I reached up to massage my temples. I was drawing a blank as to why I was in here. Trying to think made the headache worse. What the hell was wrong with me? And why ain't this fish swimming to get my doctor? Can't this broad, this nurse, see I'm in pain? I don't want to KEE KEE! *Okay calm down, Jason, she's trying to explain something to you,* I told myself.

"It's not uncommon after the trauma you've experienced. I will run and get the doctor, and we'll get you out of any pain and discomfort you are experiencing. Does that sound good?" she asked. She placed her hand on my shoulder. I opened my eyes and gave her a look that I hope read, GO GET THE DOCTOR FISH!

"Yeah," I answered taking a deep breath to calm down. Gary, my mom, and his mother came walking into the room.

"Jason! You're up babes! Oh hell yeah, thank God!" Gary said almost shouting as he rushed towards my bedside. He pinned me down. I couldn't move as he squeezed my frame kissing my cheeks and neck. He looked handsome in his Firemen's uniform. He was wearing his firemen suspenders, which always looked sexy on him. Although I was happy to see him, he wasn't the one I was hoping to see.

"Hello, everyone. If you all will excuse me, I'll leave you to him. I'm going to page the doctor and let him know he's awake," Aerie said excusing herself.

"Hey baby," I said as Gary went off on a tangent. He was still squeezing me. I placed my right arm over him to return my portion of the embrace he initiated.

"Babes! I love you so damn much. I was so scared that I was going to lose you again," Gary said thanking God multiple times in one breath.

"I love you too," I smiled. "Boo, you're hurting me though," I said wincing.

"Oh my bad! I'm sorry babes! I'm just so happy you're okay. You are okay, aren't you?" he said gripping me by the shoulders and looking me deep in the eyes. His beautiful thick full lips were quivering with anticipation and excitement.

"I can't move my jaw. And I know I look a hot mess," I said almost requesting a brush and mirror immediately. Gary reached into his breast pocket and pulled out my eyeglasses and gently placed them on my face. It was nice to have clear vision again.

"Can I hug my son please?" Mama laughed shaking her head. Gary closed his eyes and sucked his teeth. He looked at me and kissed my lips and smiled.

"Gary! Watch yur way now, child!" Gary's mother said instructing him to move out of the way. I waved and smiled at Mrs. Larrieux. She blew a kiss my way. When I focused my attention back on Mama, she pursed her lips and rolled her eyes at Gary. I didn't know what was going on with the two of them, and I didn't know if I wanted to know. For some reason that wasn't what was important, and I couldn't figure out what it was I was trying to remember.

"I'm sorry, Ms. Mos...Williams," he said rather gruffly. He released me from his grasp and took a few steps back allowing just enough space for my mother to make her approach. He didn't stray too far as she squeezed past. I noticed he gave her a quick distasteful look and then we made eye contact.

"Mama, I'm glad to see you," I smiled looking up at her.

"You alright, boy?" she asked looking back at Gary who was beaming. She shook her head and focused back on me.

"I'm sore as all get out. I'm confused. I don't remember why I'm here. The nurse told me I was in an accident, but how and why is my question?" I said.

"Yeah, you were. The car was pretty mangled up," Mama said. She rubbed my head with a shaky hand as a tear rolled down her cheek.

"Ma don't cry, I'm alright," I said as she smiled and wiped her face.

"I wasn't ready to see you in the hospital," Mama said. "I didn't know what to expect, but thank God He kept you," she nodded her head and rubbed my head again.

"I'm good, Mama," I reached over and grabbed her hand to give it a firm squeeze. Seeing her exhibit emotion was near and dear to me because its appearance from her was far and in between. And when they appeared, they could win academy awards. Not for nothing, they were rare treats that I kept safely memorized. I believe this had to be moment number eleven. I cherished them and would call on them when I needed to remind myself that she does love me, her son. Even though we don't have the typical black man/black mother doting relationship, in that moment I realized why she had to be that way. She must have known that my life wouldn't be easy to travel. She must have known that tough love would be the training tool of choice, due to this particular image of Him etched onto my spirit. Hmph, I see it now.

"Your sister and them will be here later. She's with your granny." She was still rubbing my head. I snapped back into reality when I heard her voice, but I didn't hear what she said.

"Good. Ma, can somebody please tell me what happened?" I asked. Gary kind of sidestepped my mom. She kind of flinched and cut her eyes at him. I closed my eyes just as Gary started to speak.

"Babes, like we said you were in a wreck. The cops said the guy in the truck ran the light and T-boned you on the driver side. They say you lost control, the car spun several times, and ultimately wrapped around a telephone pole. You were in and out of consciousness on the way to the hospital and were completely out when they got you here. You and I were on the phone at the time of the accident. Had me scared to death cause I heard it all on the phone," Gary intervened. How could I be in a coma, I heard everything going on.

I even saw some things I thought I had forgotten about. But I was in a...coma, so what if I'm still in a coma? I tried to get it together because this was too much at one time, then I thought about...

"Oh my God, is my car alright?" I said with my eyes bugging out.

"What you thinking about a car for? No, it's totaled unfortunately. They had to use the Jaws of Life to get you out, crazy. I was able to get some of your things out and get your keys and stuff. Once you get well, we can take care of the other stuff. It's not important right now, babes. Worry about getting' better," Gary said. "Do you remember anything before the accident?" I kept trying to pull up images from that night they were talking about in my head. I'd catch a glimpse of something here and there. What I ate, what I was wearing, and being on the phone in the car.

"A little bit. I left Shawn, and I was headed home or something, I don't really know. Why what's up?" I knew there were some details that I was missing. However, I couldn't remember what they entailed. I started going through the list of people I know personally that have my back because there was still someone that I was anxious to see.

"We'll talk about it later, Jason. Right now, let's focus on you, okay?" he said reaching over to rub my cheek. I closed my eyes and an image of a bright light and the airbags deploying caused me to jump. "You alright?"

"Yeah," I said wincing as I opened my eyes. "I'm

really starting to feel pain right now. Oh my God," I said.

"Where is it hurting?" my mom asked. Gary looked so anxious like he wanted to do something. I knew eventually I'd have to get him by himself so that he'd calm down, but I know Mama was going to make that very difficult. He kept his eyes on me and watched every move mama made like a bear watching over its cub.

"All along my left side. My head is starting to throb, Ma," I said wanting to curl up into a freaking ball. I looked away from Gary and at Mama.

"Take it easy and lie back. Does it feel like one of your migraines?" she said getting into nurse mode. I know she was probably scrutinizing everything the staff was doing. And the last thing I needed was to have both her and Gary fighting it out with the staff over my silly self.

"Where is the damn doctor?!" Gary said looking out of the room. He was starting to breathe heavily and turned a little red in the face.

"It feels different Ma," I closed my eyes and tried to relax. I figured if I relaxed, the pain would calm down and that would get them to calm down. I took a deep breath and started tuning stuff out like a true Aquarius.

"I'm about to find out what's taking this fool so long to get in here babes," Gary said rushing out of the room. I was hoping he wouldn't give the staff a hard time. He has a tendency to get hotheaded and I couldn't focus on his temper right now when I was the one in the freaking germy hospital.

"Just lie still," Mama said gently rubbing my temples easing some of the tension. "It's going to be alright. The Doctor will be in here soon."

"That feels good, Ma," I said as Mrs. Larrieux held my hand. Gary returned with the doctor literally a couple of minutes later. My nurse Aerie came in also with a tray of crystal light packets and a pitcher of water. She also had a few vials of drugs and a couple of needles wrapped in a sterile plastic cassette.

"Mr. Williams. Ladies. Gentleman. Dr. Polanski at your service. How are you feeling big guy?" he smiled. He had a serious Chicago accent.

"My head is throbbing. And my side is hurting. What's going on?" I said wanting him to get to the point already.

"Well, we are going to give you something for the pain. Do to HIPAA laws I have to ask if you mind me discussing your medical findings in front of your loved ones?"

"No sir, it's okay," I answered quickly.

"If you all have blood work, please discuss that with him privately. My mom interjected. She cleared her throat as Gary sucked his teeth and folded his arms. The doctor and I gave her a strange look and then he focused his attention on me.

"I do need to run a few tests, and I am going to order an MRI to see if you have any damage to the brain. I suspect a slight fracture of the occipital lobe. The CT scan we performed showed slight trauma to the frontal lobe of the brain, which controls a lot of your memory functions along with several different motor functions. If this is the case, then we are looking at what's known as Traumatic Brain Injury. TBI for short, in case you here that term mentioned again. Now. I want to keep you here for observation. We're getting that MRI this evening now that you're alive, alert, and awake," he smiled.

"Okay... man," I said. As he looked at my chart scribbling a few notes.

"So, some other injuries we found are two bruised ribs, and three cracked ribs, as well as a sprained ankle. Surprisingly you had no other broken bones, besides your cheek, which we were able to reset through surgery. We had to wire your jaw shut because of that, and the fact that you had a fractured jaw. I want to do a couple of simple tests right now, to test your senses okay?" The doctor asked.

"Okay," I really wanted to get out of there. I felt like I was lying in my own filth. This was humiliating to me and I work in health care as a Dental Hygienist.

"This will help me further rule out some things." "Okay," I said as he used a penlight to check my pupils. He then told me to follow his finger with my eyes.

"Alright, I want you to tell me if you can taste the flavor of this drink," he said mixing a flavor packet into some water.

"Okay," I said taking hold of the cup. I took a sip and felt the cold liquid hit my teeth. I strained the liquid through my teeth and the wires. I could vaguely make out what it was. And that's probably because I was more worried about the liquid staining my teeth.

"Can you distinguish the flavor?"

"I think it's cherry. I can't make it out completely. I don't know sir," I said starting to get irritated. I just wanted some drugs and the keys to my good gay clean house.

"Alright," he said making some notes in my chart. "I'm going to put a rush on that MRI. Okay, is your hearing distorted in any way? Can you hear the click of this pen clearly?" he asked holding the pen to each ear. I closed my eyes and sighed taking a deep breath.

"Yes, I can," I said mumbling a *chile* under my breath. Mama shook her head making me smile. "Good, I'm going to touch various areas of your body with this blunt blade. I want you to tell me if you can feel it."

"Okay." I said as he started from head to toe. I felt each poke on both sides. I was relieved at this, but now I was curious to know what was up with my sense of taste. It was off.

"Okay, I'm going to give you some Tylenol 3 for the pain via your IV. You should feel the effect of it pretty rapidly. It may make you drowsy. Which isn't a bad thing. I want your body to get as much rest as possible, so that you can heal. We are going to get the MRI around 5pm. I'm putting this in the system now. I want to see the extent of the head trauma you've encountered, and we will come up with an accurate diagnosis and thorough treatment plan for you. You up for the challenge big guy?"

"Okay," I said now wondering if I could just fight through pain after he used the word drowsy. The last thing I wanted to do was go back to sleep. I had missed enough already and was frustrated that I couldn't remember who or what was missing.

"Alright, Aerie will get you going with that. You enjoy your family. You've been one of our most got a lot of love and support," he said quickly eyeing my mother. "Feed on that. That will give you a speedy recovery," the doctor said patting my shoulder.

"Okay. I will," I said.

"Mrs. Williams, please let me know if you need anything. Do I need to give you my contact information again?" Dr. Polanski said to my mother.

"No, I've got your information. If I need you, you'll hear from me. Thank you," Mama said as if she was his boss. I wanted to hear that story later on.

"I will check on you later, Mr. Williams," the doctor said.

"Thank you, sir," I said as the nurse administered some medication to me. I tried tasting the drink again. It was still vague as to what it was.

"Ma, why can't I taste this? That's crazy," I asked. "You may have temporarily lost your sense of taste.

It should come back. Stuff like that happens when you have blunt force trauma to the brain. It might be a little swelling in the brain. We'll see what the MRI says. Don't stress or think the worst just yet okay. Let's stay positive, Jason," Mama smiled reassuringly. At that point I realized I had no choice but to be positive. Hell, I had survived a major car accident.

"Okay. I will." I said putting my mind at ease. But off top, if I bite into one of my made from scratch chocolate chip cookies or my Granny's lemon pound cake and neither makes my tastes buds explode, I'm going to die.

"Jason, I am going to go and get your Granny and Jasmine. I'll be back in about an hour. Okay?"

"Ya'll staying at my house, right?" I asked. I was hoping they weren't wasting money on a hotel. I was starting to feel better.

"Yeah, Gary gave me the key. He's been taking care of us. Audrey raised him well." Mama said referring to Mrs. Larrieux. Gary didn't even respond with a smile. I was curious to know if things between them were okay.

"Okay, Mama, I'll see you in a bit," I smiled. I was thinking maybe he just wants to be alone with me.

"Okay boy. I'll be back as soon as possible. See you later, Gary. Talk to you later, Audrey," Mama said as she made her exit.

"Okay, Janice," she said waving her hand goodbye. "Gary, I have to fetch the boys from school. I will come back and check on you two later okay?" She said referring to Gary's oldest sister Wanda's children.

"Yes, Moms. Thank you for coming. I love you," he said hugging and kissing her on the cheek.

"I love you to my sweet son," she laughed. That was a joke she shared with him in reference to his sexuality. I always thought the relationship they had together was so cool and such a blessing. And now I had my mom on my side finally. I can't wait to be on this level of love with her. "Jason, I will see you later you, beautiful boy. I am glad yur still ten toes down. Be sure to thank the Lord yur toes not up. I'm going to let you two get reacquainted," she said leaning over to kiss my cheek.

"Yes, ma'am I will. Thank you, Mama. I will see you later," I said smiling. After she walked out, Gary and I stared at each other for a minute. He pulled up a chair. I broke through the quiet space connecting us. "Gary. What?" I asked as the medicine started to really take effect. I was finally able to relax and let my body blend into the softness of the mattress.

"Babes, the man upstairs must really be teaching us how to appreciate one another. Shit I mean, it takes me falling through a floor in a burning building and then almost losing you again after getting you back in my life," he stated. He grabbed my hand and held it so tight never once losing contact with my eyes as he stood up to kiss my lips. I closed my eyes for a second wishing I could taste his lips with my tongue. I opened my eyes looking to my left observing the tenderness in his stare.

"I'm happy to be here still. I have some unfinished business to take care of," I said reflecting on all the things that I wanted to accomplish in life. I was scanning my mental bucket list.

"You know you are truly loved by me, right?" "You

love me?" I asked.

"Of course, I do crazy. Do you remember loving me?" he said with clarity and authority.

"Of course, I remember loving you, Gary. I love you," I wasn't sure if it was the drugs or another internal struggle brewing because my old military buddy Darius was who I pictured when I actually muttered the words, I love you. I pictured myself saying this to him after kissing them sexy lips of his. In this vision the background is blurry and I'm waving goodbye. I tried to redirect my focus back on Gary.

"That's what I'm talking about babes. Say that shit!" he smiled. He gently kissed my lips again and rubbed my head. The shiver affect his kiss gave me wasn't as strong as it once was. I tried to think nothing of it. It had to be the medication I was on.

"How am I going to brush my teeth and stuff?" I said beginning to feel like I was lying in not only mine, but somebody else's filth as well.

"Well your mother did that for you while you were under. And I allowed them to give you sponge baths only in my presence. So they made sure you were taken care of because your moms and me was all over everything. Babes she don't play when it come to her son. You saw how she had the doctor by the balls that's why he told her to let him know if she needed anything," Gary said laughing. He scooted closer to the bed and laid his head in my lap softly.

"Oh my God, I don't want to know what fear you two conjured up," I chuckled wondering had I been conscious, would I have been embarrassed.

"We got you, babes," Gary said as I placed my hand on his head.

"Who are all these things from? It looks like Hallmark up in here," I smiled.

"I told you that you were loved. These are from friends and family, your co-workers, and people from the spoken word set. They put the word out at the event a couple nights ago. You are a gay-lebrity according to your friends!" Gary laughed. I joined in his laughter and felt a slight pain in my side. I winced a little.

"You okay, Jason?"

"It like... it hurts to laugh baby," I said mustering up a smile. "That ain't cool."

"I know 'cause you love to laugh wit'cho silly ass," he said smiling making me laugh. "Are you hungry or anything?"

"Not really. I guess I'm good. It's not like I can eat a hamburger baby," I said as we both laughed.

"Shit, that's right. I'm sorry babes. But they have been giving you IV's with nourishment in it. The nurse was explaining it to me the other day. I forgot what she called them," Gary smiled. "You want to read some of your cards?" he asked eager to cater to my every need.

"Yeah, that's nice. I mean that will be nice in a minute, though... in a minute baby," I said as I started rubbing his head again slowly.

"Babes, yo, I was thinking about taking you away to the islands I grew up on when you get better. I think that would be so *fyre* if we went for like two weeks and just bummed out. No taking no phones, no city noises. Just you, me, a few friendly people, a drink, and the beach. What do you say...?" Gary said.

I was staring up at the ceiling letting my mind wander as the medicine I was on slowly put me in a deep slumber again. I was dancing with Darius and envisioned the two of us alone together the night of the fight between he and Gary. I remember how I've never felt more scared of my past. But the awesome thing is I faced what I needed to, and I survived it. The past is like a walking middle finger that you can't do anything about. You can't change it and it curses you in its own right if you don't leave it behind. But if you let it go, it's like a slingshot propelling you forward. I cannot change what we've done, but we can change what we do. One night I remember posing a simple question to God? Why is it fair to know our past but not our future?

I opened my eyes when the sound of the door got my attention. There stood my other close friends Shawn and Preston. They both had big smiles on their faces and rushed over to hug me and junk. Someone was still missing though, and it clicked when Preston said they hadn't heard anything from Mike before I could think to ask where he was.

Suddenly all the events from that night came rushing back together sound-by-sound providing a dramatic symphony leading up to this very moment. I was reminded of the sounds I heard the night of the accident. There was the sound of my voice yelling for Michael to pick up the phone. There was the sound of music playing in the background, followed by the sound of my tires screeching. The rise and fall of my cars exhaust note with each input of the accelerator and clutch pedals. The sound of regret in Michael's voice as he faced his truth. Then I heard the sound of my Father telling me to, *"Hold on, son!"* The question is, *What for? What if I didn't hold on?* It's amazing just how many decisions we are given in life, only to have them add up to a sum of thoughts and memories. It's even more amazing how many of those same thoughts remain dreams...

Dreams vs. Reality

During my recovery period, I put up with all kind of folk in and out of my house and my mama Janice Ann all up in through my stuff. I was hoping she didn't find out what nasty boys do with the collection of gay porn I had stored on my computer. My days recently were filled with physical therapy, sleep, and listening to the bickering from Gary about the way mama was treating him. I asked him why he wasn't complaining to her, and he said something about not arguing with women. I told him there was nothing I could do about her at the moment because she and I were still getting off on the good foot. That didn't sit too well with him. When I finally got some time to myself, I was in constant thought about life and started evaluating each of my relationships, both family and friends. I started with me first though.

Personally, I probably need to forgive myself for this, but I have often wondered what it would be like to have something to blame my sexuality on. I say that because if my sexuality is the only thing wrong with me, then why can't I pair it with its motive? The breeders can blame their sexuality on the ideal that that's the way God intended things to be. Well why can't I have that same courtesy and privilege? If they can say stupid crap like NO HOMO! Then I can say NO HETERO! The way we are designed and the things we are designed to do sometimes don't look as if they go together but partner well.

This was how I presented my case to my dad who took the time out of his nerve wrecking seventh tour of duty in Iraq to check on me and make sure I was doing well and taking care of myself after the accident. Daddy took a few moments to ponder my statement and told me he loves me and has never looked at me as his gay son but his son. He told me he was proud of me, and that being gay didn't matter anymore. It was a very emotional phone call that brought some serious tears out of not only my dad, but me as well. I couldn't believe what I was hearing, but it gave me another piece to the puzzle of why I had to go through all that hurt and pain alone.

I must have been placed here for something awesome. And judging by the balled-up scraps of metal, glass, and plastic I walked away from, I haven't finished my duties on Earth. Everything that looked as if it were lost or turned away from me was now attracted to the light I found shining through me. It's as if they now seek to be warmed by my aura, or some tea, I don't know. But what I do know is that things were looking unfamiliar to me in reality, as things were seemingly real in the dream world. Either I had a different perspective on life or my destiny was on the horizon. The crazy part about what I just mentioned is that in my dreams I belong to Darius in some strange convoluted way. These dreams were so passionate and full of vigor that I looked forward to catching some zee's any chance I got, hoping he'd pop up and grab my hand. Because the way our thighs communicated in my private thoughts was the shit. And I'm sure they had a lot more talking to do.

I met up with my boys Shawn and Preston to get some last-minute Christmas shopping done for my little niece. That night we ended up hanging out more when Shawn's boyfriend Andre, who just so happens to be Gary's best friend wanted the two of them to hang. I wanted us to meet up for drinks at my house and just get some quality friend time in. I went into slight detail about one of the dreams just to see if they thought I was crazy for connecting intimately with the dream more so than Gary...

"I'm not lying yo'! Swear to God he sent me pictures of it when he was in Kuwait!" I said to Shawn. "Oooh, Jason! Sweetie, how big is it?" Preston asked as he sat on the edge of his seat waiting for me
to answer.

"Chile, let's just say I was impressed," I said falling back on the couch laughing. Shawn took a sip of his drink. Preston reached over and gave me a high five.

"Does Gary know you got dick pics of Darius?" Preston curiously asked. I gave him a look that read, *Are you crazy?*

"No boy, of course not. Gary is from the island, mon!" I said shaking my head.

"Okay, get this, I'm not gon' ask to see the pics. But I need you to categorize this tally wacker for me," Shawn said taking another sip of his drink. "Like this, I developed some categories over the years based off of my experiences! Alright! I wrote a sermon bought, ah hah!" he said pausing for effect.

"Preach, Reverend. Ah huh!" I said tipping my glass up to him and laughing.

"Now we have four types of dang-a-to-the-lang! Alright! Turn to your neighbor, say four types! Amen?" he said pausing again.

"Yes, yes, yes. He said four types, yes, amen, ah huh!" Preston said waving his hand like an old church lady.

"Now the four types are, you ready for this Sister Jason?" Shawn said pausing again.

"Go head on, Reverend! Fo' types! Ah huh!" I said rocking back and forth and pretending I had a church fan.

"I thank Sister Preston may be familiar with what I'm bringin' to yah, this mo'nin. Well, in my experience, I've come across four types. You have husband dick. It's a nice manageable ding-a-ling you can take on the go with minimal fuss AND or… preparation. This type of dick is seven inches and below. Alright!" he said pausing as I laughed.

"Yes, yes, seven inches, yes, very manageable, yes!" I laughed as Preston and I slapped one another a high five. I took a sip of my drink.

"Then you move on up to grown man dick. Or what I simply call, GMD. Now GMD will get you in trouble." he said awaiting our reaction. "I said GMD! *WILL!* Get thee! In trouble baby!" he screeched. "Alright!"

"Come on, Reverend! Tell it!" I yelled.

"Turn to your neighbor, say trouble!" Shawn said. "Yes, yes, he said get'cha in trubba! Yes, yes, ah

huh!" Preston said in between laughing. He clutched his pearls and put on a glory face.

"Now GMD ain't nothing but husband dick that done learned a marvelous stroke game. GMD prepares you to be manhandled by the next dang-a- lang I'ma s'plain to yah! Amen? GMD HAS LEARNED! How to work with what he got! And do what others will not! To hit that good hot spot! YA'LL DON'T HEAR ME UP IN HERE! GMD feels soooooo good!" he sang. "I wish I had a few gays up in here that KNEW what I was talkin' 'bout!" Shawn said tapping his foot. "Cause if you did, you'd shout TROUBLE!"

"TRUBBA! Yes, yes, yes! I know bout me some good ol' GMD reb'rent! I know fo'mah self! YEASSS!" Preston said jumping up and down not coming out of his old church lady character. I burst into tears laughing at him.

"I'm telling you this because I don't want you to go out there and run into a husband dick thanking you got this, and it turns out to be GMD. GMD is cocky and moves with the stealth of the Panther! You better BE READY AT ALL TIMES!" Shawn said.

"That's right, Passa! Dey don't know like I know.

"Yes!" Preston said. I was on the floor laughing. "Now after you grajee'ate from grown man dick,

we have that thang I likes to call, daddy dick," he said clearing is throat as I stopped laughing. "Now daddy dick is well rounded. Daddy dick is a veteran in the sex game. It is a mature dick with a refined stroke game for every mood and occasion. It makes getting that hole plugged a very wonderful and comfortable experience. Those equipped with daddy dick range from eight to ten inches. Now I warn you! BE READY AT ALL TIMES! Cause daddy dick don't play and won't take nothing but a yes daddy for an answer. Alright!" Shawn said as I laughed at him for being so engrossed in this character. He was definitely drunk.

"Come through, Daddy dick. I like a good ol' Daddy dick, sweetie!" Preston chuckled. He balled up his face and shook his head before gulping his cocktail. I looked at both of these fools like how much dick have these two queens had?

"What's the next type, Reverend?" I said chuckling and taking a sip of my drink.

"Chile, the last type of dick I'ma tell ya 'bout is known as BSD," he said sticking his tongue out and giving the thumbs down. "Big Scary Dick, bitch! But *biiiiiitch*, she ain't nothing to be scared of. Chances are she won't stay hard for long cause she's really a bottom. Sixty percent of the time she has a weak stroke game if they do indeed get it hard cause she's really a bottom. And eighty percent of the times, they are lazy cause she's really a bottom. And one hundred percent of the time she's a bottom, gur'lt! This is the most boring dick you will ever experience and is generally anything past 10 ¾ inches and there are few exceptions. I've had one of the exceptions and if you're lucky enough to run into one of them be scared cause

I gagged," Shawn said.

"Just remember as a bottom if you see one it's unbecoming not to compliment him on how big it is because generally he has a big fat hard wallet," Preston said raising his glass. I shook my head and laughed at his gold diggin' behind.

"Chile BOO! It's unbecoming to not give her a sickening kee! Broke ass dick! She only look good in a fuck flick whore! Trust! So which one is Darius, gur'lt?" He said turning back to me. He picked up his drink and started laughing.

"I done told you about calling me girl, hag," I said pointing at him and sipping my drink.

"I know! That's why I called you gur'lt with a tee, GUR'LT!" he fired back. he cackled. "Aren't you college student? Annun'ceate!" He said imitating the character Shenehneh from the TV show, 'Martin'.

"Shut up you punk. He's...daddy dick...!" I laughed.

"Chile, he looks like it too. Do you miss him? Be honest, I mean we are drinking truth serum," Shawn said popping his tongue and raising his glass. "Climb the truth tree, bitch! I can call you bitch, right?"

"Sure, you can. Umm hmm! Now, climb it sweetie!" Preston chuckled and replenished his cocktail.

"I'm going to be real with ya'll hags. I do..." I laughed sitting my drink on the coaster. I had the two of them eating from the palm of my hands as I illustrated my point. "There are days I miss him. I really do because we used to have so much fun together," I chuckled thinking about my next statement. I covered my face for a quick second. "Yo' I can't believe I'm telling you guys this," I laughed. "But there are nights where I wish he would move home to Chicago and put it where my ribs is at," I said as Shawn and Preston burst out laughing.

"JASON! SHUT THE HELL UP!" Shawn laughed hysterically. "Bitch, was the dick that good? Have ya'll fucked before and you ain't told nobody?" Shawn was on edge holding his breath waiting for an answer.

"Shawn! NO! It's only in the dreams, boy. The closest we've ever been is that night of the fight when we slept in your guest bedroom. I only had on a towel," I closed my eyes and thought back to that evening. "I was so scared that night in that dark room because I felt like with him was where I belonged. Like my rightful place was with him," I said opening my eyes and smiling.

"WELL DO!" Preston said acting as if he was clutching a set of pearls. He cleared his throat and continued. "Hello, Gary! What about Gary?"

"It's different with Gary. I love Gary, but it's a different type of love now. It's a type that I don't have a name for, yet. That sounds bad, huh?" I smiled and shrugged my shoulders.

"Okay, Jason, this is going to pose a problem. You've got some soul searching to do, sweetie." Preston said taking a sip of his drink.

"I hope it's not that serious. Everything about Darius and with Darius is coincidental. Like how we met

46

in the gym reaching for the exact same dumbbell, how he was from Chicago, I was moving to the CHI, how before he deploys he wants to tell me he loves me the same night I tell Gary I love him. Granted, he doesn't tell me. Then off top, he just so happens to be on Rest & Relaxation Leave from the War on Terror and in Chicago the night I was supposed to go and patch things up with Gary. It's too much! It's something I feel like I need to explore. I mean, how long is this coincidental timeline going to tick on?" I laughed. The doorbell rang in that moment. We all jumped, and the room got quiet. I held my breath looking at Shawn.

"Bitch, that's him!" Shawn whispered as Batman ran to the door barking.

"Oh my God! Yo! What if it is? What should I say?" I said with a stunned look on my face.

"Okay, okay, okay. Bitch, I got it. First, run a brush over them waves," Preston paused and put on a serious face. I stopped what I was doing ready for his advice. The doorbell rang again. "Then, you should open up the door real sexy and say, how you doin'?" he said imitating Wendy Williams.

"HA HA HA! Your help is not helping, hag!" I smiled.

"Bitch, answer the door! Go get your man, whore," Shawn whispered.

"Shhhhh!" I said tripping on the rug as I hopped up. Shawn laughed. I made my way to the door and took a deep breath. I fixed my shirt in the mirror and told Batman to sit. Once he obeyed, I opened the front door with a smile. I was surprised at who the late-night visitor was. My heart skipped a beat and I sobered up slightly because this was going to be interesting. It was like I was seeing his ghost.

"Since I'm an Appletini sipping top, I figured we could talk over many of them," a voice said as I opened the door completely.

"Oh my God... hey stranger. Come on in," I said both surprised and disappointed. We gave one another a warm hug, and all was right within the brotherhood, initially. I made up my mind to give him the benefit of the doubt at least.

"Bitch! Is it Darius?" Shawn yelled. He then cracked up laughing hysterically before letting out a screech.

"YES, BITCH!" Preston joined in on the laughter. The sound of a high five reverberated through the room.

"Shut up! It's Michael!"

"Oh sweetie, that's even better! Invite him in!" Preston said. Michael took his coat off, and I put it in the closet as he walked in.

"I see you hags are already at the point of no return. What are ya'll sipping on?"

"We made some Lemon Drop Martinis. Sit down. I said. I'll go and get a cocktail shaker for this." I needed another moment to catch my breath and get my thoughts together. There was so much that I wanted to say, but I was going to be gracious enough not to go in. I opened the refrigerator as Batman came in to investigate what I was up too. I grabbed a bottle of water, twisted the cap, and chugged it to wet my dry mouth. I wiped my mouth and recapped the bottle putting on a nice face before returning to my group of friends.

"Hey whore, where the hell you been hiding?" Shawn sneered. I snickered looking back to see his face twisted up.

"I've been locked away in my apartment and I was getting cabin fever," Michael said.

"Here," I said handing Mike a martini glass and shaker. "It's some ice in that container right there," I said sitting a plate of wings and napkins out on the table. "Michael, it's good to see you," I said handing him a card I had gotten him. He had just lost his mother, so our petty differences could be put aside just for tonight I thought. Although I *really* wanted to lay into him.

"You too, Jason. I got you a card too. But I want you to read it later okay. Preferably when you are sober," Michael said. He placed the card he got for me on the table near me.

"Okay. I can do that, but you can read yours now. It's just a little prayer for you and your family. Are you okay?" I asked as he opened the card to begin reading it. He responded about a minute later. Shawn and Preston were sipping their cocktails and munching on wings like this was a TV drama about to unfold.

"Thank you, Jason. Thank you so much," he said tearing up.

"Oh my God, now you know I don't do tears," I said as he got up and hugged me.

"I'm so sorry, Jason. I truly am. I took out my own

demons on you. I'm sorry."

"It's okay, we're family man. We are going to fight sometimes I guess. I didn't know I was..."

"Jason, it don't even matter, shawty," he said sitting down.

"Chile, you hoes got me over here all misty eyed. Group hug," Shawn said dabbing his eyes with a napkin. I really wasn't feeling all touchy feely at the moment.

"Shawn, shut up. Next, we gon' start singing, "It's So Hard to Say Goodbye', or some tea," I laughed.

"I'm serious, group hug cunt!" Shawn said.

"Oh God, Shawn, hush," I said sucking my teeth. "So you a'ight?" Michael asked.

"I'm getting there. I just have to use a crutch for my ankle," I said trying not to verbally blame him for my injuries.

"Which he hasn't been using, Michael. Sick him!" Preston ordered pointing at me. Shawn then started barking like a dog causing Batman to sit up and join in. I motioned for the dog to stop and he obeyed.

"Jason, now you know you need to follow the doctor's orders if you want to heal properly and in a timely manner," Michael said chastising me.

"You sound like Janice Ann," I said referring to my mother. "I will, I will, okay. I'm going to have to hear this same speech from her when I go home for Christmas," I said rolling my eyes and waving my hand dismissively. I couldn't help but notice a void in his eyes and a heaviness that seemed to be surrounding him.

Then I thought maybe me referencing seeing my mama for Christmas was a bit insensitive.

"So what I miss. What ya'll in here kee-keeing about?" he asked pouring vodka, ginger ale, and the sour apple mix over ice. He seemed to be trying to avoid a couple of very important topics.

"How Jason wants Darius to tap that ass Tuesday," Shawn said changing the subject. Maybe being light hearted was appropriate. Besides we could talk later in private.

"See I tell ya'll too much of my business," I said pointing at Shawn.

"You messing with Darius?" Michael asked gently shaking up his drink.

"Boy! No, we were just in here reminiscing about old times, and Darius came up. Ain't no tea there. Let's get on to you, what's wrong with you? You don't seem like yourself?" I decided to steer this boat. I wasn't ready for him to question me about my personal life just yet. He closed his eyes and raised his index finger. He then poured half the contents of the shaker in the martini glass and inhaled it. He then poured the rest into the glass. I didn't want to bring up the elephant in the room, but I wasn't going to pretend like he didn't try to take his own life, either. He rested his elbows on his knees.

"What you want to know, Jason?" He said looking over at me.

"I want to know about you. This ghost that's sitting in my house," I said not missing a beat. I sized him up.

51

Dreams vs. Reality

"It's bad enough I had to put my mother in the ground, but I almost got you killed over my stupidity. That's how I'm feeling." He took a gulp of the drink. "I got some addictions ya'll. This is one of them, he said pouring a double shot of vodka and turning it up. "AHHHH! I fuck so much because I'm a stranger to myself. I don't know who I am. But I know I was a product of meaningless sex. So if I'm a stranger to me, then it's easier to be a stranger to someone else and get a good nut in the process. We're just coming together for a common goal... don't nobody give a fuck about strangers. When was the last time either one of ya'll gave a fuck about a stranger?" Michael said with a maudlin disposition. He looked up at each of us individually. He had a look of anger. I didn't know what he was talking about because this fool wasn't making sense.

"I did just now when you walked through the door. Stranger. Hello! Hi! I didn't see you when I woke up! And these two said they didn't see you one time while I was in the hospital. I was in a coma, but I was worried about you man! Even in my coma. I kept reliving that phone call in my head over and over. It bothered me that I was in the hospital sleep not knowing if you were dead or alive," I said trying to control my emotions. I stopped and waited for him to respond.

"He was probably near Belmont out at The Rocks fucking," Shawn said laughing before taking a sip and letting out a burp.

"Really, Shawn?" I said looking at him like he was

52

crazy.

"I wasn't trying to kill myself Jason," he said looking me in the eye. Tears started to fall as he took a gulp of his drink. He sat the glass back down balling his hands together staring at them intently. I only had a blank stare to offer him.

"You weren't trying to kill yourself? Hmm," I stated in nonchalant haste. I was trying to make sense of that statement. Did I hear him correctly? I mean it was good that he was still alive, but what? I shifted out of my thoughts. "Elaborate because I was on the phone with you trying to get to you. And, I'm quite sure you passed out. And you said you swallowed all the pills. I mean..."

"Biiiiitch! I wasn't gon' bring it up, but since it's on the table!" Shawn said laughing and raising his drink in the air. I looked at him almost instructing him to shut up. To me, this wasn't a laughing matter and right now all of them were in collusion as far as I was concerned. I then turned back towards Michael.

"Jason, you were right. I had way too much to drink that night, and I took my daily dose of HIV medication for the next day from my pill planner and I panicked in my drunken anger," he said. Tears escaped his eyes in pairs as I glared at him not knowing quite what to say. I felt light headed all of a sudden. I closed my eyes and shook my head rapidly for a second. "I called you because I wanted you to come back. If you were there, you would have stopped me and I'm not blaming you, but brothers take care of one another and we weren't there for one another and..."

"Duly noted," I said raising my hand for him to shut the hell up. "Now leave my house please," I said in a cool, calm, collected voice. He wiped the tears from his face with his hands.

"What?" he asked with a puzzled look stained across his red face. I refused to repeat myself as I reached over and grabbed the card he had brought giving it a perfect swift toss into his lap.

"Oop! *Biiitch*, he showing you the door, whore," Shawn laughed taking a gulp of his drink. His eyes were bouncing back and forth between the two of us. All he needed was a tub of popcorn as he sat perched on the edge of his seat. Preston looked right at home next to him chewing on the chicken he had in his napkin.

"Oh no, you two as well," I said bursting Shawn's bubble. I then glanced at him with a curt smile. He sat the glass down so hard the bottom broke from the stem. I watched him quickly fumble with the remaining piece, finally turning the glass upside down. In my head I was thinking, *Oh perfect! I got that set when I was stationed with the Marines in Okinawa, Japan, thanks!*

"What did I do, Bitch!?" he said with an appalled tone. I watched the remnants inside of the glass pool around the rim. Batman who was lying right beside me perked up and began growling. I didn't say another word to either of them. I grabbed my crutch and stood up to make my way to the front door.

"Everything ain't a freakin' kee-kee, Shawn. Dang, like seriously!" I said barely looking at him.

"Well, gag, bitch! Excuse me for trying to get you

two ol' whoopin' crane looking bitches to lighten up, bitch!" Shawn retaliated.

"Jason, come on now," Michael protested as I started walking.

"Wait a minute sweetie! Jason… Jason! What is the problem?" Preston asked as he walked up behind me. I unlocked and swung the front door open and then turned towards the closet to grab each of their coats. Batman was barking, alert to the fact that the mood in the room had just turned hostile. In my mind, I was thinking, *That's my Batty Boy! You better have Daddy's back!*

"Jason, please hear me out. I'm sorry, okay. Don't be this way shawty," Michael said. I leaned up against the wall to steady myself; I held up a coat in each hand and directed my attention to the front door.

"This bitch done lost her damn mind. I ain't ever been kicked out nobody's house," he said eyeing Preston and then continued. "Been kicked out of many a punk palace, but not a *punk's* house," he said folding his arms waiting for me to respond. "And furthermore, you only get in your feelings like this and shade us when shit ain't right with you and Gary. But at the end of the day bitch we're the ones who are always going to be here for you while you sittin' up dreamin' about Darius coming to rescue your shady ass! Say something! Read back, bitch!" Shawn said as I took a deep breath and exhaled through my lips slowly.

"I am reading," I mused dryly. Batman was still barking. I made a mental note to give him a slice of the bacon I keep stored for him when I feel he is being extra awesome.

"I guess, girl! Bye, bitch!" he said ripping his coat from my grip. He stuck his tongue out at Batman and began mumbling under his breath before making his exit.

"Shawn, wait! I'll give you and Preston a ride, you don't need to be driving," Michael said grabbing Shawn's attention. "Jason, I'm sorry, a'ight?" he said. He waited a few seconds before saying, "Would you rather I be dead? What the fuck?" It was another attempt to get me to recant my request. When I paid him no attention, he gently pulled his coat from my grip. I reached over and grabbed my keys removing the key to his apartment from my ring and handed it to him. He took it from me and slowly made his way out of the house. Preston followed suit, waving bye as he looked back at me sadly stumbling through the doorway.

I pushed myself off of the wall, grabbed the door and shut it behind them. I was so pissed I didn't know what to do. How the hell is he gonna come tell me some mess like that and try to turn the crap he started around on me? I didn't fully know why I was mad, but this crap just didn't feel right. Hell, I could have died! Preston was right about one thing; it was time to do some soul searching. My reality doesn't feel real anymore. There is only one area in my life that is so familiar to me and he's not here to hold me right now. I took a seat on the foot of the stairs thinking about two pieces of advice my dad told me before I went to boot camp. I didn't quite get what he was saying, but it resonated with me. He said, "Those you start with won't always be who you end with." He also said, "Be careful of those who want you to jump out the plane but won't do it themselves." The first one made sense, and maybe the second didn't apply just yet. Sometimes Dad can be too deep without knowing it.

Maybe this trip home would be just what I needed to cheer me up and get my head back in the game. It was going to be wonderful seeing my niece enjoy opening her Christmas presents. Maybe I could talk to Mama about this now that we were cool. It would be cool if Daddy was there and not deployed. I popped up from the stairs and started cleaning up the mess we made of my living room and kitchen. I rewarded my lil' boo Batman for having my back and dove back into the only place I felt safe, my poetry...

Follow My Directions

Don't know if I should think it. Love. Don't know if I
should speak it. Love.
So I'll be discreet and jot it down on this here sheet,
Spill ink to define how sweet you are,
How I adore you,
Want to explore you from dome to feet.
A daily forecast of sunshine is what you are.
Getting lonely thinking about how far you've come,
Yet giddy when truly feeling this is the long haul.
Finally no need to sit logged on for hours
Sifting through numerous profiles of serial liars,
Seeking only to spill the seed of man,
Wasted feelings, needs, and desires, through sexual
encounters.
Of that I'm tired as you've become my rest,
Become my prose
Become who I think, speak, and chose,
Enlightened my mind to expand thoughts of spirituality,
Transcended through fleshly reality, Reverse my
thinking,
Keep me from sinking into the bitter waters of self- pity,
Coasting and drifting further into an Abyss of superficial
play dates.
You, a life vest of hope came floating me gently against
the current
To your beautiful shores of love and sexual security. You
simply must know, you are an open notebook full of my

Follow My Directions

flows,
Mere words others haven't heard me speak,
Various pages ripped out,
Numerous Stanzas being strategically placed,
As I cut and paste thoughts once fiction,
Of you the embodiment of everything I ever wanted in a black man,
Now personified and ravaged vocally by love's poetic violence,
Something I never thought could be happenstance,
Don't know if I should ask... but that's love, right?

"That was a little something I wrote over the holidays entitled, 'Poetic Violence'," I said as the audience cheered, whistled, and clapped. Once the applause died down I continued. "Hell, 'cause love can beat that tail sometimes won't it? Literally! Um... before we bring up the featured artist, I just want to first thank you all so much for your love and support of this showcase and what Poetic Expressions has evolved into. Give yourselves a hand for being a part of this new renaissance era that represents us! 2005 is going to be an amazing year for us, so Happy New Year, everybody!" The audience clapped for a few moments and I continued. "And thank you for all of your thoughts, prayers, cards, stuffed animals, visits. Hell, my mama was even extra loving this holiday, so thank you Santa Claus." I said in a nasally gay voice to make the audience chuckle. "Oh, and whoever got me those Edible Arrangements, thank you! I feel like I owe you some booty or some tea," I said looking around the audience and rubbing my booty with a scared look on my face. The audience laughed. "Because them thangs ain't cheap! Who I owe the booty too?" YOU OWE ME, JAY-DUB! This tall sexy stud yelled standing up grabbing her crotch. "Uh oh! Ya'll know studs be holdin' on to something serious, dang!" I said looking around as if searching for sympathy. "Alright, well...come see me after the show then. Damn! And please keep in mind that I can't arch my back just quite yet," I responded as the audience broke into laugher, "Thank you! I'm almost back to normal. Hopefully, I won't be walking around here like Pops from The Color Purple for too long." I said as the audience laughed. Someone yelled out, we love you, Jason. "I love you too! So now without further ado, I am so honored and proud to present our feature to you tonight. This brotha is DOPE! I'm telling you! He has rocked all kinds of poetry slams and killed the competition coast to coast! He was the winner of this year's Peace Out Fest slam in Oakland! You may have seen him on Lyric Café back in the day, or even on Def Poetry Jam, spitting his world-famous piece, 'Not Giving a Damn'! Birth in money makin' Manhattan! He now resides in your city and his hair is oh, oh, oh, so pretty! Poetic Expressions, let's play that song! Give that energy up for Mr. Rocwell Jones!" I said as the crowd clapped and cheered him on stage. He gave me a bear hug before I exited.

"Hell yeah! That's my shit. Girl what you know

about Christion?" Rocwell said pointing at the DJ. "What the hell is up? How ya'll feeling?" he asked. As the audience yelled out, Poetic! "Chicago, I'm feeling the love and energy in here! Ya'll give it up for Jason! He's still sexy, crutch and all. Mmm mmm mmph. Boy, I tell you what; we might be able to incorporate that crutch into a few positions though. I'm from up top, so you already know I'm nasty! I got some ideas," he said as the audience laughed. "Alright, I'm going to get right into it. Ya'll know a lot of this so-called hip-hop music sucks now-a-days, right?" The audience responded yes. "If you are a true hip-hop fan, and can appreciate real lyrics, then you appreciate spoken word. That's why most of ya'll are here. Am I right?" The audience responded yes. "So since I was raised in Brooklyn, this joint is called, 'Sucka M. C's'," he said as the audience laughed.

I walked outside to take a call from Javier. We were still a team in terms of Poetic Expressions and decided to remain friends. I was glad that there was no animosity between us even though the first couple of weeks working together again on the set were awkward. Javier or Javi, was sort of my rebound guy a couple months after Gary and I broke up. I had developed a little crush on him and decided to see where it would lead. He was an awesome guy, Puerto Rican, Chi-town born and bred in the cities section called Humboldt Park. I sure did miss kissing them pretty red lips of his, dang! Aside from that, he was one of the coolest guys I knew.

He would have been here tonight, but he was working on a youth center project he was in charge of. He wouldn't give up the details and was acting all secretive about it. I went with it and gave him space to let his creative juices flow. One thing I learned about Javi is he really puts his all into whatever he set out to do in the community but can sometimes spread himself too thin. I was hoping this wouldn't be the case.

"How you feeling, papi?' Javi asked.

"I'm good, not a complaint in sight," I said. "Uh huh. How's the set going tonight?"

"It's awesome. The feature is on stage now and Jerome crazy tail is going to close out after him."

"Oh, you guys aren't going to do another round of poets?"

"I thought we'd do something different tonight. We let all the artists go first and brought the feature out last. It seems to have worked out well."

"Okay, that sounds cool."

"Yeah it was. I'll read my piece to you at a later date and time."

"Oh, you spit tonight?"

"Yup, you missed quite a treat," I smiled.

"Damn, well you definitely gotta let me hear it," he said.

"So you called to micro manage?" I laughed.

"No, papi, nothing like that. I called to see if you can do ya mans a request, por favor?"

"Oh, I see, well, it depends on what it is?" I laughed.

"You know mi abuela's birthday is coming up,

right? He asked. I was thinking is he serious right now asking me about his grandmother? Where was this going?

"What about it?" I asked.

"I really need you to go with me. She talks about you all the time because I sort of mentioned you to her when we were, you know kickin' it," he chuckled.

"Javi I don't think that would be a good idea. How am I going to explain that to my man?" I said not liking this at all.

"I don't know, but you gotta come because she caught me off guard when she asked about you and how we were doing, and she asked if you were coming and I sorta said yes," he said finally taking a breath.

"Dang it, Javi! Really?!"

"Yes, really! You can't disappoint mi abuela on her seventy-fifth cumpleanos, papito. And besides, you owe me at least that seeing as how you dogged me out the way you did," he said.

"Bogus! Oh, you gon' go there, right?" I said sucking my teeth. "Alright, when is it Javi?" I asked feeling backed into a corner. Come to think of it, Gary doesn't know about my past with Javi. So I'm good so what could go wrong? He's a poetry buddy as far as Gary was concerned.

"It's tomorrow at 2PM," he said.

"I'm kicking' your butt when I see you. Tomorrow, though? You real bogus for that," I laughed.

"I'll pick you up tomorrow. See you soon, gotta go," he said kissing the phone. It sounded like he had a big smile on his face. I walked backstage just before Jerome was about to go on stage to close. I gave him a hug and hobbled my way to the exit, trying hard not to fall or mash someone's toe with my crutch. I had my binder in one hand and the crutch in the other. I exited the club and noticed Rocwell running up behind me. I turned and smiled as he held the door for me.

Rocwell had to be one of the most naturally sexy guys I had seen in a long time. He wasn't all cut up like Darius or Gary. He had a nice natural muscle tone, encased in a smooth deep cinnamon complexion. He had a set of penetrating dark brown eyes that looked as if you could get lost in them. They evoked a sense of tenderness beneath their dark hue. He had a really nice medium sized curly fro that would be irresistible to touch. And on top of that he has this sort of bohemian meets the street type of style.

"I'm gonna walk you to your car, Jason," he said.

"I'm fine, thank you. That's not necessary," I stated politely.

"No, it's very necessary, what if someone takes advantage of your disadvantage, then what?" he said stating the obvious.

"I'm a grown man though," I smiled.

"Which is why I'm walking you to your car. I'm not into little boys. Feel me?" Rocwell said. He winked at me as he bit his bottom lip. I winked back at him and decided to give in with a smile.

"Okay, seeing as how you're not going to take no

for an answer, come on," I replied. I was thinking, boy, you look like trouble in reference to what Shawn said a few nights ago about GMD tease. And it didn't help that he had that mannish New York demeanor coupled with that accent. Give me the strength!

"I was also waiting for a 'thank you' from you since I rocked it tonight, but yo', I'm sayin'. Ya'll Chi- town kats don't be wanting to show NY no love," Rocwell stated with this boyish grin on his face.

"I'm so sorry," I chuckled. I thought to myself, *Jason, if you don't stop grinning in this man face like a little schoolgirl.* The last thing I needed was another hard leg to add to my plate. "My mind is preoccupied with some other things. Thank you so much for coming out on such short notice. I truly appreciate it, and the crew does too," I said not realizing that I hadn't showed my gratitude.

"Aww shucks, you're welcome," he smiled.

"Ah, ah! And just so you know, New York. The Bill Bellamy routine is a little played out in the Midwest. Up here fishin' for compliments and junk. I expected more from someone up top," I said laughing and shaking my head.

"Okay, Chi-town, you gets down I see, my bad Lil' Fatz," he said cheesing and admiring my boldness.

"Actually, I'm from Motown. And what's the deal with that nickname?" I said looking at him slightly puzzled.

"My bad again, shorty. I call you Lil' Fatz cause of them little nice phat packages holding the back of them jeans up," he said taking a peek. I decided to stop the direction this conversation was headed towards.

"The crowd received you well?" I asked smiling and shaking my head.

"I was feeling the love," Rocwell said. "And thank you so much for having me. It was a pleasure to meet you in the flesh. Your energy over the phone got me. I could hear you smiling."

"AT&T ain't no punk if you can hear your boy smiling," I laughed.

"Shit, that's all I'm saying," he laughed. We reached the car, and I unlocked it. He opened my door and held it for me as I put the crutch in and sat in the driver's seat. I started the car and rolled the window down as he closed the door and bent down to meet me at eye level.

"So you alright man?" he asked smiling.

"Yeah. I guess so. I'm healing; I'm taking time off from work for another couple weeks. I'm good," I said resting my head on the B-pillar.

"Cool, cool! I'm glad to hear that. You definitely gotta take care of yourself shorty. Unless you got somebody doing that for you, then yo!" He winked.

"I'm taken care of," I said listening to him spit that up top game. New York kats are charming but can lay it on a little thick at times. A Midwest kat would have been like, *so what time I'm coming to take care of you and some dinner tomorrow?* That's how you make relationships happen. A picture of Gary came to mind.

"But yo' feel me on this. I dig your energy, so I want

to invite you to my studio. We can talk, listen to a little wax from the 90's, get a feel for one another, and honestly, picture me painting you," Rocwell said.

"Painting me?" I asked, as a light wind carried the scent of his cologne past my nose. Both his statement and his sweet aroma caught me off guard. He must have read my mind somehow or maybe my facial expressions, I thought.

"Now that I have your attention," he smiled. "I got your math, so I'll use it and direct you to the studio when I have your canvass ready."

"I have to think about that. I don't..." I said as he interrupted.

"See, I like your fight," he winked his eye, wet his lips, and continued. "Don't think. Just wait for my instructions," he said.

"How you know I don't have a man?" I said.

"Oh I peeps game. Yeah, you got a man, but you don't look happy about the one you got. I know because if you were, you wouldn't have let me push up on you a second time Lil' Fatz. I'll be calling you. Get my man home safe, Lord," he said looking up to the sky for a second. "Good night," he winked without waiting for my response.

I watched him cross the street and re-enter the club. He had a confident ditty bop as if he were walking to a hip-hop jam playing in his head. I was wowed by his alpha male attitude. I have to admit; it turned me the hell on and made me notice just how attractive he was.

I knew I had to be very careful with this one. Dude

was alluring, and the last thing I wanted to do was get caught up. But *Lil' Fatz,* though? I thought and chuckled to myself. I need to stop comparing and contrasting these dudes like this and focus on the one in front of me. My first mistake, however, was not putting my foot down and saying no thank you to Rocwell's demand. My second mistake was... well... entertaining the idea of going to his studio. My third was still wondering what the next level of Darius would look like in my life...

Down Low Darius

So, I'm an officer in the world's greatest Navy, and that comes with a lot of responsibility. It's a game of politics as you smile and pretend you like and agree with shit you couldn't care less about! On top of that, my dad is a very respected doctor, and I'm following in his footsteps in many ways. So this dog and pony show and being the safe Negro is going to help me get to where I need to be.

Dad is one of the top Oral Maxillofacial Surgeons in the country. He's won awards for some of the miracles he's performed. He don't play. He started out as a Navy Hospital Corpsmen same as me and worked his way through the ranks retiring as a full bird. In layman's terms, he carried the rank of O-6 or Captain United States Navy. He instilled in me to work hard for all you get, got, and give. One thing he taught me and made sure I learned was *"Make your presence known even when you enter a dark room."* He said, *"Trust me the lights will even respond to you."* Most of my colleagues are white, Asian, or Indian. Many of the functions in the medical community that I've attended may have about 4 or 5 more black officers in the room, and out of that five, only one of them is a brotha. And he's usually mixed if it ain't me standing in the room. So now that I am in this field I understand what he meant. My dream will be attained when I am half the man my dad is.

But when I entered into this white man's Navy, I

knew what I was in for. Shit, the color of my skin and the fact that I'm from CHI-town would have me labeled before my resume was even viewed. *Oh my God, so you grew up in the hood, huh?* Usually telling someone as a black male that you're from Chicago evokes images of gang violence, Cabrini Green projects, murders, and shit maybe even Oprah. Kats normally don't know too much about the CHI in my opinion. To which I respond, *"No I'm not sure what the hood is, seeing as how I actually grew up on the Gold Coast of Chicago's Near North Side. Now if you'll excuse me."* And leave them standing there wondering what the fuck just happened.

It's funny what white people think is okay to assume and say. Now don't get it twisted, I ain't no punk. And Dad didn't tell me to be arrogant, but he did say let them know who you are at all times, make your presence felt, and keep in mind, money looks beautiful when it's invisible. A real man doesn't have to lead with something he can lose in the blink of an eye. Don't let white folks get into your mind about money. We don't have money we have wealth. There is a difference, son.

He would tell me this from time to time when he felt I was getting too cocky within my privilege. I was seven years old when I asked him one day what he meant by money looks beautiful invisible. He smiled and told me to hold that thought realizing that I was a visual learner. He didn't answer that question until one Saturday morning a week before my fourteenth birthday he woke me up and told me to get dressed.

But he said to put my fishing clothes on. It was the summer time, so that meant, just an old t-shirt, my tattered jeans which were my favorite to wear out of all the clothes I had and the fishing hat he bought me to wear on the boat. He said when you get dressed meet me downstairs.

I hurried up, excited that we were going fishing, hoping he would let me steer the boat. We always had fun on these trips because he'd let me eat all the candy and drink all the root beer I could stand after I ate the sandwiches and cut up fruit my mom would pack for us. I quickly got ready and raced downstairs. Dad was sitting on the couch with Mom watching, *The Morning Show.* I told my mom good morning and she got up to kiss and hug me before leaving the room, so Dad and I could talk. He turned the television off and said Darius, I'm going to give you two answers to a question you asked me a while back. I think you're old enough to understand this lesson now son.

He reaches into his pocket and pulls out a money clip and hands it to me. He then tells me to count it out loud. I happily took the money of course, removing the clip, sitting it on the table. I counted

$1,000 worth of crisp fifty dollar bills out loud. I noticed how each of the bills slid between my fingers easily yet were reluctant to leave the bill that preceded it. After I counted the money twice, I placed the clip back on it and handed it back to Dad. He told me the money was mine and asked what I would do with it. My response was to buy video games, and sneakers, and a watch like his. He laughed and said okay, it's your money to do what you want with. But then he told me to stand up and walk around the house holding it up in the air and to really get excited about it. I did as he asked waving it in the air saying I got a thousand dollars, woo whoo! He waits until I'm really enjoying myself doing the cabbage patch dance and snatches the clip out of my hand, yanking my arm in the process.

"What do you have now?" he asked. "Nothing," I said scratching my head sitting back down. He told me, "A man who boasts about what he has, really has nothing. He's crying out for attention, maybe help; he can't manage the little he does have. So guess what? It gets taken away either by mismanagement, or thievery. Either way you're getting robbed. That's the difference between money and wealth. You can have money all day and night and get it from anywhere. But wealth is something tangibly earned because it's acquired. That's why money looks beautiful invisible. You work hard for it; you can have whatever you want in life, Darius. Not just money. But you got to be smart about what is given to you. Ain't nothing wrong with having money, but don't limit yourself to it. You can't rely on this. He said holding the bills up. Yeah, we have plenty of nice things, and a couple of fine cars but this isn't whom we are, rather how we live. Let the world know who you are first, not what you come from. Be your own man, not the man they expect you to be. You've got to give them no choice but to respect you before you talk about your past. You understand?" I replied, "Yes," as he placed the money

back into my hand, reminding me that money makes you more of what you already were.

I said all that to say this. When I met Jason, he was the first person who didn't prejudge me. There was no need to put my defenses up with him. He truly saw me for who I was, not for the pull I had, what I drove, or what I could do for him. Hell, he's seen my dick, and I don't even remember his face showing that he was impressed like other reactions I've gotten from it. He's more than a surface type dude. Cool and calm like the deep not all over the place like my ass. He never asked anything of me but me and has never tried to change me.

Jason is an idealist whereas I am a realist. He had to work hard for everything he sought to attain in life, and I was handed mostly everything I have. The way he thinks outside the box and his view of the world makes him creative and resourceful. He was the first and only dude I fell madly in love with, but I just won't tell him. I've always wanted too much. That may be because I've been given everything my whole life. Shit, I can talk my way in and out of any person, place, or thing. But I won't allow myself to claim the one thing in this world I know is rightfully mine. Jason.

And because I know this, therein lies the problem. Remember how I told you I want to follow in my dad's footsteps? Well, I want the military life, wife, and kids my dad had when he served because the shit in my mind is damn near picture perfect. Then, Jason entered the picture, fucking my head up with a touch leading up to those beautiful bright brown eyes of his. The nigga is phyne and he don't even know it...but I digress. I'll come back to him. Mmph...

Now what I see is the traditional family portrait hanging above the oversized fireplace of me, my wife, and kids' luxurious home. I wanted to give my dad that as a gift for all he's done for me...and for losing...my mother to breast cancer. They were two days into his retirement from the Navy and she finds out she's in stage II. That shit gave her the fight of her life quickly. The way the medical community and his Navy family here in Chicago came together to support him was only something God could put together. My plan was to fall right in line with the Navy's core values of Honor, Courage, and Commitment.

This is something I've carried with me for quite some time. It's my dream, and it's not happening the way I planned it. I find out two days after I get back from Kuwait that my baby's mother Cindy fell down a flight of stairs and was in the hospital spotting pretty badly. I thought I loved Cindy and I thought she loved me. We dated in prep school and I thought yo', this could be wifey right here. She was a gorgeous bright skinned girl with long beautiful hair that she allowed me to run my fingers through even in the pool. I loved the fact that it was her shit.

She's extremely intelligent, curvy, and ambitious and I just knew she would make a great mother and wife. The only problem is she didn't see me in her dreams, so we broke up after prom. Plus, she didn't want the life I wanted to give her. A military life wasn't glamorous enough for her. I'd see her on my summer's home from college and we'd connect but break up by the fall. I thought there was promise before I left for Kuwait because she flew to DC to see me.

She got bogus as shit when she found out she was pregnant. I would call, and she would send me off. She barely emailed any progress about the pregnancy, so I had my grandmother MiMi to intervene until I could drum up a plan to get my hand around her throat. Naw, I'd never do that, but my frustration with all of this is something serious.

I was somehow able to hook up a set of family hardship orders to Chicago until she had the baby that she obviously doesn't want. I don't agree with abortion at all, and I want to be a father like my dad so bad. So I decided to compromise the full potential of my dream for the sake of this precious life she hated from jump.

I convinced her to carry the baby to term and that she wouldn't have to want for anything the entire time. She agreed until she noticed how it was affecting that tight body she got. Cindy wants to live a life of glam, throw caution to the wind, and not take responsibility for anything that doesn't pertain to her. *God, please let my baby girl be all right...at least.*

Now back to Jason. My first thought was this was a new dream. I mean, I admit to checking dudes out, but I'm a gym rat, so you're always sizing the next nigga up. I admit to gettin' a little of that sloppy head I like from a nigga on occasion. And even bustin' down with no kissin' but I do like to eat. To me, it was just two niggas gettin a easy nut. Nothing but a little harmless male attention, right? Maybe something like twenty percent or…shit I'ought know; the point is Jason changed all that. This dude made something inside of me wake up and take notice, like what the fuck! I wouldn't allow myself to touch him like I wanted to but not a day goes by that I don't want to. How can I feel like he's mine when I can't even admit that I want him? I can't treat Jason like a bust down - that's not who he is. Then there is my baby girl. How will she fit in between the two of us? Damn, without Cindy? Concluded by this Don't Ask Don't Tell shit. How do you get stuck with that hard of a choice? Life knows it can throw a mean two hitter sometimes.

I knew what it was with Jason, but I just didn't want to really give the shit a name yet. I had to fix this current situation with baby mom first and figure his role in my life out later. I mean I love him, but I love my expectations for my life even more I think. Shit, I grew up to believe one thing, but I feel another, yet the pressure to be the ideal Darius ain't coming from nobody but me.

I dozed off over thinking myself to sleep. I woke up and quickly wiped the slob off of my face when the pilot came over the loud speaker welcoming the passengers to the Windy City. I rubbed my face and stretched my arms and legs still glad that the first-class seat next to mine was unoccupied because *I died up off this mu'fucka'! I needed that sleep, ol' slobber face ass*, I thought to myself. I got off the plane, got my bags and caught a cab to the crib.

After I called to check in with my new Command Duty Officer of my temporary unit, my next stop was to the hospital to check on this crazy dame of mine. Jason was going to be next, so I sent him a text letting him know as stated, *Fuck them other niggas. Ya boy Dee is in town be available.* He shot me a text back that read, No doubt with a smiley face. I miss my dude. I made it to the hospital just in time to grab a bear and flowers from the gift shop. I know she put herself here on purpose, but I still wanted to keep the tension and stress down for the sake of the baby. I made my way to the floor that Cindy was on and strolled over to the nurse's station. One of the nurses, Rhonda, recognized me and quickly got up. She rushed to my side.

"Hey, handsome, Happy New Year! How are you, Darius? How was your flight?" she asked. Her eyes were all sparkly like I had just made her day. She had lost a little weight the last time I saw her, and I guess that must have meant she had been applying my fitness and diet advice.

"Happy New Year to you as well. It was great. How are you doing? Looking all petite and pretty," I said charming her while rubbing her back and giving her a tight hug.

"I'm well, thank you. Those tips you gave me are really helping," she blushed clearing her throat and getting back into professional mode. "Now I just want you to know she's on a sedative, so you may not be able to talk to her tonight, okay," she said. "Are you going to be okay, big guy?"

"This is the second time, Rhonda, damn. How can she do this?" I asked, taking a look around the place before shutting my eyes for a second.

"Baby, I don't know; she may have everyone else fooled, but I'm not stupid. Luckily both her and the baby are stable, but we're not out of the woods yet, so if you're a praying man, then hop on them two good kneecaps. I'm going to send some more prayer up for the little one later," she said.

"Thank you so much. We really appreciate that," she gave me a quick squeeze and I walked over to the room she pointed towards. I peeked through the window and saw that Cindy was asleep. I opened the door and walked in quietly noticing my grandmother. All of the grandkids call her MiMi. She was reading a huge Stephen King novel while munching on a container of her favorite snack, Brazil Nuts. She looked up at me and smiled broadly when she realized I was standing there. I walked over and rubbed Cindy's babies bump and covered her with a little more blanket. I then kissed her belly thanking God.

"Hey, lovie!" she said getting up to give me a kiss and hug. She stood back with her hands on her hips as I sat the flowers and bear down so that I could remove my coat. "When did you get in, just now?" She helped with the left sleeve of my coat.

"Yes, ma'am, I did, how are you?" I said guiding her back to the chair she was sitting in. I helped her get seated before sitting down next to her.

"Oh, for an attractive mature woman I'm doing well, lovie! I hope that you are?" she smiled rubbing my leg. If aging existed, you would not know it judging by Mimi. She was seventy-two years old and still had a potent dose of life and fire left in her. I loved her to death. MiMi had smooth creamy chocolate skin and had a head full of long dark hair that she kept braided up and pinned into a bun. She was a slender woman who walked with regal grace. She was a chameleon; able to rub elbows with people ranging from the homeless to the dignitaries she's met through the years. MiMi has lived her life and she trickles that zeal for life down to the rest of the family everyday she's alive.

"I am, MiMi, I missed, you!" I said reaching over to rub her hand.

"I missed you too, sweet pee. Now I'm glad you're here actually, I need to talk to you," she said as I braced myself for what was next. She was the epitome of class until she let her hair down. Literally, when she lets that bun lose, she's about to get it crackin'. But tonight, I really needed her to help me put some things into perspective.

"I'm actually glad you said that, MiMi," I said.

"Really. Well, let me get comfortable, this must be important," she removed her glasses and put the bookmark in between the pages she last read before sitting the book on the table. She sealed the can of nuts and reached up to let her hair down. I sat there looking at her chuckling with my head in the palm of my hand.

"Don't get frightened now, lovie," she said laughing. "I'm just getting comfortable."

"I'm not. I'm ready for ya tonight, beautiful!" I said. I clapped my hands in the air before rubbing them together. I peeked over to see if I had awakened Cindy.

"Ohhh, don't worry about that *stupid* little girl," she said sucking her teeth and waving her hand at her as if she were gesturing a dog away.

"Come on, MiMi, be nice," I pleaded laughing at her. "Now what were you going to say?"

"Oh, I said it. I was going to ask why you are having a baby with that *stupid* little girl. But let's focus on your other problem first. So what's wrong, lovie?" she said with a self-satisfying smile on her face. I wanted to ease into this topic with her with a little finesse because I wasn't sure how MiMi was going to react to what I had to tell her. I yelled out, *GERONIMO*, in my head and just blurted it out.

"I'm in love and I don't know what to do," I said looking her directly in the eye.

"With the baby killer?" she said pointing in Cindy's direction. Her face was contorted in utter dismay as if she were terrified. I didn't know whether to laugh or lie because I didn't know if her response would be worse with the actual person.

"No, ma'am! Not at all! I mean I love her enough for the baby, but it's not her, MiMi. I'm not in love with her," I said laughing. I leaned back in the chair and got comfortable. I could feel my mouth go dry.

"Amen to that! Darius, child! You almost made this ol' woman turn you over her good church knee. Whew, Lawd!" she said as I laughed.

"Oh, God! Not the good church knee?" I said laughing.

"Well, who is it then?" she asked finishing her laughter.

"It's my friend…Jason, MiMi," I said as her jaw dropped. She slowly stood up and walked over to the window with her hand covering her mouth. I closed my eyes not sure what to say or do next. I felt sweat steaming under my arms. She leaned up against the window frame and folded her arms. I waited for her to speak while she processed the news.

"Lawd, it don' started raining," she said in a soft somber voice.

"MiMi, did you hear what I said?" She closed her eyes and raised her head towards the sky slightly. She scratched her forehead and took a deep breath. She sighed slightly and finally began to speak.

"Lovie, I heard you," she said taking her hair out of the braid and shaking it loose. I had never seen her hair out of that braid ever. This scared me. I studied her body language looking for a way to scale this wall she seemed to have erected suddenly. She walked back over to her chair and sat down quietly crossing one leg over the other. She tossed her long dark hair over her left shoulder and closed her eyes for a second or two. Her crinkled loose hair flowed down her back and caught the light nicely in the dimly lit room.

"Jason," she said. "Jason," she repeated. That's your military... um friend, right?" she asked blinking several times and holding her head up staring at me.

"Yes, ma'am, I was stationed with him a while back," I replied.

"The same Jason you told me about that nursed you back to health in three days when you had the flu?" She moistened her lips with her tongue.

"Yes, ma'am, that's him," I said swallowing hard. I studied her face looking for a trace of compassion.

"Now I got a face to match all your war stories... hmph! Lord, have mercy, Jesus," she said shaking her head. I was trying to get a read on where this was going.

"Come again, MiMi?" I asked hesitantly, clearing my throat and trying to get my mouth to moisten.

"Ohhh, I know who Jason is. Hmph! That's that boy you hugged up with in that picture on your phone, right?" I looked at her trying to figure out how she saw that picture. No one knows the code to my phone and I allow no one to use my phone.

She was referring to an old picture I saved of Jason and I after a run on the beach we took one day when we were stationed in Camp Lejuene, North Carolina. I held his warm sweaty body up against mine and snapped a nice picture that I cherish just as much as what that day means to me. We ran together all the time after work, but that Saturday morning I convinced him to try out something challenging with me, and he didn't punk out because running on the beach ain't as easy as you'd think. But when you're stationed with the Marines, you do training like that to stay with the pack when we deploy. Damn, maybe that's when I caught feelings.

"Yes, ma'am," I said feeling like she busted me. The room felt hot all of a sudden as the rain pitter pattered against the huge glass pane window.

"You need to change your pass code. One-two-three-four is going to get you in a lot of trouble one day if you keep trying to hide what it is you think you need to hide. And if an ol' woman can crack the code on your little iPhone, hmph," she paused shaking her head again. "Why are we here with this stupid little girl lovie if you in love with some man? Just what in the hell are you trying to prove?"

"MiMi, I don't know," I said trying to remember the speech I had prepared in case this went south.

"Oh act your age, Darius. Don't start saying you don't know now," MiMi said. She stood up and pointed towards Cindy but was looking at me with a thousand-mile stare and continued, "Because this is a hot damn shit show, lovie!" she said stomping her foot twice. She waved both hands in the air and sat back down before adjusting her delicately pressed silk blouse.

"I know it is, and I'm trying to do the right thing for all parties involved," I said sounding like a little knucklehead promising not to do it again.

"But what about what's best for you, lovie?" she said giving my knee a pat.

"What do you mean? I am doing what's best for

me."

"By depriving yourself of the life you really want to lead? How is that the best thing for you, huh?" She had a point. Why was I afraid to face my feelings for Jason?

"You're right," I said looking over at Cindy. I rubbed the back of my head and took a deep breath.

"You can't relive the future your father never had by living the past you remember him having. Do you understand what I'm saying to you?" MiMi said. I nodded my head and felt like the iron coat I had been picking the lock on for years cracked open and fell on the floor. Finally!

"That's deep, MiMi. I never looked at it like that." I said nodding my head. I looked over at Cindy again and shut my eyes and lowered my head.

"Well, more people should because forcing this girl to carry your seed is not the solution to your life problems. The days of man are numbered and troubled. He already folded the right amount of trouble into your recipe, so why would you be foolish enough to add a few pinches more?" MiMi asked. I laughed as she smiled and rubbed my head.

"I know I'd be happy with Jason, but he doesn't fit my military family model though, MiMi," I said folding my arms. I knew what I needed to do, but shit, I was still frustrated with this whole situation.

"That might be true in your mind, but you may be looking at it all wrong. Ain't a such thing as a traditional family. Black folk are the first to need to admit that.

Family is whomever you feel in your heart deserves that title. Family is deeper than shared blood. What better partner to have than one that served and knows sacrifice first hand. He knows what you need doubly so because he's been there to take care of you when you were sick risking his own health. That's what you soldiers do, well, not what the two of you do, of course. But you know what I'm saying," she said clearing her throat and making me laugh. She laughed for a second and finished her thought. "I'm going to tell you like this. Gay is everywhere, you hear me? It's been *around* since it was a *twinkle* in Great Big God's glow. God makes what's called decisions about us and who we are. People make what's known as judgment calls cause of what they heard or think they know. You following me, lovie?" MiMi said.

"Yes, ma'am, I am," I said still slouched down in my chair.

"Then show some respect towards me and act like it," she said as I immediately sat up straight in my chair and directed my full-undivided attention towards her.

"Now where was I... Yes, now see, you got to live the life God gave you. Your *best* life, which is His decision. That's all your job is. I have shaken hands with people ranging from racists to Mandela himself. You know why, lovie? Because I lived my own life. I don't compare it to no one else's because it's not mine to live I have a life of my own. And you know what else? I got so much life and love to give that I was a blushing bride twice married to two wonderful men, and God rest both of their souls. Both of them gave me the world by letting me see it and taking me around it ten and seventeen times respectively. Three of them were safari trips taking pictures petting Lions. Why? Because we weren't afraid to live! And by getting what we wanted out of the life God placed in us. You've got to live your own life and no one else's. That's the only one that works for you."

"It's complicated, MiMi?" I said.

"No, that's an excuse, lovie! The fact that I think about being a lesbian from time to time all because these old horny toads in Chicago won't act right since Viagra and hussies much younger than me is my competition for men with names like Rufus and Horace is complicated," she said as we both broke out into laughter. That put me more at ease. "Rush Street is now the Viagra Triangle. Lord, am I lying?" she said looking up to the sky.

"More truth in it, MiMi," I smiled as she rubbed my knee.

"Now seriously, which dream best suits you, lovie? "Cindy or Jason?"

"Jason," I said without a shadow of a doubt. "Well, there you have it. God has something

better for you than what you had. So what's stopping you from going after it if that's what you want?"

"He's with this fool that doesn't appreciate the man that he is. And Jason doesn't seem to get it. I hate this dude with an unexplainable passion, MiMi, and I want Jason so bad, but he loves this clown."

"Hmph, I see. Well, there's no need to insult the man. Because stealing another man's most prized possession comes with great consequence and responsibility. You need to be careful. Is it worth putting Jason through all this what if and guilt if it isn't God's will? This sounds like more than just two grown men bumping uglies in a bed together," she said uncrossing her legs. I thought for a second.

"I know he's my possession and I know he's waiting on me, MiMi," I said truly believing what I had just said.

"I dare you to ask him," MiMi said. I smiled as she continued. "Where does he live?"

"He lives here in Chicago," I answered.

"Hmph. Well, when you get your man, let me know and bring him by my house. I got someone I'm going to introduce the both of you too," she said winking then smiling. "Don't you let your past distract your future."

"Yes, ma'am! I will definitely bring him by," I said. MiMi assured me that she was glad that the truth was brought to light so that I could indeed make the best decision for me. In spite of the circumstances surrounding this visit, I'm glad it brought me up to this point. I was going to have to figure out how to merge both dreams into one because I wanted my baby girl, and I needed Jason. I want to have something with him, but how when he's probably laid up with ol' boy Larry right now...

Family Reunion

"Mmmm mornin', babes! Why didn't you wake me up last night?" Gary asked in the middle of him stretching.

"Awww, 'cause you looked so cute laying here. I didn't want to wake you," I said pulling his ear. I was playing on my laptop as Gary moved closer to me and slid his hand into my underwear. He started to caress my butt. His eyes were half open as I bent down to kiss him.

"You should have woke me, babes. I had a surprise for you. I had the mood set and everything, ya' know. A preview to your birthday."

"Did you now?" I said sliding my computer over. Remembering the soft music and candles he had lit all over the bedroom when I came home. I still wasn't ready to have him take full advantage of me.

"What you doing on the computer?" he asked as I rubbed his head.

"I was looking at porn," I said. In my mind, I was thinking maybe it would help get me in the mood again if I could see what I was missing out on, just maybe that would help me take care of home.

"No, you weren't," he chuckled. "Let me see." he said opening his eyes completely.

"Here, for real, look," I said with a smirk. I turned the computer towards him, and there a dark skinned brotha' pounding out a short brown skinned dude.

"Damn, babes, you got a real man's dick right here, you shittin' me, lookin' at porn?" he said giving my body a squeeze and kissing my thigh. I shut the computer off and sat it on the nightstand.

"I know, but I'm not quite ready yet," I said rubbing his head. It's hard to be intimate with someone who hurt you as deeply as he did. I still needed to let some stuff go from our break-up. It's like this accident has shook something up in me because nothing is the way it was before it happened. "Why not, Jason! Babes, we need this, I need to connect with you. Now, you gotta meet me half way, babes," he pleaded. There was concern and sincerity in his eyes that I usually couldn't say no too. But it

didn't work today.

"I'm scared, Gary. I just..." I tried to make a point but was interrupted.

"I gotta take a shower and get ready for work." He let go of me slightly pushing me to the side and got up out of bed. Once he was on his feet, he looked at me while stretching and shook his head. "You on that bullshit. Porn," he said stepping out of his underwear before walking into the bathroom.

"Gary, I'm sorry! I *thought* you and I were talking about something important," I said pissed at his lack of interest in regard to this situation and my feelings.

"No, you were watching and talking about a bullshit reason behind not fucking your man. That's what you were talking about. Fucking scared! The fuck you scared for? I'm your man! Fuckin' woes ya'won' put me thru, no apologies?" he said starting to speak in that Bahamian dialect. I wasn't in the mood for his crabby attitude this morning.

"Really, Gary!" I said grabbing my crutch and sliding myself off of the bed. He was sitting on the toilet. He gave me a courtesy flush when I appeared.

"What ya' want, Jason?" he said tightening his jaw.

"I'm not bringing up the past, but we can go there if you keep it up because I'm not the one who changed the complexion of this relationship from light to dark!" I said really not wanting to argue about this right now. The lack of intimacy I was exhibiting towards him was really starting to take its toll on the relationship. I would clam up whenever he'd touch me. And saying I'm not ready and I'm scared was getting redundant even for me. But my body was scared to respond to him because I'm afraid he'll give me another... STD. Well, now an STI. Like that sounds any better. STI is new like this... new start with Gary. It's scary because he's unfamiliar to me somehow. I snapped out of my thoughts when I realized Gary was responding to me.

"Jason, you hear me, now? Why ya wanna hol' back on my account for? Maybe that will lead to some make-up sex," he said flushing and grabbing a magazine. I took a deep breath to keep calm.

"Gary, can we not fight today?" I asked trying to get him to empathize with me. "I'm going to make you some ham and eggs, okay?" I said trying to diffuse the situation.

"Nope! Make me some head and ass," he said turning the page not even looking up at me. He did that cocky tongue over his teeth suck thing he does. Normally I find it sexy because of the way he tilts his head back slightly and the way his upper lip moves when he does it. Today, however, it plus his good looks pissed me the hell off.

"Really, Gary! Why are you so freakin' selfish?" I said standing there in disbelief. "It's not just about your needs."

"Oh, I'm da selfish one? Yur the da one bein' stingy with the ass and throat, you know," he said. When his accent surfaces, he's pissed, and there is no reasoning with him until he calms down. I tried to bow out gracefully.

"You know what, you are an ass!" I said sucking my teeth and walking out of the bathroom.

"Yup, but not yur's. We'll fix that lil', Daddy!" he said. I decided to ignore his last comment. This definitely wasn't going to get us any further in the relationship. Maybe we needed counseling for this block I was feeling. Lord, now I'm turning into a white woman. I need to talk to my big bro, but I kicked him out of my house. Dang! All of my friends matter of fact.

I sat the crutch up against the wall, climbed back in bed, and decided to work on a poem that had been on my mind. Javi was due to come and pick me up for his grandmother's party around 1:30. I think that would be a welcomed distraction to the stress that was starting to develop between not only Gary and me but me and my friends as well. I didn't even get a chance to talk to him about that.

Gary left not even acknowledging the fact that I was alive. I sat there in bed with the computer on my lap listening to his heavy footsteps pound the stairs. I then heard the front door slam and his truck start and back out of the driveway. The tires chirped as he sped off. I wondered what if I lost him over this. I can't believe we both didn't say anything to one another just now. I sat there dumbfounded. I needed to get over our past issues like yesterday. I just didn't know how. The point in a relationship where you try to remember what it used to be like will sneak up on you without warning. I guess it can eventually push either party into the arms of another to recapture that feeling. I slipped into my thoughts imagining my reaction to the question I just posed. One-minute I was typing intently and the next thing I heard in the midst of pecking keys was Gary calling out my name…

"Jason, what up, boy?" Gary smiled at me.

"Hey, oh, shoot, what's up, Gary? How are you?" I said pasting a quick smile on my face. He leaned in for a hug. I gave a quick shady glance to his lil' date.

"Nothing, boy, bout to go catch that new Saw movie," he said with a large Kool-Aide smile. He was growing his dreds out again.

"Oh really? Yeah, that's what I'm going to see. I heard good things about it," I said glancing over at his date, which just so happened to be my rival and Gary's old boyfriend, Desjardin, of all people through my quick assessment. I concluded dude may have been cute. He was light skinned, had a nice lil' body on him, facial hair, and he was a bit taller than me. He could stand to make an investment in some Orthodontic treatment, though. And a little bump patrol.

"So, this is Jason?" Gary's date proclaimed feigning a smile just like a tired queen would do. I thought to myself, don't try me because I'm always going to have this man's attention, and both of you know it.

"Oh shit, my bad. Desjardin, this is Jason. Jason, this is Desjardin," Gary smiled at me with pride.

"Nice to meet you," I said with a genuine smile. I extended my hand out to him, sensing shade being thrown my way. He looked at my hand as if to say, *Why, bitch?* Duly noted.

"You too," Gary talks about you sometimes. It's nice to put a face with the lame, I mean name," he said with a fake smile. I thought to myself, you know who I am, HOE!

"Oh, really? Well, hopefully he left out the negative stuff? Seeing as how you may not be familiar with many of our American colloquialisms," I said. I was thinking to myself, *this ho wants me to hit him!*

"Of course he did," Desjardin said with an insidious tone of shade.

"You out here waiting for somebody, baby boy?" Gary asked me, breaking up, Mortal Combat: Bottom Edition. He looked even better than I remembered. *What was I thinking letting go of this man?* I thought to myself.

"Oh no, I was about to get some snacks for my date...and me." I replied. I reached up and gently brushed a fragment off of his shirt and adjusted his collar. I could see his lil' date seething in my peripheral. I made sure I rubbed his cheek just enough to remember my touch. The look in his eyes told me all I needed to know. I glanced over at Desjardin and then back at Gary.

"Oh, thanks, well a'ight, that's what's up! You better hurry up baby boy, you gon' miss the opening scene messing with us," Gary winked. Desjardin wrapped his arm around Gary dangling him in my face like, *'BOOM! I got yo' boyfriend, I got yo' man! I GOT EM!'* I wanted too high five that hoe's teeth straight.

"I know right. Don't be jumping and screaming during the bloody parts. You know how you do," I joked.

"I'ma fuck you up! Me no waste man, ya' know?" Gary chuckled. He bit his bottom lip and I smiled knowing I still had him.

"I know," I said noticing Desjardin ice grilling me, further reminding me just like mama used to say how much the common hate the uncommon. I was flirting within reason.

"Well, it was nice bumping into you, Jason. Cute jacket," Desjardin said trying to tie a lasso around this conversation. *This gapped tooth ho is trying it!* Never let a queen who isn't used to having anything see you being fazed. I heard this Mary J. Blige Impersonator named Misty Blue, I knew in my head reminding me:

Family Reunion

"Chocolate Drop, I encourage you to stay the sweetheart you are by placing this word in everything you do. Because it goes a long way and will get you the appropriate attention you deserve from any man. Subtlety. I'm going to give you this little phrase: Subtle is your tea. Remember that, Chocolate Drop." All of a sudden, she was on the stage singing, 'Ring My Bell'. Next thing I knew, my phone chimed several times waking me out of my daydream...

I grabbed my phone and viewed a couple of text messages from Javi. I responded back letting him know that I would be ready to go on time. Just as I was about to sit the phone down, I received a message from Darius. Saying his name in my head echoed causing a shiver to run down my spine. He let me know he was in town and instructed me to be available. I quickly responded with a No doubt and added a smiley face. Maybe seeing him would help me get to the bottom of my feelings concerning him. All of a sudden, my day was a little brighter. I just had to do this favor for Javi real quick.

I jumped up showered, cleaned up, walked the dog, and finished getting dressed just as Javi pulled up. He blew the horn and I grabbed my keys and crutch making my way down to the car. As soon as he pulled off, he confessed that this wasn't his abuela's 75th birthday, but it was his uncle's homecoming party from prison. Her birthday was last weekend. I laughed and told him that at this point it didn't even matter. We engaged in a conversation about family on a cultural level. It was funny because neither of us could relate to what the other was saying.

"Jason, I don't know why I'm nervous. I haven't seen my uncle since senior year of high school. What do I say?"

"All I can tell you is you'll know what to say when you see him. That's your blood. You all at least talk and are close. Come home with me to Detroit, and then you will see what not knowing what to say means," I stated as a matter of fact. I felt like everyone in the family was out to crucify me for liking dudes.

"What are you talking about, papi?" he chuckled. "I always feel like I'm being judged or looked at as

the demon child because I'm gay. I love my family, don't get me wrong, but I feel like an outsider. More so on my dad's side of the family though. They're very religious, so it's like you get beat over the head with scripture before you can say hello," I chuckled. "POW! You didn't say hello in the name of Jesus!" I laughed.

"Jason, I know it ain't that bad, pa?" He said joining in on the laughter.

"Next time I go to Detroit, you're coming with me to meet my abuela, bruh," I said as he laughed. "My grandma always gives me this look like I have something on my face. I don't know. It's like everybody knows I'm gay but won't directly come out and say anything about it, let alone ask me about my life," I said.

"Wait! You suck cock, kid?" Javi asked jokingly. "Who better than you to answer that question," I smiled hitting him in the shoulder.

"I know right! Don't make me pull over," he smiled.

"We don't have time for that right now," I teased. "There's always time for durbin," he said using a

Chicago term for giving head.

"I'm not going to fall into this trap. Keep driving," I smiled fixing my eyes on the road so that I wouldn't think about how phyne he was when he licked them pretty red lips of his.

"I'm just sayin'. A dick in the mouth beats one in the hand. But I digress, finish your story," Javi said.

"Anyway! My mom's side of the family is a little different. You have the pretentious side, and the down to earth side. It's like night and day. But I don't feel prejudged. I always felt uncomfortable when we used to go around my dad's side of the family," We came to a light and I looked out of the window at the basketball court. A few kats from the Monte Carlo car club were playing a game. In Chicago, the Monte Carlo Boys and them Box Chevy boys from the South Side were some of the hottest brothas cruising the city. Preston had the pleasure of actually messing with one of them Monte Carlo Boys. I was trying to see if I saw the car he showed us in the picture when the light turned green.

"Damn, well I'm sorry about that, pa. You alright?" he asked gripping my leg.

"Boy, please, I got over that a long time ago. Them Negroes aren't feeding, freaking, or financing me. You on the other hand will be fine. From what I have observed, your family is close and demonstrates unconditional love. The Blacks could learn a thing or two about family from the Latinos."

"Why you say that?" he asked glancing over at me.

"Because Black folk sweep stuff under the rug so much that we get left behind the power curb on so many things. We don't like to acknowledge and vent and address our issues. It's all about appearances in most Black households. Let's gossip about the issue rather than address it, and we'll ignore it in the name of Jesus. If that ain't using the Lord's name in vain, I don't know what is. I just wish someone would ask me, how my personal relationship with God is going, instead of the nonexistent relationship I'll never develop with a female. If gay is so wrong, what conversations do you think I have with God about me being his creation not mistake," I said feeling good getting that off of my chest.

"You sound bitter," Javi offered as an observation.

"Perhaps, but the image of a black homosexual man is shameful and less revered than that of the dope boy with three illegitimate children he only sees when the baby mama's start tax time ballin'. Black folk put too much stock in appearances. Let's not talk about it. Let's make it look pretty. It's like how the architect of the Civil Rights movement, Bayard Rustin, was not acknowledged simply because he was gay. You know the story," I said waving my hand and taking a breather.

"Yeah, I know it. Jason, we Latinos have our issues

too though. And trust me, having your family know all your business can be frustrating sometimes. Being close-knit has its drawbacks. There are pros and cons to everything. And that's the reality of it," he said shrugging his shoulders.

"But that's not my reality, they think they know all my business, but won't find out from the source. It's too taboo a subject in most Black homes," I said trying to harness my anger.

"So, why not force feed them. Blind them with who you are," Javi said. I thought about what he meant for second and came up with nothing.

"Just how would I do that?" I asked looking at him with curiosity written on my face.

"Just walk through the door holding your man's hand," he said shrugging his shoulders. "You'll be surprised what the element of surprise can stir up." I shrugged it off thinking how crazy that sounded. Hell, maybe it was that simple.

"Anyway, the point is, your uncle is back, and you will know exactly what to say when you see him. Why has it been so long since you've seen him?" I said changing the subject.

"Uncs told me that he wanted me to stop coming down to visit him. He didn't want me to see him locked up anymore. I was seven years old when he told me that. He has this heavy Puerto Rican accent, right," Javi laughed. "He said, 'Papi, I won'ju to think'o this as... my going away on sabbatical. I'm saving my life for ju' papi. This is like rehab, papito. You write me, and I write you.

Don't come back here. It hurts me for you seeing me like this. I won you to be a big boy. You better than this, papito.' Javi chuckled. "I cried for a couple of days thinking he hated me, until mi Abuela explained in her own special way why it was important for me to respect his wishes. I swear we wrote each other weekly. It's going to be good to see him after all this time. Till this day no one tells me why he was locked up. None of us kids know."

"You shouldn't be nervous," I said smiling. I was glad we could still have open dialogue with one another.

"Yeah, it's going to be like seeing him for the first time, pa? Fuck my uncle Julio is back. You know he was the first one I came out to."

"For real?"

"Yeah, even though he told me to stay away from the prison, I begged Mommy to take me down to visit him the summer of '95 when I turned fifteen. I wrote him and told him that I had something to tell him in person and he needed to make an acceptation to his visitation rule. He honored my request and sent word to Mommy to bring me on her next trip down. He had some business to discuss with her first, and then it was my turn. She left so we could talk. I was fidgeting with a piece of paper. You know because I still ain't know what to say, right. Back then, you could sit face to face with them at a table in a room full of guards." Javi laughed. "Uncs reached over and snatched the paper from me. He goes, 'Papi, what you got to tell me. I got like five minutes.' He was smiling. And I just spit it out. Like BLAUU!"

"What was his reaction?" I asked chuckling at his little sound effect.

"He took a deep breath, and then told me that he was the last person to judge anyone. He told me not to deviate from the way God made me. He said he loved me regardless. This big muscle head Boriqua cool with his little sobrino being gay. He told me not to ever be scared to talk to family, and if anybody had a problem with it they deal with him some way somehow."

"That's what's up!" I said. That added strength to my faith that things will change in my favor if I hold on to the dream of both my parents truly being on board with Jason living his own life.

"Yeah, that's what's up. I've always been able to talk to my family about anything after that," he said as we parked the car. We each grabbed a case of Corona from the trunk and made our way inside. The first person to greet us was his grandmother.

"Abuelita. Como estas?" Javi said bear hugging this petite well-seasoned woman.

"Bueno Javier. Come in, papito. Who's your friend?"

"Jason, this is my grandmother Rosita. Abuela, this is Jason."

"Ah, this is him? He's handsome. You picked a beautiful man. Look at those dimples," she gushed. She gave me a hug. "I get a good vibe," she said winking at Javi and releasing me from her embrace. I smiled. "Jason, you call me if he gets out of line."

"Yes, ma'am, I will," I said getting into character. I had a feeling this was going to be an interesting afternoon.

"Don't you ma'am me. Abuela Rosita to you. Okay?"

"Si, Abuela Rosita. Encantada de conocerto." I said. "Ah y tu. Muchos gracias! Javier, I like this one, very nice. You teaching him Spanish?"

"Yes, he's picking it up pretty quickly," Javi winked. "Well, come on take off your coats get comfy. Let's get you something to eat. I made all of Julio's favorites. Carne Frita con Cebolla, Carne Guisada, Arroz con Guandules. Plantains, Flan. It's too much food. You name it, I cook it. Come eat," she said leading us out of the foyer. "Look who I found," she said as we made our way through the living room.

"Where is Uncs hiding?" Javi said looking around. "Oh out there in the back playing dominos.

Gracias a Dios por mantenerlo." She said. She outlined a cross in front of her body in true catholic form. In English she said, thank you God for keeping him.

Everyone was so festive and inviting. I felt very welcomed and was being pulled left and right talking with Javi's cousins and being asked all sorts of questions. Javi's mom walked in with a plate topped with a mountain of food and a drink for me. I told her that this was too much, and she said that I could work it off in the gym later. I laughed as she made it a point to let me know that I would offend her if I didn't eat every bite. It was amazing to see how everyone got along and came together. It reminded me of Thanksgiving and Christmas in Detroit when I was younger.

We would have two sides of family to visit. We would spend time over my granny's home, and then my Grandma's house. All of my cousins would be eating at the children's table eavesdropping on the adults. My cousin Kesha and I were the same age. We'd often imitate the adults by talking about things that we overheard our mothers and aunts saying on the phone to each other. We would then disappear somewhere in the house and talk until later when it was time to go to the basement and listen to our aunts and uncles reminisce about their childhood, past whoopings, and tall tales. The old 45's would be pulled out, and we'd hear the sounds of Al Green, the Stylistics', Bettie Wright, Ashford and Simpson and the like.

Those old folk would dance, play cards, and have the kids showing Granny and Grandpa the latest dances. My uncle Charles would give me his video camera, and we'd all take turns getting our five minutes of fame. Ah good times. This get-together made me miss how my family used to be when all of us lived in one city. Now we're spread about the country and seem to only come together during times of bereavement. Javier was definitely blessed to have this in his adulthood. It's a wonderful feeling and blessing when you have your whole family on one accord and in your corner, especially when it's not a lie.

I was able to sneak away to use the restroom. Afterwards, I walked around to see if I could find Javi. He was in the formal living room staring at an 8x9 photo encased within a beautiful ornate silver frame. He was studying it intently. The photo revealed the image of a beautiful younger looking lady with long straight dark hair, full painted lips, perfectly arched eyebrows, light-brown eyes, and a seductive smile. Her body was swath in a tailor made form fitted violet dress. She had one hand on her hip with the other at her side. She was standing in front of the same fireplace that Javi was facing.

"She's beautiful," I said. I placed my hand on the small of his back and stood next to him. This seemed to startle him.

"I didn't hear you come in, pa," he said glancing at me.

"I didn't mean to scare you. My bad," I smiled ready to tease him.

"Oh no it's all good kid," he said trying to smile. "So who is she? I don't see her at the party," I
smiled.

"I don't know, Jason, this is the first time I've seen this picture," he was really studying the photo.

"Oh, really?" I said quietly observing how lost he looked at that point.

"Yeah, but I see myself in her smile. And she has the same mark over her eyebrow as me," he said touching and studying the photo.

"That could be something in the picture. May I?" I asked extending my hand out. I looked at him as he handed the picture to me. I took a close look to investigate what he'd observed.

"You see it too, don't you?" He asked almost immediately.

"I do see what you're talking about. She does have the same mark," I said thinking maybe she was his long lost sister or something.

"Not just the mark, the resemblance. We have the same eyes. I'm the only one in the family with light brown eyes like this."

"Maybe that's you in drag. I mean you and Jerome are best friends," I laughed. Javi didn't find this humorous. I switched back into serious mode.

"Something's weird about this, Jason," he said as his Uncle Julio walked in.

"Fellas, what's going on? Did you find the gift?" Julio said putting his arms around both of us.

"Oh yeah, I sat it on the table. Uncs, who is this woman? I've never seen this picture before at Abuela's house."

"You probably just overlooked this one, papito. No big deal," His uncle kind of looked at both of us and tried to hide the uneasiness in his gaze.

"Maybe, but that doesn't answer the question Uncs," Javi said standing his ground. He had an intense look on his face. He was determined to get answers to the questions in his head.

"It doesn't matter, cabron. She's an old family

member; let's go grab a beer, ay? Play a little dominos," He was trying to change the subject and avoid a confrontation. He looked at me hoping I would help him deflect because Javi wasn't backing down.

"I have her eyes, Uncs, and this scar. Look!" Javi said pointing at the picture. Julio backed away from us. He rubbed his face with his hand.

"Let's go party Javier, we talk about dat later, papi." he said in a firm voice. He started to walk out of the room.

"Uncs! What's the big deal, I'm just asking who she is. Why are you avoiding the question?" Javi replied in just as firm a voice. Julio stopped at the entrance.

"GODDAMMIT! Javier! Ella es su Madre!" he said punching the wall. He turned to look at us. Javi started shaking his head.

"Mi Madre? Que quiere decir?" Javi said.

"Justo lo que dijo. Ella es su madre, y yo no soy tu tio. Yo soy...tu...tu padre. You're my son," his voice cracked on the last statement. He looked up at Javi with tears in his eyes. "That's your real mother. I put that picture up today when I got home."

"This is my mother, which means...wait I'm not hearing this. This is fucked up. How can you be my dad? What the fuck do you mean you're my dad?"

"Miro tu boca y el tono," Julio said.

"Forget about my tone! How is this all possible?"
"Mira! Ju were young papito! I was going to Ju didn't need to know why. Ju wouldn't understand. I wanted you to grow up with a normal upbringing."

Family Reunion

"So you lied to me? All this time, you knew you were my dad, and you just let me go through life thinking you were my uncle. So Paula is my Aunt? Explain it to me. Why lie?" Javi said. I was stuck in the middle. I didn't know whether to leave the room or stay there for Javi's sake. I was mortified. Paula, Javier's quote unquote mother walked in.

"What's all the yelling about?" she asked. "Julio, what's wrong?"

"Believe me, I wanted to tell you so many times. I didn't want you taking on my mistakes. So I lie. Your mother was strung out papito. She kept using fucking heroin. I tried to save her... I loved her... things were fine when you were born, she cleaned herself up, she was getting back on track. I was working, she was home with you. Taking care of the house. We were a family. Mi familia bonita. I come home from work one day. I had been calling and calling. She had every light in the house on. The TV was loud. You were sitting in front of it with a box of cereal. I remember picking you up in my arms, wondering where your mother went to. I walked into the kitchen. The bedroom. Finally, the bathroom. There she was. My angel... needle in her fucking arm... sitting on the toilet. She OD'ed Javier. Your mother left us... I tried to revive her... she was so cold... and lifeless... I held her... rocking her... I called for help... but it was too late for her... I will never forget that night. I knew exactly who she was getting that shit from. I grabbed the steel and walked the street until I found him and his punk ass friend. I killed

110

that fucker. Pulled out my piece and shot him in the streets like the piece of shit he was. I ran after his partner. I pistol-whipped him within an inch of his life. That's why I went to prison. Those motherfuckers showed me no love. I lost everything, Javier. I was ashamed. I couldn't tell you, my son the truth. I'm a killer. That's not the example I wanted for you. I didn't want you to know your mother... that beautiful sweet woman... was a junkie. I sorry, Javier," Julio said with such sincerity and hurt in his voice.

"Javier. I'm sorry," Paula said crying. She walked over to try and console Javi. He was breathing heavy and displayed no emotion. I don't think he knew how to process what he'd just heard.

"Don't touch me," he said backing away from Paula. "Let's go, Jason."

"Javier, por favor espere! Please!" Paula pleaded.

Javi snatched the picture out of his father's hand and stormed out of the room and made his way to the foyer. He rambled through the closet and grabbed our coats. He grabbed the keys out of his coat pocket, tucked the picture under his arm, and he made his way toward the car. His grandmother and cousin Roberto came to investigate. They asked me what had happened. I hugged his grandmother and thanked her for having me. I heard Javi scream my name demanding that I come outside and get in the car. I abruptly made a b-line out the door. I shuffled as quickly as I could over to the car in spite of my injuries and got in. Javi sped off, cursing in Spanish. He didn't say anything to me and I didn't know what to say to him to console him. I didn't know what would be appropriate to say. I knew that if he needed to talk, then I would definitely be there. He pulled in front of my house.

"Javi you want to at least..." I asked before he raised his hand and interrupted me.

"Jason, I just need to be by myself for tonight at least. I'll call you in the morning, pa. Thank you for doing me this favor, okay?" He looked over at me and tried to smile. "I'll talk to you later." I didn't say a word. I just nodded my head and gave his hand a squeeze. I opened the door and made my exit. I watched him put the car in gear and drive off into the night. If I felt helpless, I couldn't imagine how he felt. It's amazing how someone else's life can look so much better than yours, until you start looking behind the curtain. I guess my family situation wasn't as bad as I thought. You never know the problems of others you wish to be or the lives they live. The cost to be in someone else's shoes could be more than you're willing to pay...

Paint by Numbers

"It's open, bruh! Slide the door hard to the right," I heard Rocwell yell through the enclosure.

I took a deep breath then slid the door open as directed and closed it behind me. I walked into the huge loft and noticed all of the various pieces of artwork he had either on an easel or hanging on his walls. He even had dozens of his work leaning against the wall in stacks of seven. His place was pretty inviting and very artsy. It looked like a very eclectic and abstract art gallery in the making.

I was mesmerized by the powerful images depicted in his work. There were all types of emotions conveyed on each canvass. I came to a painting of words on a canvass with a gold background. The words were very familiar to me, and I realized it was one of my own poems. My eyes rested on his and I was a little embarrassed for greeting the artwork before I greeted him. He was standing there staring at me with a paintbrush protruding from his mouth, and a jar of yellow paint in his hand. I waved at him and smiled without disguising my embarrassment.

He gave me a sinister grin as he sat the paint down on a TV table. He placed the paintbrush into a tin of fresh water. I couldn't move. I just observed him and took in his natural beauty. He was a sexy dude carrying a physique that hours at the gym could not match. He walked over to me and without saying a word, took my coat off, and threw it on the couch. He then turned me around by the shoulders and lowered his mouth to my ear.

"Do those words look familiar to you, shorty?" he asked in that sexy New York accent. I shook my head yes. "Yeah, they should, huh? I heard you spit that in DC last year. I personally thought it was amazing. Somehow I remembered every single word."

"I don't know what to say," I smiled.

"Speak what's painted," he said. He moved in closer to me. "I'm the audience." I debated on whether to relax and move into him or not. The thought was tempting.

"You're pretty close to be an audience," I said taking in his warmth. I decided to relax just a little bit.

"Think of me as an intimate setting," he said as he widened his stance and wrapped his arms around me. "Let me hear it." I closed my eyes and held his arms in my hands. I took a deep breath and was relaxed by his fragrant cologne and the tightness of his embrace.

Okay,
So first you knew my name,
But didn't know me.
Carrying on like nothing's wrong.
Lost some place between the notes of some break up
to make up song, Kind of confused, When all this time you were my muse,

Paint by Numbers

But we chose to sit there used. Not letting guards
down,
In fear of feelings being abused. But like you said,
We earned each other.
We had to go through that to appreciate the
blessings we are to one another.
A secret petition of the heart,
Exposing antiquated guilt of two black men
foolishly in love from the start.
Rearranging some plot thickened and placed in a
Hughes or Nugent piece,
Of black gay love handed out in the open as
personified
Indulging Kindred Spirits removing the ribbons off
each as
Gifts.
How sweet you are the sugar of my shaft.
The rigid cane they fear from men whose backs they
tried to
Bend and break globally over fathoms deep fudge
packed forward and aft.
Black male love a rocky surface of fluid intensity
with me your compass and you my raft.
Funny how I never thought about or even cared if
they'd laugh.
I'm seeing there is more to you than I could have
ever imagined.
We similar in so many respects yet too different.
You so dope adding fresh colors to my
kaleidoscope,

So that the artist in me can type away about the vivid,
Romanticized view of the world I see and again believe in.
Dare to dream in because now I can be your muse as well,
I'm just hoping you can still love me behind the fail...

"My man. Damn, thank you, Jason," he released me from his embrace. I could still feel his presence wrapped around me. It felt so right, yet I knew I was wrong for letting him invade my space like that.

"You're welcome. How in the world did you remember each word like that, and what made you do this? I'm speechless," I said not taking my eyes off of the painting.

"I was attracted to you and moved by it. I didn't get a chance to step to you in DC, so this was my way of keeping the memory of you alive."

"Damn," I smiled shaking my head. "I shouldn't be here dude."

"Do you want to be here?" he asked. I looked out of the window and then at the door.

"I do, but..."

"Then get comfortable," he said. I walked over to the space he was working in.

"I'm doing a sketch of a mural in my head for my homeboy. He owns this trendy coffee shop up top for the young black urbanite. It's going to be sort of an ode to hip-hop through the years since NY is the birthplace of true hip-hop."

"Sounds nice. I'm liking it so far." I said observing what he'd painted.

"You know how to stroke the canvass?" he asked seductively.

"Umm, I haven't painted since junior high I think," I chuckled.

"It's not hard. Grab this and I'll guide you," he said placing a paintbrush into my hand. Once again, he got behind me, wrapping one arm around my torso. He encircled my right hand within his. We dabbed a little paint onto the bristles. He then lowered his mouth to my ear. "Now. Relax. Think of the canvass as the skin of someone you have a strong desire for. The paintbrush becomes an extension of your fingertips. You stroke the silhouette ever so gently in some areas and apply firm steady pressure in others. You feel that? You know how to make love, don't you?" He quietly said with that New York growl.

"Yeah, I do," I said trying to control my smile and erection.

"Good. Then that means you're going to do it right. That's all you, don. You like how that feels?"

"Yeah, I do. So how long have you been seducing, I mean painting?" I said with a chuckle.

"Better question? What's going on in your relationship?"

Those words echoed in my head waking me out of

my slumber. *That was a hell of a dream*, I thought as I rubbed my eyes and looked at the clock. It was 12:17 in the morning. Batman came trotting into my room whimpering for me to let him outside. I grabbed my phone and put on my glasses. Batman followed me down the stairs as I made my way to the front door. I strapped him into his doggy harness, threw on a coat, grabbed a plastic sandwich bag and headed out the door.

I went through my phone to see if I had any messages from Javi. Nothing yet. There were a few texts from both Shawn and Michael, which I didn't read but deleted instead. I tried to call and speak with Javi, but the phone went straight to voicemail. I checked the phone logs again observing that I hadn't received a call or text from Gary. He was really acting childish, so I decided to boss up and reach out to him. It too went straight to voicemail. I left a message for him to call me back and let him know that he was on the brain. I walked the dog around the block a couple of times before heading home. I discarded the sandwich bag of Batman's excrement into the dumpster and wheeled it out to the curb as a bright yellow sports car with the latest hip-hop jam on 100 decibels sped up into my driveway. I immediately knew who it was. The man got out of the car and Batman ran over to him jumping up and down like he was his owner.

"You gon' let the dog show your boy more love than you?" he said picking Batman up and walking over towards me. I was so happy to see him and dropped my crutch as he scooped me up with one arm and kissed my cheek. He had on his uniform and looked sexier than a mug! After we hugged, he picked my crutch up and handed it to me and then grabbed a bag out of the trunk and helped me get situated.

"Ewww, don't be bringing your bust down bag in my house," I said smiling. And what you doing in uniform this time of night? And I know you ain't rock them crisp Air Force One's across my Quarterdeck shipmate?!"

"Shut up, fool. I had to go check in and pick up some things. I threw these on, on the Drive. Damn, it's so good to see you, Jason. I really needed to see my boy tonight," he took a pause to look at me. It made me blush a little bit.

"It's really good to see you too. I've been looking forward to it," I worried about him so much when he was deployed. Every time I got a chance to see him in one piece, smiling and walking erect in his right mind, I could rest easier at night.

"When did you get this? It's definitely you," I said shaking my head yet admiring the car.

"This my Chi-town whip. I bought it in Cali right before we flew out and had it shipped to my dad's house. So I can have my own shit to drive when I'm home. You like?" he asked rifling through a folder in the seat.

"Of course this is pretty nice, Dee! This is that car from the X-Men movie. That Mazda RX-8, right?" I said admiring the car.

"He may be a fag boy, but he know his cars. It's a stick so I'll let you drive it later," he said looking at me and winking.

"Shut up, punk! What's in the bag?" I asked. He closed the door and walked into the house with me.

"I brought us a couple of Jew Town polishes, the fat body shrimp from that Greek spot you like on Clybourne Ave. I sampled one on the way here. They taste so fresh. I got a gallon of MiMi's fyre sweet green tea, and some of that Kush from So Cal! And I know you got the junk food happenin', so we straight!" Darius said sitting his bag on the kitchen table. He walked over to the sink and washed his hands. I opened a bottle of water and poured some into the dog's dish and sat my coat over a chair.

"Aren't you scared to pop on a piss test?" I asked smiling looking at him sniffing the container of weed. The scent hit me long before he even got the top open. I was glad to see him but trying to conceal my excitement for some reason. Maybe I was feeling guilty about what I was feeling for him. He looked so good with his dark chocolate self. He looked like he had gained a little more muscle mass since the last time I saw him. He was still a gym rat.

"I'm in charge of Urinalysis for the unit. So I ain't worried. You gon' smoke with yo' boy?" he said grinding up the weed. "Whew! This is the care package to end all care packages Jaws! Sitting three boxes down from CO's secondary mailbox. Nigga, this gon' be good!" Darius said with enthusiasm.

Paint by Numbers

"I'm scared of that stuff Dee, I don't know about this," I said laughing. I really wanted to try it out to see what the hype was about.

"Don't protest; smoke with your boy, I got you, this is going to ease any tension you may be feeling right now. *It's me, Jason,* come on," he said stretching his arms out. "I need you right now. You have no idea how much." He looked at me with that look of sincerity that he knew I couldn't say no to. Even I was not exempt from his charm.

"I'm down," I said offering Darius a light smile. His face lit up like a Christmas tree. It was something about the way he said, it's me, Jason, that really resonated with me.

"That's my baby boy right there, come on let's go into the living room, I'm gon' light this incense and we can get you relaxed. Ain't nothing like a chest full of weed. We 'bout to get down on this Geedunk and get these sea stories poppin' like we some old salts in the Chiefs Mess back in the day! You do remember how to be a Sailor there HM2?! Right?"

"Yeah, I remember. When you cross the Equator, come holler at me shipmate, I got the tea and glasses," I said as I walked right behind him referencing my stint onboard a ship when I was stationed in Okinawa, Japan. It's something I really don't get a chance to talk much about. Some days I missed the uniform and using all the terms and lingo.

Darius went from start to finish initiating me into club 420. We got comfortable by one another on the couch, smoking, eating the food, and laughing about random crap we've been through while Do or Die blessed us with that Midwest flow in the background. I couldn't believe I was smoking *weed*. It was a much different feeling than alcohol and it made me feel so free and relaxed. My head felt as if it was floating and I could feel a peaceful smile on my face with a slight tingle tickling the base of my skull. The thick smoke filled my lungs in a way that fresh oxygen never did. All of my senses were on ten joining hands with the vibrations and sounds coming from the music playing. I started laughing as Darius shared a story with me about a restaurant he visited in Dubai...

"Darius, I mean what did you expect? You can't always get what you want boo!" I laughed. I took a small hit of the blunt he rolled.

"Jay, I expect and demand to be accommodated as I see fit," he chuckled rubbing his beard. "Bottom line! Period!"

"That's because you're spoiled! You weren't in Chicago proper. How the hell are you going to demand bacon...?" I burst into laughter. "It's a Muslim country, fool!"

"Jay, we were in Dubai, I figured as an American, I'd be able to get a few slices with my fuckin' pancakes. I was so pissed. What real man do you know eats turkey bacon? That's like eating a fuckin' turkey burger! The fuck..." he laughed taking the blunt from me.

"I do," I said raising my hand trying to sound serious narrowing my eyes letting out a giggle in the process.

"That's because you're one of them white black boys. Ol' Chicago proper white washed face ass," he said taking a puff. "That ain't real bacon, fool. It's one of them white boy tricks to experiment with cancer research later. It's a conspiracy. I'm telling you, Jaws!" It was cute hearing him trying to kick knowledge to me. But I didn't want to be serious right now.

"Have you tried it? You want me to fry you up some now," I smiled.

"Hell naw, if it ain't pork, it don't belong on my fork," he coughed before we both laughed. I shook my head as he looked over at me passing the piff in the process. "Yo' lame ass probably put the turkey bacon on your turkey burger, don't you?!" He said bursting into laughter.

"Anyway fool!" I said cackling and coughing up smoke at the same time. I was guilty, and I had just given myself away by that statement.

"You are such a white boy! I knew it! Give me the blunt, back; I'm stealing two of your pulls! Because that's that bullshit, right there," he said trying to sing it in a song.

"Darius!" I paused and looked over at him.

"What up, doe?!" He said giving me the nod and a smile.

"Shut up. I must say this... I commend you dude, I mean, yo'," I said exhaling and handing off to him. "Not many brothas would do what you are doing. I'm proud of you, man," I said giggling at how he wrapped his lips around the blunt when he took a pull. "Don't be laughing at me, nigga," he cheesed.

"Ol' new smoke to the dome face ass!"

"Your old wanna be ghetto baby out of…um…baby out of…" I said snapping my fingers trying to get the phrase off the tip of my tongue.

"Wedlock, nigga! Wedlock!" he laughed. I took a second to think and then responded.

"Hell yeah! Wedlock! Baby out of wedlock! Dang! I need to stop smoking weed, Dee," I said as we both laughed so hard we bumped heads.

"Ouch! Watch where you fling that big ol' blond Flintstone head face ass of yours," he joked. I took another pull and passed off to him.

"Yo' mammy!" I said.

"Hey, watch it, new smoke! You only get one of those a year. Real talk!" he said trying to sound serious. I gave him a look that exuded the phrase, Negro, please! He started laughing once he glanced over at me causing me to laugh as well. I then cleared my throat and raised my right index finger.

"You only get one of those a year. I'm Bill Bacon, rejecting turkey bacon with Real Talk, ABC hickory flavored news, signing off!" I said imitating Jonathan Capehart and rendering a hand salute! He died laughing. "Was that how I sounded?" he said putting the blunt into the ashtray. He sat back on the couch.

"Hell, yes, that's how you sounded," I said pushing him on the shoulder.

"That's some dog ass shit!" he laughed. "That must

124

be on channel 420," he laughed as I snickered. He looked over at me and wet his lips. His face caught the light making him appear to be in high definition. "So check this out."

"You know I didn't mean anything by that punk! So what's up?" I said noticing something in his eyes I hadn't seen before. He unlocked some feelings in me that I had only dreamed about. He felt like reality in my dreams and now he was here in the flesh. Suddenly this felt right. Plus, being high felt awesome. Hell, maybe it was the weed.

The future involves so much guesswork, my dude. I'm not so sure I can be like my dad, Jason," he said looking over at the table.

"I think about that from time to time. But listen, did he ask you to be like him, Darius?" I asked. I had a strong desire to rub his face because he looked like a scared little boy, but I refrained.

"Damn!" He took a minute to think and rubbed his beard. No, he didn't," he said looking back at me.

"You are the first son I've heard that wanted to be exactly like their dad, but who's dad doesn't expect him to. I don't know how that feels. Because I used to want to be exactly like my dad, but when I found out I had to eat pussy as a prerequisite, welllllll…" I said as we broke out into laughter.

"You a fool, Jay!" Darius said shaking his head. "No, but for real. I didn't like or desire women like

he did. Things changed. I couldn't even relate to him as a man because we both couldn't get around the sexuality issue, therefore I knew I couldn't live up to being what he wanted me to be because I wasn't him and I am not who he thought I was going to be. I can only be Jason without fail," I paused and glanced over at him. He seemed to be pondering what I was saying. "Was that too much?" I chuckled.

"Naw, I totally get what you're sayin'. You always got an honest answer for me. I've always appreciated you for that," he smiled and gave my cheek a rub with his hand. His thumb grazed my lip before he returned his hand to his side of the couch. "Yeah, but it comes down to this being a choice though, right?"

"The only choice we have in this is whether or not to let this portion of God's reflection in us shine through or let them extinguish it. We only get one shot at this. Shoood! I'm going to live out the complete life He gave me. You gotta agree with me on that?" I said folding my arms. "And hopefully I'll be with the one," I said wishing I could have retracted that statement. In that moment, my jam 'Get It Wet' by Do or Die came on and hearing that beat drop had me feeling that way.

"When you expect your man to be home?" he asked not breaking eye contact with me.

"This is my house, so I don't know when he'll be here. He hasn't called to check on me all day," I said glancing over at my phone. Darius needs to stop asking the right questions 'cause he gon' get what he wants.

"Damn, I hear that. You all right?" he asked leaning back on the sofa.

"Yeah, we got into a fight about why I won't have

sex with him," I said as Darius burst into deep hearty laughter. He brought his fist up to his mouth and raised his knee in the air and everything. I looked at him in disbelief but couldn't help but laugh myself. "I shouldn't have said that."

"Nigga! Is he serious right now? Clown! That's because you don't belong to his lame ass." When he said that, something inside me nodding yes in agreement blew my mind. I stood up.

"What made you say that?" I said, for certain I would be more scared of the verbal answer than I was of the thought. He sat there and propped his foot on the table.

"Can't you tell?" he said.

"I'm tired of going through this with you," I said sucking my teeth. A flood of courage broke through me. "Will you stop playing charades as it relates to something you say about you and I. Just this one time! For me! PLEASE!" I said folding my arms. My heart and adrenaline were pumping now. And the effects the marijuana had on me were strong, but I was still aware of my surroundings and had control of my own faculties.

"I'm jealous of him because he has something that belongs to me, Jason. He's borrowing you and I can't stand to see it anymore."

"Darius, what are you talking about?" I said. The thoughts and questions in my head were piling up like Tetris as I tried to figure out what was going on.

"To answer your question if I agree, all I can tell you

is this. Homosexuality is linked to Him spiritually just as heterosexuality is. Homosexuality more so because we have to depend on Him more for protection just for being brave enough to be who we are. A straight boy takes that for granted and probably will never even think about it or know God the way in which we do. Shit, I've met some legit pastors and bishops both gay and straight who are actually real about Kingdom business," he said going off on this weird tangent.

"Darius, I don't get where all this is coming from?" I asked rubbing my head.

"This trip is to remind you that he's only borrowing you. That nigga is practice for you until I get this shit figured out for the two of us. Be ready when I come back to take you home, Jason."

"Darius, all you gotta do is..." I said before he stopped me in mid-sentence.

"All I gotta do is WHAT?!" Darius said jumping up in my face. His muscles were flexing causing my dick to jump. "Do WHAT, Jason?! I fucked up and let you off the leash, but you know damn well who to come home too, Jason! Don't you?" he said nodding his head and stretching his arms out. He was literally a fists distance from my face.

"What...? Let me off of... what the hell does that even mean?" I said staring up at him in utter oblivion. I stood my ground not sure what these urges were erupting in my body. I felt most of this energy surging within the confines of my underwear.

"All that shit talking! Shit! I know how you feel! Let

me come to terms with how I feel! Quit talking!" he said as I looked down and noticed that he started to unbuckle his belt and was unfastening his jeans in one swift motion with his right hand. He took his other hand and gripped my head with a firm mind crippling clench. My jaw dropped when I saw him reach into his pants and pull out that beautiful dark dick. He then maneuvers the front of the striped forest green underwear up under his massive balls.

"This is how I feel! Fuck it!" He yelled pulling my body closer to his.

My body responded in a way that cannot be described once Darius's lips came in contact with mine. All I know is the urges raging throughout my body caused me to disrespect my first mind. My heart and my ass were in trouble and were about to get a serious beat down. I gripped his head tightly as we kissed devouring one another in a way that was out of this fucking world. It was overflowing with chemistry, with rhythm, causing me to mentally prepare for him to redeem his prize. He tilted his head side to side kissing me with confidence. Our lips skillfully massaged their opponents as our tongues glided along playing tag with one another. Our bodies melded together with Teutonic precision. I loved the way it felt like we were supposed to be doing this. Hell, it felt like we were supposed to have done this a long time ago. Every flashback in my head of being intimate with him felt like and became reality in that moment.

The more we kissed, the more he kept reaching

into my jeans gripping and roughly caressing my ass. He ripped open the shirt I was wearing exposing my bear chest. In the middle of kissing, he slipped his middle finger into my mouth allowing me to wet it. He then reached back into my jeans to grip my ass securing me close to him with minimal strength. He bends down to suck, lick, and kiss my nipples while simultaneously rubbing and piercing my tight willing hole with his moist middle finger marking the spot he wanted to drill. I gripped his hard biceps and with all of my strength pushed him onto the couch. He had a sly smile on his face as he lie biting his lip before slipping that same middle finger into his mouth. I tore off what was left of the shirt he destroyed. He removed his shirt, as well as his navy trousers and socks exposing an expertly chiseled body from pedal to crown. I let my jeans fall to the floor and he slid my underwear down and laid back to observe me. I slid my hand across my chest, stepped out of my garments and zeroed in on my target. I fell to my knees to grip his thick dick in the warm safe care of my hands.

I cupped and massaged his balls with my hand, then wet my lips before bringing them to rest on the tip of his dick. I licked my lips again relishing in the taste of his precum. I looked him in the eyes, winked, and took him into my mouth slowly getting the shaft nice and wet for what I was about to put on this dude. He had a sexy grin on his face as he bit his bottom lip. I closed my eyes and heard him demand I suck his dick before gripping the back of my head. I withdrew his dick from my mouth circling the head with my tongue making his body shake. I told him I got this and held his hands down before bending down, sucking him back into my mouth, and clocking in on yet another thing I do very well. In the middle of my zone, he yelled out, "Damn nigga! That tongue trick is what I been missing?! FUCK!" he said as if we'd done this before. He pulled me off of his dick before sitting up to kiss me. "Jason, you can't give that lame ass mothafucka this premium head game NO MORE!! That shit's mine!" he said before kissing me again. "You hear me? It's mine!" he said as he gripped my ass tightly.

He stood me up and we kissed feverously. He moved behind me and pulled me into him maneuvering his dick between my legs with one quick stroke. He kissed and sucked on my neck before bending me over and lowering himself down to my ass. He went in for the kill working his tongue and moist flavor into my center. He playfully bit and sucked each cheek causing me to go crazy. It felt so good I started to ride his face wanting this sensation to never end. He worked his tongue so damn good that I shot three healthy streams of life all over the couch. He rubbed my body down allowing me a few moments to enjoy my release.

As he gripped my waist, he kissed my neck distracting me as he slid his rigid dick deep within the cozy confines of my body. His touch and the way he knew what my body needed at every given moment felt so familiar to me. This was beyond passionate lovemaking. It was something so celestial I had to have done this with him before. I rode his dick like it belonged to me, and he drilled my ass like the heavy duty machines found at Ace Hardware as he whispered in my ear...

"It's always been mine. Ain't nobody but me beating them drums from here on out. You hear me?"

"Yes," I moaned. "Nobody, you hear me?"

"YES!" I moaned loader. He clinched my body tightly against his, grabbing my head turning my face towards his. His muffled throaty war cry intensified as his soldiers invaded the territory his love muscle deeply carved a space for filling me up with a warm silky essence. We collapsed on the couch, our bodies sweaty, hot, and writhing in ecstasy. I suddenly knew who Darius was to me...

Gary and Darius Cross Paths

Damn, I just dicked Jason down. I want to say... we made love, but two men fuck, we can't make love. That shit was... fucking incredible. I mean unlike anything I've experienced with one of my dames. Damn, I still got my dick in this nigga, and he feel so good wrapped in my arms. What am I doing? This can't be what I've been missing; this can't be right. I mean I've got it in with a few kats but this right here.

I looked at Jason and pulled him in tighter and realized I was still high and needed to calm my mind down so that I could get my thoughts together. I needed an exit strategy. Damn, I wonder how he's feeling. This shit is wrong yo'; he fucking up my dream man. I'm a military man. *Dee! Dee! Dee! Shut the fuck up man! Calm down, bruh!* I told myself. *Yo' chill out and see how this really feels for a minute and enjoy it.* In my head it's wrong, but this shit feels so right. I just had sex with my boy... Jason!

I felt all right once I got control of my thoughts. I relaxed a little and sat up to take a few hits of the herb. Jason maneuvered his head in my lap and looked up at me with them big brown eyes he uses to manipulate me with. I handed the blunt to him and he shook his head no. He had this satisfied look on his face. I hadn't planned on this happening. I had to get up out of there. This was a lot to deal with right now as I thought about Cindy and the baby. I needed to figure this shit out and I couldn't do that laying up with this dude tonight.

I kissed him on the lips, and it felt so good. I shook it off and got up to get dressed and gather up my shit. I packed my bag up and told Jason I'd get at him. It was around 2:30 in the morning when I stepped outside the door. I saw a truck that looked familiar drive by and park. Whoever it was turned the lights off and didn't get out. I was too high to figure out why the truck looked familiar to me.

I got in my ride, backed out of Jason's driveway, and made my way past the truck that had parked. I leaned and looked over and realized that it was Jason's ex. Damn, it was well into booty call hours and I hoped to God I ain't just get that boy into some shit. A part of me wanted to turn around and make sure shit was cool, but instead I just kept driving because my head was all over the place right now based on what just went down.

Damn, how am I going to be a father to my baby girl when I... like... I can't even say it tonight. I quickly turned on the radio to avert my thoughts from consuming me. Damn! And that nigga saw me leaving his crib, and my ol' bogus ass should at least go and see about Jason real quick. Damn...

After this shift, I gotta go and see about Jason. Lately I've been a real asshole to babes. I don't know if it was because he went home to visit his mama for Christmas leaving me to fend for myself, or the fact that I still wasn't getting no ass. I guess I could be a little more understanding but jacking off just don't do it for me. I didn't have to yell at him and say the nasty shit that I said to him, but he pissed me off. Damn, how I sound? If I was him, I'd probably say fuck you too.

I'm sure he'll come around, I just need to approach it from a different angle, and once I get it in that angle, I'm wearing it out! He gon' remember who daddy is. I rubbed my face with my hands and took a sip of the coffee that had now turned warm. I needed some action on the job and at home. There hasn't been a fire in the city in a few weeks now. I'm tempted to go and start one just to have something to do.

I grabbed my mug and got up from my desk to go and see if any of the other overnighters were up. I walked into the galley and Schneider was frying up some eggs and sausage. I nodded to him and poured myself a cup of Joe.

"Long day Lieutenant?" Schneider asked? He scooped the eggs out of the frying pan onto a paper plate.

"Just gotta get used to nights again, that's all. When you make rank, you start over in some respects, so I'm paying my dues." I said adding creamer to my coffee. Schneider was the youngest guy on my crew. I was glad the fellas finally stopped hazing his ass. He took it like a gee though. I remember them days. As an officer I couldn't participate in such fun anymore.

I had at least 11 years on him and I wanted to take him under my wing because he has the heart for the job and the potential to be a good Ladder man. And that's what my station specializes in, the monkey bars.

Gary and Darius Cross Paths

We operate the best Ladders in the city. I've loved these trucks since I was a kid and my dad let me do a ride a long through the city with him. It was amazing how he made that long red truck whip in and out of traffic like a small hatchback.

"I understand that. It's been kind of dry lately. Is this normal for this time of year? Or period?" He asked. He held up the plate of eggs offering me some. I declined, and he started fixing a plate. I sipped my coffee, shook my head no, and grabbed the remote to turn up the news.

"Nothing is really normal when it comes to a fire happening. So all I can say for now is some weeks we're hot and some we're not, young'un," I wished I would have said something a little more motivating, but I decided I didn't feel like talking. I think he got the hint and ate his food in silence.

I was becoming a zombie just staring at the TV, so I decided to work out since nothing was going on around the station. I couldn't take my mind off of my issues at home, and that was not a good place to be. I needed to come up with a quick fix to solve this problem, and I think I know just what to do to get it poppin'. I made a mental note to hit the West side after work. Maybe choppin' it up with my little brother Timothy's knucklehead friend over the holidays about being a fire fighter would pay off tonight.

My Captain came in and let me cut out early. A part of me wanted to stay, so I slow poked around for a little while, made a call to the West side connect and cut out.

Gary and Darius Cross Paths

I wanted to call Jason, or at least answer one of his many text from the day, but I was still pissed at him, so I wanted him to sweat and miss me for a change. As soon as I see his face though, I'm going to be all right, and the shit we beefin' about won't really matter. As soon as I handled biz out West, I took a slow ride to my spot to shower and relax while I got my plan together to make my move tonight. How the fuck was I going to do this, I thought, as I remembered I needed to find a liquor store.

I took a shower and shaved and dried off before walking into my bedroom. I laid across my bed naked and grabbed my dick. I pictured what it was going to feel like with Jason wrapped around my shit. I started to get hard as I dozed off for a few minutes thinking about it.

My phone rang waking me up from my nap. I checked the time and reached for my phone. It was someone calling from an unknown number. I sent them to voicemail and stood up to stretch. I grabbed the bottle of lotion off of the nightstand and started to rub it over my body starting with my feet. I looked myself in the mirror on the dresser and took a close evaluation of my muscle tone. All this stress was making me lose weight. I couldn't be losing size. I opened a drawer and grabbed some underwear and put them on. I put some deodorant on, sprayed some of Jason's favorite cologne on my chest and put on a wife beater and sweats. Yup! The bust down uniform.

I grabbed my coat and keys and bag of tricks and

headed to the truck. I took a deep breath and headed to the liquor store and then to Jason's house. I was all smiles when I turned down his street until I noticed this yellow sports car in his driveway. None of his friends have a car like that, and these are certainly booty call hours, so something wasn't right about this shit right here. I had to be on the wrong street, maybe; just maybe, this is not his block I said as I stopped in front of the house.

I pulled off, getting pissed at the thought of another nigga touching him. I had to see who this was, but first I needed to make sure I was on the right muthafuckin' street. I wish this would be somebody up in his spot and I can't even get a scratch and sniff. I came to a screeching halt at the end of the street. Sure enough, it was Levitt. I did a U-turn and drove past slowly as the nigga I fought in the club last year came ditty boppin' up out babe's house like he just had the time of his life. I swung the truck in a spot a few houses down and turned the lights off as he walked to his and got in. A few minutes later, he drove past me speeding off down the street.

I thought about what I was going to do next. I was HOT! I started to sweat a little. I tried really hard to stay cool, but I wanted to explode. I don't believe babes' is fuckin' around on me with ol' boy. But they are just friends. Maybe the fool just came by to visit, I thought. Naw, he lettin' that nigga fuck. I ain't stupid. Yeah, it's bout'ta go down. I got out the truck and grabbed the bag of booze. Of all people, Jason, though. Damn! This nigga had better just been over here visiting. I walked up to the door and heard the dog bark. I rung the bell, wiped my face with my hand, and a little bit later heard Jason running to the door. He quickly opened it.

"What did you forget, Dari..." he stopped in mid-sentence. I glared at him and took a deep breath. I could see terror in his eyes all of a sudden.

"Surprise, sunshine!" I said as he looked at me not sure what to do next. He had a, *Oh shit, I'm caught look* on his face. The dog stopped barking. I stood there looking at him in his fucking skimpy ass draws, ass all out, eyes red like he was high or some bullshit like that. I pulled him back into the house by his arm and slammed the door.

"I'm going to go... and put some pants on," he said trying to run off.

"Did you have pants on a few minutes ago, Jason? Don't bother on my account," I said still holding on to his arm.

"It will just take a minute, then we can talk, okay?" he said looking like he had just been caught stealing. I let him go and told him to hurry up.

"I'll fix us some drinks; you cool with that?" I asked. He shook his head yes and ran up the stairs looking embarrassed because he had been caught. I walked into the kitchen and opened the bottle of Grey Goose and took it to the head for a minute. I couldn't believe this lil' nigga played me. I mixed up some drinks and took them and the bottle into the living room where it looked like the party had begun. I took everything into the dining room instead and sat at the table. I sat his drink in front of the chair across from me and took the bottle to the head again before recapping it.

"Gary, where are you?" Jason asked searching downstairs.

"I'm in the dining room, babes. Bring your ass here so we can get some things straight," I said feeling the intoxication mix with my rage.

Jason walked into the room shaking like a leaf. I glared at him and told him to have a seat. I took a swig of my drink and watched him do the same. I didn't know what to say, and I think he must not have known what to say either because he took a big gulp of the drink and looked over at me searching my eyes the way his moms did when it was just the two of us there.

"Gary. I don't know...how to say...I don't know what..." he was slurring his words and couldn't form a complete sentence. All of a sudden, the dog ran over to him and started barking. Jason reached down to pet him, but I kicked him away. He yelped and ran back to me and bit me on the ankle.

Jason tried to get up but fell out of his chair reaching for the dog. I got pissed and grabbed the dog and walked him into the bathroom, locking him inside.

"It's time for you to start paying your man some attention Jason! And I mean that shit!" I pulled him up out of the chair trying to figure out what the hell I was doing and what was going on? In my mind, he ain't have no business letting no other man parade around my domain. I remember him slurring an apology and things

Gary and Darius Cross Paths

got a little fuzzy after that...

Soiled Linen Sheets

I am lying here wrapped up oh so tight in the arms of Darius Westbrook. The one constant in my life I can count on like the need to blink. This can't be real; I'm lying comfortably nude with Darius fucking Westbrook, way past IHOP's closing time, warm and naked in the spoon position, producing a quiet rumble in my ear, arms locked around me, with his dick in my booty. *Wait, no it's not, I paused to clinch and thought, oh my, yes it is, and it's still hard. Think Jason, what are you going to do next?*

I took a moment to focus and regroup. My eyes were dry, and my head started to swim. I tried to get it together but couldn't get my eyes to focus on the nightstand so that I could turn the lamp on. Something didn't feel quite right about this particular situation all of a sudden as I noticed there were no arms holding me. My left arm was a little soar as I reached over in a failed attempt to pull the chain from up under the tall lamp shade. I couldn't reach it because a pain shot from my ribs that didn't feel quite like they did after the accident. I let out a deep grunt and it became hard to breathe. It felt like something sharp was trapped inside my body trying to cut its way through my flesh. My eyes started to mist, and beads of sweat multiplied instantly across my brow.

It took a minute for me to catch my breath. I licked and rubbed my lips together noticing the sting of a freshly swollen lip. Panic started to ensue as I lie there wandering what had happened the night before. I nudged myself from under the big pillow lying across me. I pulled myself closer to the lamp reaching towards the string with my eyes closed fighting though the pain searing from the left side of my abdomen. When I felt my fingertips catch the tiny ball between them, I pulled and laid back down tired and sweaty from the level of discomfort my injury was causing. I was breathing shallow puffs of air and became a bit light headed. I didn't feel like myself either.

I took a little time to try calming down. I opened my eyes noticing that in my left eye, my vision was clear, but in the other it was blurry. My right eye felt dry and hurt when I looked to the right. I slowly moved my lower half towards the edge of the bed. A twinge of pain from my rectum shot through me within the depths of my body. I propped myself up blinking several times as my body tensed up into a cold sweat steadying myself in preparation to try to stand up. I focused really hard and observed towards the foot of the bed the red fitted underwear I had on the night before with the elastic band ripped across the beltline. A couple of sweat beads found an entrance into my left eye. I collapsed from the pain slashing through me as I rubbed my eyes trying to rid them of the stinging sensation.

I gripped my left side while concentrating on my breathing. My ribs were hurting so bad that my body began to feed off of the adrenaline pumping through my system as soon as it was released. Something wasn't right in my own damn house. It was time to boss the hell up. I heard Batman whimpering loudly downstairs. I was wondering why he wasn't running around freely or curled up in his bed in my room. I swung my legs over the bedside and slowly pulled myself up. The room was spinning all around me making a well-played attempt to keep me disoriented.

I gained control of my breathing and looked down at my foot noticing the pocket to my favorite Jeans and my wallet were propping my left foot up. I did a quick scan of the room and noticed my jeans were resting on top of the Sony Flat screen I had on my dresser. My inner thighs were blood stained and felt clammy as my ass jumped onboard the pain train. My Navy survival skills quickly unfurled in my head as I took a deep breath and thought to myself, *Pain ain't nothing but weakness leaving the body.* My instincts were telling me to get up out of there. I picked up my wallet, grabbed my phone, the sweats and t-shirt draped across the chair near the door, and headed out of my room pushing through the pain.

I made my way down the stairs as fast as I could. I took a breather and sat down on the bottom step. My teeth gnashed together as I slid the green sweat pants on. I almost cried when it was time to put the t-shirt on, it hurt so bad. I grabbed my side and stood up motivated again by the desire to escape this nightmare. I slid each foot into the high top sneakers waiting at the end of the staircase. I rubbed my eyes trying to ignore my blurred vision and the pain radiating throughout my body. I could hear Batman whimpering for me to come and free him. I hobbled my way towards the sound of his cries. He was locked in the bathroom downstairs. I opened the door and noticed he was tied around the toilet. He was skittish and became timid when I approached him licking his chops and shaking violently.

It took all I had to unhook him. He wasn't his normal hyperactive self and I figured he obviously had a rough night as well, poor thing. He was hot on my heels as I took a snail's pace to the front door for my keys and a jacket. I opened the closet and pulled a black jacket out and put it on slowly. Batman whimpered and scratched at my leg. I pulled it together and shut the door. I looked over at the hook where I keep my keys and noticed they weren't there. This was the only spot I *ever kept* my keys and they weren't there. My breathing became labored as I tried to get my scene together in preparation for a painful scavenger hunt. *Why do the stupid rental car companies put all the keys to the rental on ONE RING!* I thought to myself.

I walked into the kitchen to see if they were on the countertop with no luck. I quietly opened the drawers trying to make as little noise as possible. I became nervous when I coughed up a mouth full of blood on the counter top. *Yeah, I needed to get out of here,* I said as I wiped my mouth and said a silent prayer to God for help out of this house. The pain started to intensify the more I fought back. Batman began wining and circling

Soiled Linen Sheets

around me. I leaned on the countertop, so I could muster up more strength. I could feel the sweat running down my back swiftly into the comfort of the baggy sweatpants I had on. I grabbed a sharp blade from the block along with my left side again as I made my way out of the kitchen, I coughed up another mouthful of blood. I tried not to think about it as I wiped my mouth again before seeing what looked like the keys on the living room floor next to an overturned plant. Batman was sitting there and started wining.

I smiled and made my way over to retrieve them. I braced myself for more pain as I reached down to pick them up. I wiped some of the sweat from my face, gave Batman a pat on the head, and we made our way towards the garage. I opened the door and fear gripped my soul at the unexpected sound of what I thought was my name being called. I looked behind me and didn't see anyone. I closed the door and reached over to push the switch that opens the main garage door. If I could have avoided breathing at that moment, I would have because it hurt so badly. I unlocked the doors to the car and opened the driver's side door. Batman, whimpering, barreled his way into the front passenger compartment and began barking at me as I maneuvered my way into the car. The inside door swung open. I gripped the knife tightly and frantically found the button to lock the doors. Batman started to bark as if he'd lost his mind. I pushed the button to start the engine and slammed the car in reverse. I hit the gas abruptly backed out of the

147

driveway and sped off to another location.

Once I was a safe distance away, I noticed Batman was lying in the seat panting quietly exhibiting confidence in the fact that the worst was over. I had to piece this thing together. The last thing I remembered was a visit from Darius turning into a night of passion and his confession of love. Was I dreaming that, or was that real? Did Gary catch us in the act and exact revenge? What the hell was going on? I pulled over into a METRA Park and Ride station. I found a parking spot and put the car in park. Batman jumped into my lap and began licking my face. I was exhausted from the super rush of adrenaline and the pain running through my body.

It all hit me at once. I looked at my phone trying to think who I could call on at a time like this. I had kicked my friends out of my house and I didn't know if it would be a good idea to call Darius about this, Ma was back in Texas, my dad was fighting the war, and... Gary... well... My head started to throb, and I was feeling light headed again. I started to cough and almost choked on what was rising to the surface because my breathing was so intense. I rolled the window down and spit out another mouth full of blood. I wasn't going to be able to drive anywhere in my condition especially with my head spinning the way it was. It was like I was on some drug I couldn't shake, and everything was intensified. While I still had a somewhat logical mind, I swallowed my pride and made a phone call that probably saved my life. I drifted off to sleep after the call. My body was hot, and I was soaking with perspiration. No matter what I did, I couldn't get my breathing under control. The next thing I know, I was laying in a hospital bed with an IV infused into my arm. I was a bit confused but grateful to be in a safe location. My vision was blurred in both eyes now, and this scared me more than anything. I lay their realizing that I didn't feel any pain. I was relieved and began to relish in the fact that I could finally relax my muscles. I looked at the blurry image of the ceiling and let my mind wander.

My reality is a total contradiction. It's like, I'm the odd man out. I'm too gay to be straight and too straight to be gay. I straddle the line on so many levels. I'm my own fucking cheerleader and worse critic because it's not easy being me. I reflected on the time I was the pimply-faced thick eyeglass wearing scrawny gay boy who got called Urkel. All I know is I had a desire to change the worlds thinking about boys like me. Like Darius said, we're brave enough to be who we are. There is an amazing power in us that once tapped into, shows us that we have no choice but to be strong enough to live as who we are. In the midst of my thoughts and daydream, I opened my eyes to a familiar face...

"How are you doing, Jason?"

"You tell me," I said noticing my ribcage was secured tightly with ace bandages.

"You're going to be okay Jason? You have been though some serious shit. Did you see what these fools did to you? Or at least the fool I think did it to you."

"I have a general idea of what happened, but I don't remember how or when it happened. I feel it though," I said.

"Jason, you were raped okay, we discovered that when we did your initial assessment. They found two traces of semen in your... rectum."

"Michael, you're telling me it was two of them?" It couldn't have been both Darius and Gary. All I could remember was seriously feeling like things took a turn towards lust when Darius came to visit and waking up feeling like I saw Gary that night also.

"Jason, do you know who did this to you?" Michael asked. "If you do, you need to tell me?"

"Mike, am I at your job? Is this the Naval Hospital?" I asked ignoring his question.

"Yes, you called me, and I came and got you because you said you were coughing up blood. I'm glad you called me because I got there just in time man," he said pulling up a chair. I was reluctant to tell him who the two men could have been until I made more sense of this.

"Thank you," I said. My body was so soar. "Whoever did this to you drugged you with a mixture of the date rape drug and ecstasy. It had to be crushed and laced with something that seriously irritated your stomach lining, one of your once fractured ribs is now broken and set to heal, we had to stitch the inside of your lip, treat your eye because of a burst blood vessel, and they had to... fuck... Jason, you had a series of anal tears, man. If you know who did this to you, you gotta tell me, shawty?"

"Michael, I don't know man?" I said not wanting to take the foolhardy approach to public accusations. I took a mental inventory of the extent of the injuries inflicted on me. Did Gary do this to me? Did he attack me because of the argument we had earlier? My gut was telling me that Darius had nothing to do with this. I was hoping to wake up at any moment. But I wasn't dreaming this time.

"I know Gary did this to you, Jason. You just say the word, baby, and I got this nigga handled for you," Michael said slapping his fist into his palm. I looked at him and then up at the ceiling.

"I don't know," I said getting upset.

"Jason, this motherfucka' poisoned you, and damn near crippled your ass, not to mention what the fuck he did to... have you seen your fucking face boy? Come on let's go look in the mirror and I bet you'll tell me then," Michael said carefully easing me out of the bed. I grabbed the IV cart and wheeled it beside me. He walked me over to the sink and steadied me against his right side. I let my eyes rise from the floor to my sightline in the mirror. I was in awe at what I saw. The whole right side of my face was bruised and swollen to include my upper lip. The whites of my right eye were a bright red surrounded by a dark puffy ring cradling the lower lid and corner. I stood there thinking, could he be that mad at me that he would explode like this. I can't go to work and see patients looking like this. I felt like that white chick in the movie, *Set It Off*, when the chick from Roc got up on her and asked her to identify Cleo as the murderer of Luther.

"Dang," I said shaking my head. That was all I could say as I looked away. Michael slowly turned me around and walked me back to the bed. He assisted me back under the blanket where I let my head fall onto the pillow. I was dumbfounded. A part of me wanted to call Darius and have him by my side to tell me that it was going to be all right.

"Jason, who did this to you? Please tell me. Either way it goes, I'm going to get arrested so at least give me the right motherfucka' to handle," Michael pleaded.

"Michael, you're not helping right now, okay. Shut the hell up! Let me think," I said needing a moment to collect my thoughts now that I wasn't in an illegal drug induced state. "Hell, I don't even know if we're still friends."

"After all we been through together, that's how you feel?" he asked. I looked out of the window even though the image was blurry.

"I don't know what I feel anymore dude. Nothing appears to be what it seems these days. And it seems like everyone is playing with my emotions just because. Here I am trying to hold it together and be what everybody wants me to be in the midst of... hell, I don't know. I got psychos sending me amateur porn tapes starring my man, drunk drivers destroying my dream car, soul stirring sex in my dreams, bisexual love

152

triangles, being raped and gay bashed or some tea. I don't know what's happening anymore. I don't know where I lost sight of who I was. I don't know, Michael. I just... I just need a moment," I said pausing still looking out of the window. "Yo! And I forgot the botched suicide attempt," I said laughing until it became uncomfortable, "Hell, maybe all ya'll did this to me. The test showed that I was a cum dump, right?" I said sucking my teeth loudly.

"Are you done?" Michael asked.

"Only if ya'll are," I said looking in his direction. "I don't know how I got lost in my own reality not knowing where I belong," I chuckled.

"Tell me about it, I know what you mean about not belonging. If you didn't notice, I'm the only light skinned person in my family. I do know what it's all about being the odd man out, Jason. I envied them because they looked unified; they all looked the same and were there for one common goal - to be a family. That's one of the reasons I joined the Navy. I've always valued uniformity. I was so glad they accepted me," he smiled and nodded his head before proceeding. "My male cousins envied me because I was always told I was the cutest by the girls in the neighborhood. 'Ooooh, he got that good hair.' 'Oooh, you gotta use sun tan lotion, huh?' 'Ooooh, since you white, you can show us how to ski, huh?' Followed by the adults, 'He ain't shit but a half-breed,' 'He a bastard child, that ain't his real daddy.' This is the fuckery I heard and put up with for *years* growing up. I hated being light skinned because it set me apart from those I loved in a major way. They saw me as a threat." He rubbed his hands together and sighed. "My momma always made me feel normal. Whatever that is. She would tease me and tell me that I was just as black and beautiful as she was. I think I was seven when she first told me that," he paused smiled and continued. "It took me a long time to figure out what she was talking about. I actually realized what she meant the day of her funeral. I figured out I fuck around because I'm hoping to find myself in the pleasure I give to them boys that's darker than me. I love how dark skin feels to the touch, with its smooth, evenly rich, unmistakably black tone and texture. This is confusion," he said holding up his arms as if he were inspecting them. "Ask me why, Jason?"

"Why?" I said learning a new side of him. I sat back with my focus on him.

"I'm a product of rape. I represent what was done to our ancestors for years," Michael said nodding his head and huffing.

"Oh my God, Mike, I didn't know."

"How could you know, Jason?" he shrugged. "The story goes...my mother's car broke down on the side of the road one-day driving through Tuskegee, Alabama, on her way to her new life in Atlanta, Georgia. From what I was told this white man stopped, offering his assistance and thought in exchange, she would pay the only way a "nigger bitch" can pay." He paused and closed his eyes. "That piece of shit was positive and passed that shit off to my momma, who passed it off to me. I was undetectable when I joined the Navy. At the time, that was another word for negative, and I was cool up until well… you know. I have never had a first boyfriend to get this shit from. I lied, Jason, but you are the only one who knows this."

"I'm so sorry, Michael. Dang, to be honest, that story about the boyfriend giving you HIV never made sense to me," I said being blunt but still offering my sympathy not only for his loss but for the hurt he endured as a result of this. I couldn't imagine. Michael was able to join the military at a time when being undetectable was that gray area leaning in favor of circling a negative status. He had been doing fine until he found out he needed to start a medication regimen. He got his thoughts together and continued his story.

"See what happens when you lie?" he said poking me in the chest. "Momma gathered her sanity and went on about her business. The family didn't understand why she wanted to keep me, but she said I was her miracle baby because she was told she'd never be able to have kids because of her fibroids. Momma was of a particular age when she had me. I was her only chance at motherhood because all of her other attempts before and after me with my father failed. The man I know as my dad raised me as if I were his own," he said looking up with tears in his eyes. "And all she wanted for Christmas this year was for me to bring my ungrateful ass home to run up her light bill a few days. I could hear something in her voice crying out to me, shawty, but I ignored it," he took a moment to gather more thoughts. I listened intently to all that he was saying to me. I felt he needed an ear to bend more than anything. "If I square off face to face with my momma's attacker, my father, I wouldn't know what he looked like. I don't know what white pasty-faced asshole to take my frustrations out on for being different. There is a part of me I may never know, man. When the family looks at me, they see a mistake wrapped up in white privilege. The messed up part about life, man, is that you can have everything and not notice, but still want everything. Them fools thank being light skin is everything." He paused again shook his head and looked me in the eyes as a couple of tears fell from them. He wiped his face quickly. "But for you, Jason, all you got to do is say the word and it's a wrap. I admire you, man, 'cause you take full advantage and control of the person you are not giving a damn, shawty. I love you for that so much, man, because you've helped me more than you know. You opened the window to my faith that day when I thought I was outta here, shawty! When I thought this shit in my veins was going to kill me like it did my momma. I thought about the tough love you showed me when I was on my couch." He wiped his eyes and continued.

"Jason, it takes courage to pull somebody out of that mind frame. You take chances where it counts. You've helped me face my reality and learn how to love myself alongside my momma. You, I gotta protect no matter the cost, Jason, 'cause people aren't blessed with people like you for just any old reason. You are my blood more so than my own blood. How do you suppose that is?"

"Well, Michael, I never liked to color inside the lines and I hate ties. So therefore you can't constrict me to just one thing. I guess." I was amazed, humbled, and blown away that he felt that deeply about the simple man I was. Words truly escaped me. "Damn, shawty," he smiled nodding his head. "Thank you, Michael. Can you forgive me?

Brother?" I said trying not to let my emotions take control of me.

"No, thank you, and forgive me for my part in this whole mess, brother," he said with a slight smile. "My friends and my dad are all that matter to me in this world now, Jason. And I know you don't like getting mushy, but please believe that, okay?"

"No doubt, hag," I said as he squeezed my arm. "Oh, and by the way that little guard dog of yours is safe at my place," he winked.

"Thank you," I smiled taking everything in.

"Well, hey, I'm going to do my rounds for the afternoon," he said getting up from his seat. "If anybody comes in here, you are a reservist who got into a car accident on duty. Don't fuck up the important part of this lie, Jason. Excuse me, this story, one of the nurses will probably stop by to check on you after the shift change," he winked. I smiled and nodded my head yes.

He left my room so that I could get some more rest. Before he left, he informed me that they did draw some blood work on me and that everything was negative so far. He told me he'd come and get me so that we could go to his place when he got off. I was going to call Darius as soon as I woke up again. Maybe he could help me get some answers.

I took a moment to just lie there silently praying for the wisdom to know what to do next because this was all beyond me. My heart couldn't feel anything but felt everything at the same time. I was awash with so many boxes of compartmentalized emotions. It was as if I was going through them box by box looking for the answer to this riddle we all live posing the question of, why? I was thankful my brother from another mother, Michael, was still on my side.

Seven-Year-Old Tears

Falling asleep now was fast becoming a chore of mine. Since these bodily injuries were my reality, I felt safer being awake than being medicated and living in my head. At least I would be able to see danger coming. I was thumbing through a magazine lying on my back staring at the wall. I wasn't reading it, but listening to the sound of the pages sweep over the ridges of my thumbprint. I wiggled up in bed slowly to sit up so that I could read an article, any article that would either bore me to sleep, or at least take my mind off of my situation for a moment. I surrounded myself with the pillows Mike had given me to make my stay at his place comfortable and opened the magazine up to the last page. Me, being the weirdo I am, have always read magazines backwards. I don't know why I do it, but I feel there is no wrong way to read one because magazines give you the option to pick up anywhere you damn well please. It's one of the last rebellious forms of expression outside of the mouth.

I flipped through several pages and sneezed gritting my teeth at the slight discomfort this caused as my diaphragm expelled air and a light mist into the air. Batman, who was lying next to me peeked his head up, licked my arm a few times, and lay back down. When I looked back at the magazine, I noticed an ad for a hair care product proclaiming to be *"the savior for your hair."* I laughed to myself and had a flashback of

Sundays past at Canfield Church of God and Christ. I remember being there for hours clapping and mimicking several of the grown folk in the church each taking their respective praise breaks. This part of the service was routine and calculated as the Holy Ghost swept through the sanctuary. They were heightened moments just before alter call. I can't tell you the number of times I walked up and asked to be *saved*. The intercessor would cup my head gently in their hand and anoint my forehead with a heavy thumb full of holy oil. I'd then be instructed to *tarry*, meaning to repeat the phrase *Thank you Jesus* over and over until alter call had ceased. I remember being scared to wipe the oil from my forehead until it was time to take my nightly bath. I'd even avoid the temptation to touch it as it oozed its way through the tiny hairs of my baby face tickling my senses.

I felt like if I removed it too soon, I wouldn't be saved. Going up to get saved always brought sort of a welcomed pat on the back from my dad's mom. My grandma is the mother of the church and sadly, I wasn't that close to her. It wasn't my fault though because I always felt like she looked down on me as if I were not worthy of the blessings of God. No matter how much I would sing, be attentive in Sunday school, paid close attention during Wednesday night bible study, learned how to pray, volunteered for the plays we'd put on in church, recite spiritual poems and bible verses, and I tried Sunday after Sunday to be the best penny marcher the church had ever seen; I didn't feel holy enough in her eyes. The penny march was something the kids had to do after Sunday school just before the pastor got up to deliver the Word. We would come up from the basement of the church boldly singing, "Yes Jesus Loves Me." I could care less about the prize consisting of six quarters tightly wrapped up within a dollar bill. The prize for me winning the penny march was to get the smile and proud approval of my grandmother. I'd always be disappointed when my name wasn't called, and of course beam with pride when I was announced the winner.

It's funny how one's priorities shift with wisdom as you transition from a boy to a man. As I got older, I ultimately gave up competing with my cousins and the other kids in church for her approval. It became tiresome and pointless to me as I started to understand and seek the approval of Jesus, so that I may be deemed worthy in God's sight, not man's. So I stopped trying to get close to her. Now don't get me wrong, I love her dearly, but I realized she doesn't have a Heaven or hell to place me into. I am justified through Jesus Christ, not anyone else. No one knew what I was going through as a child and I know my parents could sense a disconnection they never asked me about it. They didn't know that I would hide from Pastor Aldridge's son because he tormented me every time he saw me. He hated my guts maybe because he probably saw something in me that was in him as well. I wouldn't be able to tally the number of times he called me a faggot, or sissy, or tell me that I was nothing but a bald headed girl. He called me everything but a bitch. Maybe, it was because we were in his dad's church.

No one came to my rescue even when I told my dad what he was saying. He brushed it off as "boys being boys." When Isaac caught wind of me being a tattle tale with no repercussions, this made the taunting worse to the point of him putting his hands on me from time to time, pushing me and punching me in my chest or shoulders. One time he pushed me up the church stairs in the basement so hard I skinned my knee under my dress pants. He then dared me to cry calling me a "faggoty punk sissy" and laughing in the process. He was a little bigger, a year or two older, and that intimidated me. I guess me telling was like admitting the secret no one wanted to address. I gritted my teeth through the pain and held back my tears not wanting to prove him right. And finally I was able to fight back when I found my own blood seeping through my pants. I stood up and pushed that fool down the stairs and watched him fall flat on his back. I was ready for him to retaliate, but to my surprise, he rubbed his head, stood up and walked up the stairs past me into the main sanctuary. I triumphantly poked my little chest out thinking to myself, *Who's the faggoty punk sissy now?* I never hated myself, and I never hated my enemies because I loved myself even when I was at my lowest point in life.

I think the poison they feed us about who we are in God's eyes is sweet causing many of us to conform against who God designed us to be. What they don't know is I'm not a choice. This was part of a conversation my dad and me had when he said he's always known I liked dudes. I would have never guessed he did. So, I have to give the old man more credit than I felt he deserved because ironically, I'm just like him...

"All I know is when a man see's a woman he wants to claim as his, he'll do whatever he has to do to protect her, to provide for her, and cherish her. I don't know what two men do for each other... line each other's mustache?" Daddy said as I burst into laughter. "I mean help me to understand. Why don't you like girls?"

"Be honest, huh?" I chuckled. This was kind of weird because for so long I was unable to speak freely about this.

"Yes, did I do something because I... "

"I can't explain it, Daddy, it's like we protect one another I guess, and provide something to one another that can't be explained in regard to masculinity. And if cherish is to love, then we do that too. I mean love is love when two spirits on the same page connect."

"So what about that lil' girl you took to your homecoming dance that year? I was so proud. I think that was the dance you went too. I was thinking my son bout to get a lil' trim," he said laughing. "Did you?"

"Well, that was actually her senior prom. And no I didn't. Nothing happened with her either," I smiled wishing I were having this conversation face to face so I could see his reactions. It was awesome to have a genuine conversation with my dad.

"Well, did you at least grind up against her on the dance floor and grab a titty or something?" he asked.

"We did dance and got sweaty on the dance floor. She grinded on me, and I did feel her up...she put my hand on one of her titties," I laughed recalling how spongy it felt. I was embarrassed thinking, *Am I really about to sit on the phone with my dad and kee about a set of teenaged titties?*

"And? What did you think? Spit it out son," he laughed.

"I mean, Pops! What do you want me to say, I mean, it was interesting?" I laughed.

"Interesting?" Dad chucked.

"Like, it was soft. Fleshy, even. Her cheap perfume didn't make me sneeze, and it was cool grinding up against her on the dance floor. She had a lil' phat butt to throw, and she made all the dudes there give me props."

"But...?" He asked.

"But to tell you the truth, she was a prop," I stated as a matter of fact. "She asked me to the dance and I thought, why not. It helped reduce my nerd image a little. Plus, the fact that Mama found my journal and told you about it, I had to play the role to survive. What I do wish is that we could have talked about those feelings I had. I mean I didn't get to explore me until I left the house."

"Well, I wasn't gon' sit up there and help you date no man, Jason. I don't know how to do that."

"Daddy, that's not what I'm saying," I said taking a deep breath and sighing. "That's not what I was getting at."

"So nothing I did *made* you this way?" he asked. "Nothing you did made me this way, Dad, but the

things that you said made me question my existence." "How so?" I could hear him shuffling some

papers around in the background.

"You remember when you asked me if Uncle Jesse touched me?" I said crossing my arms.

"Yes, I do. I needed answers," he said clearing his throat. The sound of him swallowing something to drink found its way to my ear as I began to prepare my statement.

"I know you did, but somehow, I suppressed that memory. It wasn't a big deal to me then because it was the truth. He didn't do anything to me. But when Jas had Aaliyah and I had to take her to the bathroom for the first time, and be left alone with her for the first time. I was scared because I thought to myself, what are they thinking when I'm alone with her. Do they think I'm a pedophile just because I like men? Do they consider me a pervert? Or is it just everyone else? Folks always couple the two together. I got so self-absorbed with where my hands were on her body, even to the point of thinking about her butt to my crotch ratio when she'd sit in my lap. The first year and a half of that little beautiful baby's life, I barely wanted to touch her. My niece loved coming to me, but I barely hugged her wondering if ya'll were looking at me with disdain and would one day ask her the same question." I paused... He was quiet. "Daddy...?"

"I'm here, son..." he sighed.

"It got so bad that I made Jas cry when I had to explain to her why I would no longer be holding her child." I closed my eyes and let my head fall against the headboard. A twinge of pain on my right side made its presence known.

"Damn, that's how you felt, son?" he asked in disbelief.

"Yes! That's how I felt. I mean Jas and I talked and she said she didn't feel like that and that she knew I would never hurt her or Aaliyah. And that made me let all that go. So it was never about what you did that made me gay, but what you said almost made me completely walk away from even an innocent baby who shares my blood," I said. I have wanted to get that off of my chest for so long.

"Jason, I never meant to hurt you, son. I hope that you can find it in your heart to forgive me for not being the father you needed."

"Daddy, I'm actually grateful for you. It doesn't even matter to me because I forgave you a long time ago. I had faith that you'd come around, no matter how slight."

"I'm glad to hear that. I always felt like we were fighting each other. Some days I didn't know how to deal with you. But you are my son and I had to at least try."

Seven-Year-Old Tears

"What does that mean?" I asked out of curiosity. "It means, being gay isn't what I had in mind for

my son, but I love you anyway. I don't know how I'd react if you brought home... a boyfriend... or... you know what I'm saying... but if I can get over this, then I can get over that and love you no less," he sighed.

"That's good to hear," I smiled like I've never smiled before. To hear those words come from my dad's mouth was incredible. But we'd definitely need to have some heart to hearts in person once he got back from Afghanistan. It took a lot of courage to be transparent with my dad. I was a bit apprehensive about it at first, but realized that he was probably just as scared to approach this subject more so than me.

"This is a lot to take in. This is still hard for your old man. I can't help but feel like I didn't do something right, main man."

"Dad, let me put it to you this way. Some of us are molested into this. Others like myself just are and know that we are early on. God doesn't give us a choice in which shell He merges us with. For you to say you always knew that I was gay shows that you were in denial about it my whole life up until this point. I wasn't molested, and I didn't choose to be gay."

"So you feel you were born this way?"

"I'm saying this was what I naturally progressed into as my sexuality matured, Daddy. To be born gay would be like saying I was born black. I had two African American parents who came together to produce a child of flesh and bone. My spirit was already predestined for this body and this walk long before you two decided to come together for my conception. I'm who God made me to be. Being gay wasn't something forced upon me like some of the folks I know."

"Well, what about those people you just mentioned?"

"Okay, so like, I have friends and a couple of guys I know who were molested at a young age. They don't feel they were, for lack of a better phrase, born this way because some confusion still lies there as it relates to their sexuality. I feel like when you force sexual behaviors on a child, it tarnishes their innocence and will put feelings and ideals in them prematurely that they are too young to comprehend. I think it can give that person a skewed image of themselves and how they will grow to relate to others on an intimate level. We all know sex is a learned behavior gay or straight, but sexuality like yawning, is innate. I hope that makes sense?" I said.

"I hear what you're saying? So everybody who is gay isn't gay?" He chuckled.

"Yes, something like that, it may be debatable. To be real Dad, the only choice I had in this was whether or not to let this portion of God's reflection in me shine through me. I'm not a mistake and I am not a signal for the end of the world."

"Anyone lacking wisdom, let him ask... in all of our relationships, we should enter them in the realm of a covenant not a contract. That's how God works, so I as a man, should not put stipulations on the love I am supposed to have for you as my son. The bible doesn't speak of contracts but of covenant. Therefore, we should handle one another as Christ does. I'm proud of you, Jason. And I see you in a different light now son," he paused and sighed. "My son is no longer my lil' main man," he took a deep breath before expressing, "I love you. I'm your dad. Don't ever think I won't be there to lace up your tennis shoes. Just be patient with me as I adjust to... reality."

"I love you too, Dad, and thank you?" I said, thanking God that I now had my dad's full love.

"I still need you to find a church and know that churches are like hospitals. Sometimes even the physician gets sick. I mean, I still don't agree with this... gay thing... and I want you to be happy and all... and live your own life. God knows, but just promise me you'll at least consider being..." he said never finishing his statement. There was a slight pause as I searched for my own words to say. "Main man... say this was a choice... what would you choose?" Dad asked with hesitation in his voice.

"That's never been a question for me to consider answering... there is a purpose for this that only God can bring logic too. I'm just the vessel, Daddy..."

After talking to my dad that night, I began to think about what motivates us to press on when we're stuck being human. To be who we are called to be, that two percent that never stops even when those close to us think we are crazy for playing the cards we're dealt. Motivation. Motive. Reason. These are all one in the same, yet considerably different dynamics. Life is a motivational factor. What we do with it is our motive. And the result of the doing is the reason. What does one choose to leave behind? What mark or impact do we want to represent us after we leave these shells we inhabit? What motivation will you pass on to others as you stake your claim in this world? What relationships will you build? What will you bring to those relationships? What image will you leave behind?

No one can answer the question of what life means. No one can fully understand either side of judgment, nor explain its relevance. It seems it gets harder and harder day-to-day, yet easier and easier as you learn to calm down. I'm beginning to learn from my mistakes and simplify my surroundings. I'm trying to eliminate negative forces including people out to hurt me. I think I have reached a point where I want to make every effort possible to figure out and hold on to what really matters.

What I've learned so far is that there are many of us who are spiritually conflicted. We are all put here to help open each other's eyes and minds to see a side of God that the world would place in a box, never to be found. Better yet, a lost time capsule of His truth with no date to be exhumed.

I got my dad to listen to me finally and it felt like he respected me for standing my ground as a man. It was interesting to hear my dad breathe a sigh of relief when I told him again that Uncle Jesse didn't touch me. No one turned me this way. I guess every parent needs to know who did this to my child? It was awesome hearing an awakening in his voice as we talked. I can't remember the last time my dad and I just talked. I prayed we'd have many more of these talks not just about this but also about whatever 'cause I need my dad. I wonder if this is how Darius feels when he has conversations with his dad...

A Matter of Time

If you don't pay attention to yourself, you'll lose yourself in habitual monotonous bullshit. And my bullshit, maybe my weakness smells like validation. I let my own arrogance of thinking I had life figured out keep me from facing my own intimidation. What the hell was I thinking? Jason and I haven't spoken for a couple of weeks since we...*did what we did,* I don't know. I have been avoiding talking to him because I don't know how to bring this up. *I need to let go of my pride and stop being a, Shiiiid! That fool can call me too, though. Damn, Jason!* I thought to myself.

I know we both need to address this situation and figure out what this thing between us is. I always have a great time with Jason, but the night we... damn... that night we... shit, I still don't know if I should call it fucking or making love. What we did, yeah, let's just say what we did that night was "fuck love." I have never connected sexually with someone like that before... not even Cindy when I got her pregnant. I can't stop thinking about it, and him. I gotta see him face to face rather than call him on the phone. I think I owe him that much.

MiMi told me to carefully consider the possibility that his feelings may have changed or that he may stay with ol' boy, but I feel otherwise. A lot has happened within these last two weeks that have made me put a lot of things on the table to look over.

A Matter of Time

Namely, that Jason is the one person on the face of this Earth that gets me and will be my ride or die. I just hope the sex didn't change all of that. Sex with Jay was definitely more than a bust down between two homies.

Why wasn't this fool calling me? Shit he might be saying the same thing. I took matters into my own hands and I headed to his place with the biggest shit-eating grin on my face. I was all geeked up and stopped to get the boy the biggest, freshest, and most beautiful bouquet of red roses I could find. Flowers always worked with my dames.

When I arrived at his crib, I checked my breath, and gave myself a once over in the mirror. I stepped out and made sure the roses weren't lopsided. I didn't give a fuck if his man Larry was there. I could handle that nigga if need be. This was my time to make a move. And I couldn't explain why.

I rung the doorbell a couple of times and waited patiently for Jason to answer. I gripped the vase with a suave stance, tilted my head slightly, and put on my come to Daddy smile once I heard the door locks being unlatched. Jason opened the door with the chain attached and peeked through. His dog was in the background barking viciously. I could immediately tell something was wrong because he had on his eyeglasses in the middle of the day. Something was up 'cause Jason hates wearing glasses.

"Jason, you gonna let me in, baby boy? It's me, what's up?" He stood there for a moment just staring

174

at me like he was calculating a strategy in his head. I had seen that same look in the face of many of the soldiers I looked after in Iraq. He abruptly shut the door and removed the chain. A few seconds later, he slowly opened it hiding behind it like a shield of protection. "You alright, baby boy?" I asked walking inside cautiously. His house was quiet as shit. I've never known Jason not to have music playing. Nothing was out of place of course but there were no sounds of any kind echoing around. The smell of Pine Sol and Bleach hit me like a ton of bricks when I stepped all the way inside. He poked his head out slowly, and then shut the door locking it, placing the chain back into its cradle.

"What's up?' he asked as he half-heartedly smiled. He didn't move from the doorway as I walked over and tried to hug him. Batman who was close to his heels started barking uncontrollably not wanting me to get close to him. I could since a bit of fear yet relief in Jason's eyes as he studied me for a second. He nodded his head no and raised his hand motioning for me not to step to him.

"Jason, what's going on, baby? Is everything alright?" I asked as he placed a long sturdy knife on the small table close to the front door. He snapped his fingers and the dog shut up.

"Umm hmm, why do you ask?" he said still trying to smile. I noticed his eye was blue under the lower lid, and looked to have a blood clot in the white area. He pressed a few buttons on the keypad of his home security system. He was wearing a loose fitted tee shirt, with a pair of basketball shorts. He walked slowly into the living room holding on to his side. I followed.

"Because you don't seem like Jason. What happened to you and why are you carrying a knife?" I asked. I knew I should have turned around that night. This mutha'fucka done went too far putting his hands on Jason like this. If he confirms my suspicions, I don't know what I'm liable to do now that my feelings are wrapped up in him.

"Because my gun isn't in just yet," he stated in a smart tone. He curled up on the furthest end of his couch away from me and wrapped up the lower half of his body in the large fleece Lion blanket I had gotten him from overseas. I took that as a good sign that it made him feel safe. Maybe it brought up thoughts of me. I was caught off guard when I noticed a solid wood baseball bat sitting upright within arm's reach of where he was seated. Batman jumped up on the couch and curled up at his feet as if standing guard. I placed the bouquet of roses on the table, sat on the couch, and removed my jacket.

"What you need a gun for and what's with all these weapons, and dead silence, and the house being locked up like Fort Knox? Why is it dead in here?" I asked trying to get him to start talking.

"Well, when you get the shit beat out of you, drugged and raped, with no recollection of how it happened you get a little defensive," he said removing a Gerber knife from under the blanket. He tossed it onto the table. "Will that answer suffice?"

A Matter of Time

"What the fuck?!?!?! Are you serious?" I asked moving closer to him. He flinched as I rubbed his leg causing the dog to start growling. He looked over at his knife for a few seconds as if calculating another what if scenario. "Jason, I'm sorry yo! What happened?" I felt bad all over again leaving him alone that night. Damn, I should have turned back around that night. Batman started barking at me and snipped at my hand. Jason reached over and grabbed the knife.

"Batman, chill out, I don't think he's a threat. Come here, batty boy," he said as the dog rushed up into his lap. He began petting him to calm him down. "Chill out, okay? It's all right, okay? He hasn't left my side for one minute," Jason said looking up at me. He was rubbing on Batman with love and a lot of gratitude. He placed the knife next to his leg.

"What happened, Jason?" I asked trying to follow and deal with what he said to me. I felt guilty for getting him caught up.

"Didn't I just say I don't know?!" He snapped. "Well when did all of this go down? Stop bullshittin' and talk to me, man!"

"The night you and I linked up! Okay! I don't know too much after that except I woke up half blind and in pain! My clothes were ripped, my house was trashed from what looked like a struggle and I..." he closed his eyes and rubbed his face with his hands. I stood up and pulled him up off of the couch. He tensed up at first but then buried his head in my chest allowing me to touch him. I held on to him for dear life.

"It's okay, Jason. I'm here, baby! Damn, I should have stayed with you that night. I'm so sorry I wasn't there to keep this shit from happening to you. I'm here, baby. You hear me?" I said squeezing him and rocking him in my arms. I knew that couldn't change shit, but what else could I do at that point. I'm killing that mu'fucka! What kind of man does this to somebody?

"You're the only person I've told this too. I feel stupid for letting this happen. But I really don't know what happened. I must have did something wrong, like why couldn't I stop this from happening? What did I do, Darius?" he asked.

"Listen to me. You didn't do nothing baby boy. Alright! You're not stupid, alright, chill with all of that, yo!" I said trying to fight the anger and sadness battling each other over what was done to Jason.

"I haven't even told Michael," he said as I rubbed his back.

"You can trust me Jason," I said reassuring him.

"I never knew the definition of scared, Darius! I'm so frustrated and confused and I don't know what to think," he said as we sat back on the couch. I lay back as he laid his head in my lap. I started to rub his back and stroke his head. Like I did before I left the night we had sex. He let out a deep sigh as he got comfortable with me being there. The tension left his body.

"Have you seen that mu'fucka since it happened?" I asked clinching my teeth together. I said trying to get him to say if it was indeed his ex.

"He stopped by drunk a few nights this week. I

didn't let him in. I had the locks and the garage door codes changed. I just been at home cleaning and laying low the last couple of weeks. I had to go and pick up the car I ordered. Thank God I'm still on sick leave for a few more days... I mean I definitely can't see my patients and clean teeth like this. And I'm glad I took out that income insurance policy, so I can keep the lights on. I haven't really left the house. Mike and Preston have been coming by to check on me and make sure I'm eating and taking my medication. I haven't heard from Shawn at all. Then I didn't hear from you and I was like maybe these two fools were in on it together. But my spirit was telling me that wasn't the case," he said wiping his face.

"How is your body healing?" I asked giving him a once over.

"I'm fine, my ribs are still soar, and my eye is getting better according to my doctor. He said I should have full sight and be able to wear my contacts again in a couple more weeks. For now, I'm in these ugly things."

"I'm going to find out who did this to you. I promise you that," I said kissing the nape of his neck. I already knew who.

"Don't make me any promises. And what the hell did you bring these red roses for? You showing me what you taking to your baby mama?" he said.

"Those are for you, asshole!" I laughed.

"Roses for me? If you know me so well, then you would have gotten tulips," he said rising up slowly. He maneuvered himself upright on the couch reaching over to grab the vase. He closed his eyes, bringing the flowers up to his nose gently taking in the perfume of the floral arrangement. It looked like my plan was working.

"Yeah, I came here to tell you that I love you. I've always loved you, and that I am in love with you. That night wasn't just about sex for me. And this is my small way of breaking the ice so to speak," I said. He took a deep breath and sat the bouquet back on the table. He then turned his body towards me and sat Indian style placing a pillow in his lap.

"Hmph! Here you go," he chuckled. "People use that word so loosely. Sometimes when it's too late," he said shaking his head.

"Jason, I'm not using it loosely, and it's never too late," I said in an attempt to defend my character. "So what is your point?"

"I'm glad you asked, Dee. You see, people always tell you at the very last minute when you've given up hope of the love you have for them ever being reciprocated. It doesn't mean as much at that point. My mom waited until I left for boot camp until she said it meaningfully to me. Gary screws his ex before he realized quote unquote just how much he loved me. My dad risking his life in Afghanistan hearing the news that his son was in a coma finally has a change of heart and professes his love for me. Michael, probably one of the best friends I've ever had up until this point, writes this crap in a hallmark card about how much he loves me. Whatever that means." He turned his head towards the roses sitting on the table. "Now you, years later. You come up in here with a fifty-dollar vase of stinky red roses, two weeks after you fuck me, mind you, leaving me without a response...now get this, for two whole weeks!" He stopped to look back up at me. "There was no carrier pigeon, flare gun, smoke signal, a simple hey, just checking on you, to any of my texts or phone calls."

"Jason, you of all people know this is a tough pill for me to swallow and I didn't know how to approach this... " I started before he interrupted me.

"So you approach it with red roses, five years and two weeks later as if you've done something spectacular to romantically make all right with the world. I'm sorry, but these sweet gestures of love based on delayed after thoughts are a bit redundant to me. Take those to that chick of yours carrying your child on the Southside because *clearly* that's who you wish to have a romantic love life with. I'm tired of waiting on all of you idiots to get it right. So forgive me for not being sensitive to your needs right now. I have had enough of you people. I promise you that. I cannot count on none of ya'll to love me like I can! You love me?! Whatever!" he said. He folded his arms and looked at me like he hated me.

"Jason, I'm being as vulnerable as I can be right now. I'm being fucking honest and you're cutting me off at the knees here, baby boy. What do you want from me?" I said looking for the right words to say.

"Is that right?" he said unfolding his arms.

"What the fuck am I supposed to do, Jason? I can't just let this go!"

"Why not?! You let it go over and over again, so what you're supposed to do is what you always do. Why don't you go back to your greener pasture and help her raise your baby girl, Darius? I'll be fine."

"Because I'm in love with your ass! Don't you see that? I always knew that shit now that I look back. You never judged me, you never held shit over my head, and you never let me down! You know the beautiful thing about you, Jason?! You never look at anything that way! You see people for what they can be, not what they are. And I love you for that shit! Somehow it's been you all the time, so don't sit here and tell me that you've given up on who you are to me and the rest of the world because its bullshit. You hear me? It's bullshit, Jason!"

"Do you love the man you are becoming? Because you do understand what responsibility that carries, right?" he asked folding his arms again. He still had the same look on his face. I didn't like it at all.

"Yes, I do because I had you by my side this whole five years and two weeks, shit maybe even longer than that. You're the only one who truly knows me!"

"Hmph! Really?" he scoffed. "When did you become so bitter?"

"Now I'm bitter? Darius, I'm hurt, okay, both mentally and physically. I'm drained. I'm... I'm... depleted! I'm hurt... I'm hurting! ME! I'm hurt! I give a piece of me to *EVERY-FREAKING-BODY* but myself. And look what the result is?" He stood up slowly off of the couch, holding onto his side. He removed his glasses, then his shirt. There was a rigid body brace enveloping his torso. "Does that answer your question? Everybody I've ever loved has hurt me. My dad had the gall to tell me he accepts me for me for being gay, but in the same breath asked me to consider not being me. How the hell does he propose I do that, huh? Am I still your second daughter Pops?! Huh?!" he said yelling up at the empty silence in the room. "I deserve to be selfish right now. I'm not bitter! This is pain talking! I'm hurt. Literally, shit, get it right!" he said as a tear ran down his face.

"Come here, Jason. Please, I'm sorry," I pleaded as I reached out for him.

"Don't touch me," he said not moving a muscle. He wiped his face. "Yeah, I'm done crying over ya'll too. Do not come any closer. I don't want to be touched by you right now."

"Okay, that's fair. Well, what do you want me to do?" I had to change the tone of this conversation ASAP. He glared at me for a few seconds, rolled his eyes, and shook his head.

"Give me five years and two weeks to figure it out and then we'll discuss it. I want to be left alone right now until I get my sanity back. I can't even prove who raped me because I'm losing my mind it seems," he said.

"Well got-damn!" I said. I couldn't think of a better

reply to issue. This was a side of Jason that I never thought was in him. Jason has never been like this.

"I'll show you to the door. And please take those. That's just another dead thing for me to try to bury in my mind," he said without looking at me.

I grabbed the vase of roses and my coat without saying anything else. He turned towards the couch and grabbed his baseball bat and followed me through the foyer. The dog trotted close to his heels. He punched in the code to disarm the security system. I turned towards him opening myself up offering a hug. He shook his head slightly motioning a subtle no. I unlocked the door, gave it a tug, and walked outside pulling it closed behind me. My heart sank with heavy emotion as I heard Jason latch the chain and turn the deadbolts securely. Damn, what was I going to do with these feelings? Did I just fuck up the one constant in my life? My phone began to ring as I made my way down the stairs towards the ride. I checked the time and then looked at the caller ID reading, Cindy Ballard, hoping she had good news to share about the baby...

Masculine

Preston noticed that I stopped wearing my favorite wristwatch and asked me about it. It was a unique silver watch my mom gave me the Christmas before I left for boot camp. I told him, ever since the coma, time has become just another thing that comes and goes that I can't get back no matter what state I'm in, so why carry time with me. This got me to thinking what if I could though? Like, what if I could wind it back and forth like I do my watches. I'd go back to my most embarrassing moment because I've often wondered what my life would look like had my mom never walked in on me wearing her canary yellow heels that day. Would I have been a big ol' drag queen? Would I still have a subtle distaste for the effeminate?

Have I subconsciously smuggled homophobia into my own existence as a result of being reprimanded for an activity that "boys" should not engage in? When the bottom line is, I was adhering to the principle of not lying with a man as you do a woman. For one I'm not attracted to women, so how can I lie with a man like I do a woman if I am not attracted to one sexually? And two, two men don't approach sex and relationships the way a man and a woman do. I'm same gender loving.

It's like sexuality is one thing, I get that, but what steers us into the directions we take once inside of our sexuality, as it relates to our own personal tastes, traits, and proclivity? If mama hadn't caught me sashaying in her heels, what would I be like today? If being effeminate and carrying out things like a female is not what a man is supposed to be, why am I the submissive one in the relationships I partake in? I enjoy being male. I enjoy the company of men, but as of late, I feel like I have submitted my masculine energy to the men in my life without even knowing it. On the outside, I'm all man, but on the inside, I'm this nurturing humble guy with a passion for humanity. A man that got my ass kicked by my ex- boyfriend for not passively submitting to the sexual demands he expected of me.

It's been a fight most of the time for me as I present what the world expects me to be. Ever since that day I got caught in the heels, I decided never to be typical. I didn't want to be a stereotypical black gay man, and I seriously never wanted to be the stereotypical black male. I learned early what type of drama that could bring. But I've always been different in my own right, never wanting the focus on me, but the focus has always been on me. I was always watched, and so I had to watch my every move, my every word, and my every movement. I concentrated on walking masculine, speaking masculine, especially when needed. I'm from Detroit, and in certain circles, you can't call attention to yourself by being soft spoken. You can't switch; you have to assert yourself. The fact that I was constantly evaluating and tweaking how much of it I was doing always made me feel awkward around people.

That seems to be my issues with guys who do drag

or black women who speak fluent fag. Am I in straight drag or is this really me? Like, female impersonators and the androgynous boys of today go the extra mile to be feminine. So every move is heavily dramatized, and so well-rehearsed that it becomes exaggerated and overdone. The days of the effeminate male are coming to an end as this age seems to be watering down the lines of masculine and feminine energy. There may be a lack of balance that seems to be brewing as we pretend to live more progressively than before. But what is the cost of this shift in boys vs. girls? The interesting part is that a number of black women seemingly aspire to imitate these types of behaviors by taking on the characteristics and behaviors of their gay brethren. Men who unabashedly teach them to be new age women with a contrite undertone towards their natural feminine ability. These women become androgynous in their own right impersonating what is exaggerated to be feminine rather than being feminine.

However, I digress; the motives behind my mystery are not my own. I am at a place now where I am again, unpacking all of my compartmentalized junk trying to figure out my place here in this world. I'm the oldest grandchild, the oldest son, and the responsible one. I was the one who was always too white for the black folk, and too pro-black for the white folk. And too masculine a bottom for the gay kids, but too soft for the straight kids. I am all of these things for other people, but who am I to myself?

Masculine

I sat on the passenger side of my moms' car staring at the heels she was wearing when she picked me up from the airport. I remember staring at her feet hit the pedals the day she confronted me with my journal. I studied the way she walked with the grace and beauty only an accomplished well to do woman of her pedigree could showcase. She was a strong woman who didn't like to show her softer side, but she had her moments of tenderness that only a mother in love with her child could execute. She didn't say a word when she quickly tipped towards my direction as I slowly made my way to the baggage claim of the Dallas airport. I mustered up a smile as she embraced me in her arms. It was the best hug I had felt in a long time.

She rubbed my face and kissed my cheeks as we exchanged a few pleasantries. I guess I just needed to get out of Chicago for a minute, so I decided to spend the last weekend before I returned to work with my mom. We retrieved Batman and the small suitcase I had packed. She placed her arm around my shoulder as we made our way to the car. This would make that the third time she's hugged me with such gentle sincere care. I have searched for that feeling in the arms of so many for years and she was the only one I knew could provide it.

The first time she hugged me like that, I was seven years old. I had made my way back up the remainder of the church stairs after I faced my bully. Our eyes locked as she saw me coming up the isle towards the pew she and Daddy sat on. She excused herself and made her way over to see about me. She kneeled down to look at the damage done to my knee under the large rips of my dress pants. She rolled my pant leg up and took me by the hand so that she could grab her purse. I remember trying to be a big boy and not cry in front of the congregation as we then made our way to the bathroom so that she could clean me up. When I told her what happened, she embraced me and rocked me so gently in her arms that time paused to record that memory and gave God a chance to smile upon us.

The second time she hugged me like that was when I left for boot camp. Here I was broken and bruised, and she does it again. She gave me exactly what I needed. I guess I needed to know she wasn't one of those people who would feed off of my weakness of restored hope. I observed her dainty feet luxuriating within the plush contours of the beautiful designer heels she wore, helping her manipulate the pedals of the car. I drifted off to sleep as she took a phone call on the way back to her house.

When I woke up, it was the next afternoon. I didn't even realize that I had gotten into bed. The sun poured into the room as the wind made the tree just outside of the window its dance partner. There was a nice balanced temperature from the warm bedding and the cool air being pushed down by the ceiling fan. I rubbed my eyes and rolled over to grab my phone. I observed the time and noticed that it was 3:20 in the afternoon. I slowly got up, put on a t-shirt, grabbed my hygiene bag, and walked into the bathroom. I brushed my teeth, showered, and made my way towards the sounds coming from the television in the family room.

My niece Aaliyah was playing with both Batman and my mother's dog, Kirby, while being entertained by the colorful puppets on the screen singing about how sharing is caring. I snuck up behind her and tickled her as my sister Jasmine looked up from the large nursing book she was reading from.

"Uncle Jason, you finally woke up!" she said, laughing as I picked her up hugging and kissing her. Both of the dogs jumped up and down around my legs and then focused their attention back on one another. "Yes I am finally up! How is my little big girl doing?" I asked placing her on my hip and walking

further into the room to sit down on the couch. "What's going on big head?" Jasmine said leaning

over to hug me.

"Nothing, heffa, what's up with you?" I said laughing and placing Aaliyah on my knee.

"Now as nice as it is for you to come home to visit, how in the world are you going to come and sleep the day away?" my sister asked.

"Because I was tired. Shoot, that's what working people do," I said.

"You almost slept your life away," she laughed. "It's about to be 4:00. What happened to your eye, why is it all bloody looking?" She said starting right in on me.

"Nothing, I had a bad case of pink eye," I lied.

"As germ phobic as you are, that ain't from

nobody's pink eye boy!" Jasmine said.

"Hey, Mama," I said looking in her direction and ignoring my little sister. She was putting together what looked to be a care package. She had some of me and Dad's favorite car magazines, canned tuna, Sardines, bags of candy, toiletry items, socks, undergarments, and other non-perishables surrounding a box made ready for shipment. It reminded me of the boxes I used to put together for Darius.

"Umm hmph," Jasmine mused.

"Hey, boy, you alright?" Mama asked.

"Yes, I feel better I guess. I really needed to get some rest. I haven't been able to sleep all that well lately," I replied.

"Hmph, I see," she said lining the box with bubble wrap.

"Uncle Jason, I made you a picture," Aaliyah said, speaking really well now.

"You did?" I gasped. "May I see it, please?"

"Yes, you may! It's on the table. I'll go get it," she said sliding down off of my knee. She ran over to the dining room table. She was getting so big and I looked at her in amazement, as she came back to me holding the picture behind her back.

"Uncle Jason, you ready to see my picture I made for you?" she asked with the sweetest little smile on her face.

"I sure am skootah bootah! Let me see it," I smiled looking at her with excitement in my eyes.

Masculine

"Okay, hold out your hands, and close your eyes please," she instructed. I followed her directions as she placed two pieces of thick yellow construction paper in my hands. "Okay, you can open them now."

"Wow! These are really awesome! You did these all by yourself?" I asked as she nodded her head proudly. "So this is me right here?" I said pointing at the male figure she drew. It was of me in a Navy uniform and she also drew one of Daddy in his Army uniform. There was a ship with water in the background of mine, and she drew what looked to be a tank and a helicopter in the background of the one of Daddy.

"This one is for you, Uncle Jason, and Mommy said we can send this one to Grandpa with the other stuff. You like it, Uncle Jason?" She asked sweetly.

"I love it, pretty girl. I absolutely love it. You know where I'm going to put it?" I asked her as I hugged her and kissed her chubby cheek.

"Where, Uncle Jason?"

"Well first, I'm going to buy a really expensive frame for this priceless work of art my lady bug drew for me. And then I'm going to take it and put it in my living room at my house. This deserves to be on my wall," I smiled.

"Do you think Grandpa will like his too, Uncle Jason?" she asked.

"I am sure he will love it just as much as I love mine. Thank you so much," I said kissing her again. She took the picture of Daddy and gave it to mama before going back to watch the television again.

"Uh, Ma. Is there something you want to tell me?" I asked with a puzzled look on my face, she laughed and stopped what she was doing.

"You care to do the honors, Jas?" She smiled looking at Jasmine and then me. Without hesitation, Jas piped up.

"Gladly! Mommy and Daddy are getting back together, Jason! Isn't that great news?" she said with utter delight.

"Are you serious? Wait, I've been having regular conversations with him and he didn't mention that to me. What do you mean? Are you for real?" I asked still shocked at the news.

"Well, you make it sound like you want us to stay apart," Mama said. "I thought you'd be happy about this." She sounded as if I had burst her bubble. I just wanted to know which one of them set aside their ego to restore the relationship.

"Yeah, Jason, you want them to get divorced? Boy, boom!" Jasmine asked. I see she had been hanging with some ghetto girl name Qua or some tea, by that last little comment. I thought to myself, *you just don't bring baby number two up in here.* I personally didn't know if I cared if they got together or not. I hadn't thought about it until just then.

"No, but this is just... wow! Okay, well how did all of this come about?"

"Well, we have been talking about working things out since before he left. We both have been stalling the divorce process and we recently made the decision to work things out seriously before, well when he gets back from Afghanistan. We've been married too long to throw everything away like we did."

"Wow! I am...wow! Well okay, that's...wow!" I said.

"Will you shut up with the wows? Use your words, Jason," Jasmine said as we all broke out into laughter. "Be quiet, heffa!" I said quickly glancing at my sister while I got my thoughts together. "So wait a minute, Ma. You guys have been talking about what,
exactly? May I ask?"

"Everything, Jason. We had to acknowledge the fact that the blame game isn't an effective way to communicate. He said some things that hurt me, and I did the same thing and we both needed to hear those things to move forward. It was like we became two different people over the course of our marriage because we never got to decide who we wanted to be, if that makes sense? Our growth was stunted," mama said studying my face.

"It makes perfect sense, Mama. I get it. Wow!" "Really, Jason?" Jasmine and Mama laughed. "What?!" I chuckled, this is...wow...I don't know
what else to say. Congratulations though. I'm happy for the two of you and I am so glad that we are going to be a family again," I said still trying to revisit the idea of them under one roof again.

"Well, it's going to take a lot of work and effort on both of our parts. Maybe things would be different all around if we weren't so messed up," Mama stated plainly.

"Ma, what does that even mean?" I asked taking a deep breath.

"Nothing, Jason, forget I said that. I'm just thinking out loud."

"About what though, Ma? We are all grown, and we need to be able to talk, Ma," I pleaded.

"Fine, let's be grown and talk. What happened to you in Chicago, Jason? Why are you here in the middle of the week surprising us with this visit?"

"Ma, I just needed to get away for a minute while I healed. I needed a change of scenery," I said looking down at my feet.

"You're not a good liar, Jason. And when I left Chicago, you weren't wearing a body brace. And you weren't as frail as you are now."

"Ma, I just... got it to help with the healing process. That's all," I said hoping that she would drop the subject.

"Jason, don't sit up in my house and disrespect me by lying to me. Like I'm one of your little friends," Mama said in a stern voice.

"Ma, I got... it's hard to talk about because..." I said rubbing my face trying to hold back my emotions. I didn't want to bring my problems to her doorstep because I had been so used to handling my own issues. She would not be ready to handle what happened, but it was my own fault for coming here in my current state of mind and condition. I just needed her right now.

"What did you get into a fight? Is it AIDS? What

happened?" she said coaxing me for an answer. I wanted to read her to filth for that last statement. AIDS, though?!

"No... Ma... I was raped, and I think it was Gary," I said in a low tone. I was breathing shallow breaths as if I were standing in a pool of deep water applying pressure around my torso. Jasmine covered her mouth saying, "Oh my God" in the process.

"Boy, what did you just say to me?" she asked as I looked into her eyes.

"Ma, I was raped and beaten up, and I think it was Gary! It's not my proudest moment, okay," I said finally owning up to what happened.

"Oh my God! Jason, I'm sorry, are you alright?" My sister said as she scooted closer to rub my back.

"Jasmine, take the baby into the room and close the door, okay," she didn't take her eyes off of me as Jasmine honored her request. When Jasmine disappeared with my niece in tow, Mama grabbed the remote and turned the television volume down significantly.

"Ma, I didn't want to tell you," I said hoping this didn't turn out the way it felt it was going to go.

"Jason, how could you have let some... man... come and do this shit to you?" She had a look of disgust on her face. The same look I remember her giving me when she confronted me in high school.

"Excuse me Ma? I didn't let this happen so much as I don't know how this happened," I said looking at her trying to understand where she was going with this.

"You let another man overpower you and rape you? I thought Gary was your lil' *boyfriend*?" she said as if saying his name was beneath her.

"Ma, are you hearing yourself right now? So you just think I just let... some man do this to me? *Some man!*" I said shrugging my shoulders. "No, I didn't let anyone do this to me, but it happened Ma, okay, it

happened!"

"If you weren't like this, Jason, would it have *happened*? Huh?!" she said as tears started to well up in her eyes. Everything around me seemed to fall deafly silent as the thunderous sound of my own heartbeat rang clear in my ear. Her eyes darted back and forth as the anger rearranged the soft features of her beautiful face into a mask of vengeance.

"Am I a disappointment to you, Ma?" I said waiting for the answer I already knew. This was confirmed by her silence and the pursed lips attached to her face. "Well, Ma, if I were *like* what?" I said seriously wanting her to really tell me how she felt once and for all.

"If you weren't some little... faggot... like the rest of these weak ass men walking around here switching and carrying purses, and wearing make-up, and wearing dresses, and all kinds of bullshit," she said as I looked at her and smiled briefly.

"And there it is. Yup," I said shaking my head. "You don't look like them, Jason! You don't act

like them, Jason. Your daddy and me didn't raise you to be like them, and here you are, up in my house, telling me that you been raped like some female or worse. Like you some prison bitch! Hell, you may as well be in jail! What did I do so wrong to make you be like this? What did I do, huh?" she said letting the tears fall. I looked at her in disbelief thinking to myself I must be dreaming. This was not the same women who told me that she didn't want to lose me or that she was okay with her son being gay. This was not the same woman who met my friends and even my *boyfriend.* Excuse me? *Some man?!*

"You know, the word faggot never affected me until now," I said still looking her in the eye. I didn't know what to say or do. I now knew what disappointment felt like very eloquently illustrated before me. "So this is how you truly feel? I knew it was too good to be true. I shouldn't have gotten my hopes up. For every move I make I get pushed back further than before. But there's a reason for it, and I'm cool with that. The bigger the struggle, the bigger the blessing."

"Well, I'm sorry, but I don't want my son to be like this anymore and this should be a sign to you that you need to leave that lifestyle alone before you end up with that AIDS virus! You don't got it do you?" she said. She was really on one today.

"No, I don't, Ma," I said not really caring about my tone.

"Good. That's one more chance to change because that gay thing ain't right, Jason. Maybe if your daddy and me had set a better example for you, then you'd be normal," Mama said. Batman came running up between my legs. I picked him up and decided to make my exit towards the hallway. "You better sit down while I'm talking to you. This is for your own good boy. I'm not just talking for my health. I'm trying to get my family back to normal," I stopped and looked at her.

"Mama, there is no such thing as normal because everybody's normal is a little different than your own. And if AIDS is the best thing you can come up with... Ma... I'm tired of arguing with ya'll about this, so I'm going to do you a favor and leave before I disrespect you in the manner to which you disrespect me because, Lord knows..." I said as she jumped up from her seat and stormed over to me.

"Look at what that lifestyle has done to you, Jason, and you gon' still sit up here and tell me that it's normal for a man to get fucked in the ass?" she said very agitated.

"Ma, unlike your materialistic keeping up with the Jones mentality, being gay is not a lifestyle! You don't even know how to be a mother. I shouldn't be able to count the number of times on half of ONE HAND that you've ever told me you loved me!"

"You get this one thing straight boy, I am your mother and you only get one! All the sacrifice I've done for you was out of love; everything that you are and ever will be is because of me. You got that?!" Her eyes were rapidly darting left to right scanning my face.

"Yup! Even the faggot that stands before you, huh?" I replied with cavalier haste, and I probably had a slight smirk on my face when I said it. She drew back and slapped me so hard I saw stars. Batman wiggled and jumped out of my arms and started barking beside my feet at her. I felt a warm stream of blood ooze from my nose. I chuckled and dabbed it with the tip of my tongue before wiping it away with the back of my hand. She didn't say a word as I snapped my finger once to quiet the dog. She put her left hand on her hip as if she dared me to make a move towards her. I turned around and walked back to the guest room to collect my things, so that I could get the hell up out of her house. She followed behind me yelling a few obscenities before retreating to her bedroom. Jasmine came in to check on me as I rushed to pack my suitcase.

"Jason, please don't leave," she pleaded. She handed a Kleenex tissue to me from the box on the dresser. I took a moment to blow my nose, still feeling the sting of my mother's hand on my face. "Jason, I didn't mean to start this, it's my fault. I should not have brought up your eye. I'm sorry, L.J."

"Jas, this is not your fault, she has been indifferent towards me since I can remember. This ain't your fault, baby sis, okay?" I said unzipping my hygiene bag to make sure that all the contents were inside. Once I was satisfied with the arrangements of my clothes, I zipped up the suitcase, put Batman in his cage, and grabbed my cell phone to call a cab. I grabbed my belongings and went out on the porch. Jasmine lay her head on my shoulder and waited the 15 minutes or so with me in silence until the arrival of my cab. I stood up and walked towards the curb as the driver got out and grabbed my bag to place in the trunk. He put the dog cage in the back seat and returned to the driver side just as Jasmine came rushing back out of the house towards me. I hugged my sister goodbye and told her that I loved her and wished her good luck in nursing school.

"Give her time, Jason," Jasmine said. She placed the picture Aaliyah created for me in my hand and hugged me.

"Her time is up, Jas. I'll call you when I'm back in Chicago, okay," I said trying to let her go. She clenched me even tighter pulling me closer to her.

"I still love you, Jason. No matter what," she said as I tried to get her to release me. She let me go and I began to get into the cab.

"I know you do. I love you too. And I appreciate that. Just know baby sis, we may not always get love back the way we give it, but you will always get it back. Somehow. I gotta believe that. Now I gotta go. Kiss the baby for me, and tell your mother this is one faggot she won't have to worry about," I said closing the door. I instructed the driver to deliver me to the airport and looked up at Jasmine one last time before we pulled off. She was sobbing. I looked away, determined not to let my emotions bring me to the point of tears. I forced myself to man up. Tears are a thing of the past for Jason.

I started to think about the relationship my friends have with their mothers. That awesome relationship and bond that countless black men I've seen have. My dad even has it with his mother. Well, I don't know what I did to not have that. I'm envious of my dad and my friends for that one thing they take for granted. Ironically, as much as she claims to hate this "thing" as she calls it, she's never put me out, so I know she loves me and I'll always love her. I pulled my phone out of my pocket and sent her a text message that read: *For the record, I'm not a disappointment. I love you, but I can't be shamed into what you want me to be. You just procreated what God spoke...*

Little Him the King Bee

Somewhere over the course of a few months in the midst of my melodramatic melancholy attitude, Chicago Black Pride made its cameo appearance into the lives of the Same Gender Loving population. It was one of those rare Friday nights that Michael convinced me to get out of the house and join him and Preston at the Prophouse. I reluctantly went and demanded to be the driver so that I could regulate the time we'd spend there. I was starting to outgrow this whole club scene, and could only give it a couple hours of my life if any, now days. The newness of the flashing lights, the endless possibilities of finding the man of your dreams, the flow of sugar infused liquor and the latest song putting you in beast mode was becoming something of a nostalgic memory. Maybe because it reminds me... of how it all began.

My boys and I used to spend hours in the mall after work searching for the right looks accented by the perfect sneaker. Oh, and let's not forget the accessories. We'd discuss who we hoped to see there that night, what deejay would be spinning, how much life we were going to get, what club to go too, and what shady queen we dared to say one single crass word to either of us. The scene would always end up going as follows: Michael turning into a porn star from the pressure of having to bust multiple meaningless nuts before last call, with ummm... yeah, what's his face; Shawn trying to live the life of a video vixen on the dance floor; Preston smiling sweetly while being manipulated by the enticing sex appeal of some homo-thug while checking in with his jealous boyfriend every 10 minutes via text message or live conversation. Oh yeah, and me as the designated driver, nursing a weak cocktail rolling my eyes ready to go home after some fool grinds his sweat soaked body on my beautiful brown skin in an attempt to feel on my booty. And while he's groping my back shots, he's stepping all over my nice clean sneaker. And I promise you it was ALWAYS the left sneaker. AGHHHH! Just once, I needed some excitement. I felt like I needed one reason to make this all worthwhile again. What happened to the allure of everything when I first came out?

God! I am only twenty-five years old, and I'm having what my dad calls one of life's "epiphanies." He told me your first one happens at twenty-five if you have your head on straight, and more will follow every five years thereafter. He said my greatest one would be when I hit the big three oh!

"Jason, at that age a man is too old to be young, but too young to be old. All the things I've taught you are going to come to challenge your character. You'll see all the seeds you planted and the ones I instilled in you manifest into a harvest of useful wisdom as you begin to look at the world with a more serious eye. Your primitive side takes over allowing you to be more aware of your innate ability to man up and survive," he said.

Little Him the King Bee

I don't quite know the full extent of what he was saying to me, but I did tell him I didn't feel like my friends anymore. And looking around this club, I see dudes who were pushing my generation to the side waving Beyoncé banners high in the sky as *that bitch*. What happened to the reverence surrounding the Asiatic black queen of the 90's where Lauren Hill was the dime piece empowering the natural beauty of our black women? When black people wanted more while actually wanting to look black and be black? What happened to the voice of Common and Nas, who predicted the fall of an amazing era of music that expressed the importance of self-identity and social-conscientious awareness?

Looking around this place, the caveat is self-righteousness and cookie cutter emulation. These kids who I'm not much older than, are on a whole new level of shade. It's all about me type of shade. The show me, look at me fags, as I like to call them. Peacocks, with an ambiguous flair rarely found in my generation. They go all out for self not caring who they hurt or exterminate in the process, professing, *those are your feelings, not mine.* I'm not judging, this is just my observation, and it's their turn to start taking over the scene, I guess. But who's leading the sheep now offering them a sense of purpose and worth. This may be the alcohol talking, but things change too fast in the gay community. We're a popcorn society always bored and begging to be entertained at all times. *This can't be life, God! I need the DJ to spin some joints I can dance too. OH MY GOD! I thought to myself.*

I was practically a wallflower all night and decided to let Preston and Mike close the club. Who am I to stop the show? I picked the right bartender tonight. I kept my buzz going with several Malibu and Cranberry cocktails, and got my life finally when the deejay decided to play a few examples of some real hip-hop by night's end. Watching the floor transition from the vogueing Beyoncé generation into those who still held Lil' Kim as the real queen bee was awesome! She reminded us that she, like the rest of us, used to be scared of the dick! Preston and I rapped every freakin' solitary word as if we were on stage right behind her. So I eventually got out of my head hopeful that as long as there were real kats like myself around, the balance of the socio-sexual hierarchy within the Same Gender Loving world would always be there. These young dudes will be pondering this same thing if they are lucky enough to live through the crimping cogs of sex, drugs, and delusions of grandeur found within the natural habitat of the children. Alas, the infamous clubhouse. Such a façade, but a place of refuge to relax and be free.

The lights came on like clockwork at 3:45AM and the music was turned down halfway as the bouncers prepared to kick all of the horny intoxicated patrons into the city streets. The invigorating aroma of expensive cologne and testosterone was all of a sudden heavy as Mike walked up behind me wrapping his arms around me thanking me for not being a party pooper. Preston, nose buried in his phone, laughed walking beside me as we joined the sexy herd heading out of the door being cattle prodded by security. I felt like all that was missing were they telling us, *we got your money faggots, now go home! BOOO HA HA!*

My buzz had me feeling right and Mike made the corporate decision to join some of our mutual associates at the IHOP in Boystown. A Friday night at the Prophouse would not be complete if he didn't get his proverbial dick sucked religiously by this gorgeous dude named Tavares in the small IHOP restroom. You'd think this was ol' boy's sole purpose in life because he was always there standing by when we arrived as Michael discreetly excused himself from the table. We knew what to order him, so by the time the food arrived he'd be finished with a satisfied look on his face ready to eat.

We walked slowly back to my car and Preston dialed Junior Mafia on my iPod and turned the stereo up. I was smiling watching him and Mike dance and rap along with Cease and Biggie as we inched our way towards the intersection avoiding the crowd walking and congregating in the streets and parking spaces.

The night got so much better as I looked over to my left noticing what looked to be a very familiar face. I rolled my window down to remove the dark tint out of my line of sight. I needed to make sure he wasn't a figment of my imagination. I giggled and made a rash decision to jerk the wheel to the left and pull up alongside dude's car blocking oncoming traffic. My heart rate increased, and I knew exactly what I desired to do. I slammed on the brakes, being as dramatic and stunning as possible. I threw the car in park, unbuckled my seatbelt and swung my car door open arrogantly. Mike and Preston stopped their antics trying to figure out what this was all about. The horns of oncoming traffic blew as one of the patrons yelled out asking, "What the fuck is wrong with you?!?!?!"

"I promise you this is going to be SO worth it, bruh! Just watch!" I yelled looking over my shoulder at him. He was hanging out of his car window in disbelief.

"Jason!" Michael yelled. I ignored him and walked right up to the dude I had eyed across the street. He was sitting on the rear deck lid of this raggedy green Pontiac Sunfire, chit chatting with a couple of his friends.

"You remember me?!" I asked not giving him a chance to even think about answering. I clenched my fist tighter than Vivica Fox latest facelift in that 50Cent video, and delivered a swift solid hit to his razor bump filled face.

I hit him so hard that tooth number nine, root and all, popped out of its socket and landed on the trunk lid. A fiery red rage shot through me as I climbed up on top of him and his car. I heard some queen in the background yell out, *"DAAAAAMN! HE FUKIN' HER SHIT UP GURL'AH!!"* I was completely out of character, but this had to be done. And for once, I had the spotlight! This was awesome! I straddled him and wrapped my left hand securely around his throat and began beating the crap out of this dude with my right fist. He gripped my left arm and started kicking his feet flailing about as he struggled to rid himself of my chokehold. I heard Michael in my ear after he fought his way through the crowd of folk standing nearby astonished by my attack. I was breathing like a savage as Michael gripped me like a vice and pried me off of dude. I started to come to my senses after I realized what I'd done.

"You'ought know him like I do. But you're finally my competition... stuck up, bitch!" I heard Desjardin say between coughs. I saw a smile on his face. I didn't quite understand because this wasn't a game. This was my life he played with.

"COMPETITION! What the FUCK did he see in your little filthy looking ass anyway, punk?!" I yelled out letting Michael pull me away from the situation. He pushed me into the back seat of the car as dude slid off of his trunk wiping his face and staring up at me coughing and gasping for air. I rolled the window down and started laughing as adrenaline pumped through my body. "Go brush those two teeth I knocked out your mouth, you dirty bust down! That should make it easier for you to suck somebody else man's dick, right?! Consider it a favor you shaft scrapin' HO! Cause he *love* how I do it. Start being my competition in that arena with all thirty-two!" I gave this stranger a high five as he stood there laughing. Michael was trying to safely maneuver the car around the crowd and out of the traffic I had blocked.

"Damn, bruh! You fucked his shit UP!" The dude

who I originally told would be worth his while stated. I reached out the window at the same time he did and gave him a pound. Michael rolled my window up and sped off around the corner up Elston Ave towards the freeway.

Preston turned the music down and he and Michael were quiet as I sat in the back seat feeling exhilarated from what just happened. I felt like all of my years of holding in this primitive side of myself were well worth every minute. I took out every single dose of anger I ever had in my life on the one person who ruined my happily ever after with Gary. All of my hate, and frustrations, and anger surrounding anybody who ever hurt me had been taken out blow by blow on ol' boy.

"Why ya'll turn the music down? Hell, we still partying right? " I said opening and closing my right fist. My knuckles were slightly swollen and reddish. I checked my hand for cuts.

"Uh, sweetie, what the hell was that all about? I'm kind of scared right now. Subtle was not your tea," Preston said turning to look in my direction.

"Screw subtle. Subtle got me Syphilis! That was Desjardin. You know, Gary's ex! Ol' dirty nasty whorebag!" I said laughing. "YES SIR!!! THAT WAS AWESOME! God Mike, I should have taken your advice and done that long time ago! I GOT THAT HO! YOU HEAR ME?! I GOT THAT HO! My DICK is hard right now dude!" I said gripping and jerking his shoulder. I remembered I hadn't told Preston or Shawn about my STD development with Gary, so I tried to glaze over it and I hoped Mike would too since he was the only one I told.

"Jason, I feel some kind of way about your inner nigga coming out. Damn, what were you thinking?" Michael said chuckling and finally breaking his silence. I rolled the window down and yelled out at a couple of females standing at the intersection waiting to cross the street as Michael came to a complete stop.

"DETROIT! WHAT! I'M FROM THE MURDER CITY, BABY GIRL! TELL YOUR MAN TO GET AT ME! HAPPY

BLACK PRIDE!" I winked and laughed rolling my window up as the two females giggled. "That's what I was thinking about! Swear to God! And where the hell you going? I need a short stack with some freakin' hot syrup to be happening in front of me like right now! Turn this ho around!" I said swirling my finger in a circular motion. I looked around checking traffic through the rear window. "You good on my side."

"Jason, change of plans, I think we need to get you home, so you can get some ice on your hand, okay? You are aware that you make your living with your hands, right Mr. Dental Hygienist?" Michael said.

"Mike, I'm fine. If need be, I'll use a... uhhh... Gracie Curette, and crank up the Cavitron. It was just a few punches to a ho's face, a few teeth on the trunk, no biggie," I laughed. "They got ice at IHOP. So let's get there. Boystown. Dick suck! Now!" I demanded, trying to persuade him with the standing appointment he has with Tavares.

"Jason, you've flexed your nuts enough this

evening, alright? You may want to lay low for at least tonight, okay?" Michael said in a calm voice.

"I agree with Mikie, sweetie. Let's just grab some food from a cute little drive-thru window and head back to my place? What do you have a taste for?" Preston said tying to reason with me as he opened the sunroof and smiled.

"IHOP, HAG!" I yelled.

"We ain't stopping past da IHOP, Jason! Nah, be a good lil' bottom and sit back and enjoy the ride," Michael stated plainly letting his accent creep out. "Put'cha seatbelt t'on!" I sat still and quiet in the back seat for about twenty seconds looking out the window as we traveled further and further away from IHOP! I thought to myself, *Oh, I am about to reeeeeeead these two HOES all up and through my Ultimate Driving Machine!!!*

"So I let ya'll hoes close the club without complaint and I can't get served a plate of pancakes? Either take me to IHOP or pull my joint over right about here so I can run this. This is MY car!"

"Shut up, Jason! I'm running this!" He said hitting the steering wheel. "Nah, dis whas gon' hap'n, a'ight?! I'm drivin' your drunk ass and your car to Preston's place and that's final, shawty! Now we can either kee about what the fuck just happened back there and listen to Kim while you bask in the victory of your first fight EVER in life, or you can jes' hush an' chill da fuck out, nah!" Michael said in a very serious tone. "Because you ain't gon' win this fight! H'ea what I'm talm'bout, shawty!" he said blowing his gum into a big bubble. Michael only did that right when he had reached his limit. His Georgia accent would also come on strong. It was like his way of warning you. I had seen him snap many a jaw in some of our Pride travels over the simplest of things. Mike always had gum in his mouth, even during Uniform inspections. But when that bubble was blown, that meant chill out.

"Umph! Psssshhhh! Well, excuse the Detroit out of me! Big brother has spoken, huh? Take me to Wendy's then since I can't get a gotdang pancake up in this piece! I want a single with cheese. Oooooh, or something manly, like a ummm... Baconator or some tea! And Preston! Will you stop sittin' there all prissy and dignified and let's rock to 'Big Momma Thang'! TURN IT UP!"

"Thank you! ATL trumps the Murder City right now, shawty!" Michael said as we all burst into laughter. "We'll get you some ice at a service station. I owe you some gas."

"Boy, anyway! Hush the entire hell up and work this stick, Mike. Aren't you a Top? This is a German automobile, so drive it like the engineer intended! Go to the Wendy's on Western! That's the best one in town at this hour punk!"

"Yes sir, Mr. Williams, will there be anything else the boss bottom would like to demand or address at this time?" Michael said speeding up making a sharp right onto the onramp to the freeway.

"Yes! You better drive! Guess what?!... *I used to be*

scared of the dick. Now I throw lips to the shit! Handle it like a real bitch! Heather Hunter! Janet Jackme! Take it in the buttttt! Yeah that's what…!" I rapped as Preston joined Lil' Kim and I turning the stereo up again. For the first time I felt like I could tackle the globe with a headlock. And that felt incredible…

Poets and Brushstrokes

It was déjà vu like all of a sudden when I slid the large heavy door hard to the right. I was greeted by exposed brick walls and numerous canvass paintings mounted on either side of the long corridor of the spacious loft owned by one of the most intriguing men I've had the privilege of meeting. Okay, that may be overkill. I didn't know what to expect but I did know that I was going to go with the flow and enjoy myself. I can't say that I was back to my regular self because the only thing that stayed the same was my residence and my occupation. I was in a much different headspace.

I generally wouldn't have entertained the idea of taking the train and following a set of directions given strictly via text but after reading, *Hey gorgeous, the door will be open if you slide it hard to the right because you've officially been summoned to chill with a good brotha' out in Bronzeville...* several times, a smile swept across my face turning into laughter when the voice of the white woman on the subway train in the movie Coming to America blared a mighty, "*Go ahead, honey! Take a chance!*" I took my time showering, shaving, primping and selecting the right outfit to wear. I didn't want to come off as a ho by wearing basketball shorts and a wife beater. And I didn't want to look too clean cut, but I wanted to sort of match the artsy flavor of Poetic Expressions so that I would be in a cool calm and mellow mood. Hell, I even told lunch it was a wrap and cleaned the *"chit'lins"* because if it was going down, I wanted to be ready.

Once inside his place, I sauntered through the entrance taking in all of the incredible artwork on display as if this loft was an extension of the Museum of Art showcasing a glimpse of Africa. Deborah Dyers' voice filled the space acoustically, elevated through two large old school house speakers. I leaned up against the wall and relished in the smooth fragrance billowing from the Black Love scented incense making love to the aromatic cloud of marijuana. There was a large leather sectional positioned in the center of the room, facing a large flat screen television mounted on the wall. An easel was set up in one corner next to the large windows cradling a large canvass with the start of a fresh new piece ready to join the line-up against the wall. The other corner encased a life sized wood carving of a very detailed naked male figure of African descent, arms extended palms up, head lifted towards the sky, feet firmly planted on a cylindrical base. His chest stuck out firm and strong. The brotha's place was pretty dope, like no other home I'd seen before. It was so eclectic, yet simplistically sparse in traditional creature comforts. But the best part of it all was the king of this castle, Rocwell Jones, lounging comfortably enveloped by the plush midsection of the sectional sofa. He had his eyes closed lost in a world of his own, head bobbing as if his mind was riding the waves of the melodic notes invented by one of my favorite singers. Once the song playing came to an end, I cleared my throat still standing in the entrance of the room. He opened his eyes and smiled. "Gorgeous! Don't move, shorty," Rocwell said as I smiled at him. He reached over to grab his camera, and snapped a photo of me. "That's one of your portraits I'm going to paint," he said sitting the camera on the makeshift table. It was a square thick glass tabletop supported by a wide retrofitted tree trunk.

"So you're just going to catch me off guard?" I asked.

"There is nothing like capturing pure emotion. I'ought like rehearsed poses. Plus, you saw me grab the camera," he said getting up. He walked over to me and grabbed my hand leading me into his lair. We both sat on the couch next to one another. "Take off your shoes and get comfortable with me," he said rubbing my head. He moved a tall upright ashtray over to his side of the couch.

"Your place is amazing, Rocwell. Oh my God, you did all of these?" I asked in awe of his talent.

"Yeah, I sculp and paint. Now you see how I eat. I'm my own boss and with your writing skills man, you will too soon as you take yourself seriously," he said nodding his head. I smiled and rubbed my head avoiding eye contact with him. "You cut off all your hair? Why? What's so wrong in life that you'd have to liberate yourself prematurely?"

"Who said anything was wrong?" I said removing my shoes I placed them neatly to the side as he uncorked a bottle of Riesling and poured us each a glass.

"Because you seem to be carrying yourself with a little more boldness. The timid Jason I met a few months ago is long gone," he said stretching his arm and motioning his hand towards the horizon. "Am I right?" He handed a glass to me. I looked into his eyes for a second and found solace there.

"You picked up all of that when I walked through your space?" I asked kind of wanting him to tell me more.

"Me noticing your exit from your previous youthful disposition is going to help me bring you back to your passion, Jason. That's all I'm here for. Salut!" he said as our glasses clinked from the toast. I thought for a moment and found myself unaware of what my passions were these days.

"So are you a counselor now, Mr. Jones?" I smiled trying to let him know he didn't intimidate me.

"Just a man whose undivided attention is all yours. You're safe gorgeous, so you can let your guard down," he concluded as I took a sip of my wine. Somehow, I felt like this was true. "You chief?" He asked referring to the weed he had in an airtight container.

"Oh, no thank you. I... umm, had a bad experience the last time I did," I chuckled.

"Damn, that's pretty unfortunate," he said sounding a little upset about that. You tap into a whole different perspective if you channel the mood right.

"That very well may be," I smiled.

"Well, if you change your mind, I have plenty to share," he smiled. I was glad the option was still available because it did make you feel good, I thought, pondering if I had learned my lesson.

"It's been pretty rocky these last few months for me! I mean, starting with my accident the end of last year," I said, listening to the song playing in the background.

"Lay up wit' me and listen to this track right here," he asked cradling my head as I laid back on his shoulder. I let my body relax against his as we chilled in silence. I closed my eyes and steadied my glass on my lap. I let the acoustic sounds of the British rock band Skunk Anansie's track "You Do Something to Me" relax the questions, the fears, the ideas, and the bull crap buzzing around my head. "You listening to it?"

"Yes, I am. I love this group. This song has such an honest feel to it," I quickly answered.

"Yeah, it does, doesn't it? If the world listened to this song once a day, I promise you it will be all the better for it."

"Yeah, but they never released it; they just perform it as a cover. You are the only other person I've met who is familiar with this group," I smiled liking the fact that he was more than mainstream. But he seemed to be trying too hard to be deep. Maybe it was because I wasn't high with him.

"When did you discover them?" he asked taking a gulp of his wine.

Poets and Brushstrokes

"I was a 16-year-old kid in Germany when I saw Deb expressing herself on camera with the rawest emotion ever, dude. It was umm, that track 'Brazen'. It was exactly how I felt at the time. It was crazy."

"Damn, so how has the world treated you, Jason?" he asked as I laughed. I took a moment to sip some of my wine.

"Like there is some promise I reneged on," I answered shaking my head.

"Can you live happy being spiritually you and not what the world says your physical anatomy promised you should be?" he asked.

"Rocwell, the better question is will I ever be happy?" I chuckled and took another sip from my glass. I hadn't eaten yet, so the cool wine was taking its effect on me as I finished the last of it. "What should I do when I feel like it's no longer fun being me? I am so tired of fighting and defending my type of masculinity. And sometimes I don't even know what I'm defending. Who am I defending? Like, is it freaking worth it? Because people don't care, my family don't care, hell, gays don't even care."

"It is, Jason. It's very much worth it. You are supposed to show up to the fight because it's your duty. So many of us need healing so we can unite and call one another family because we're all we got sometimes, bruh. And once we realize that, then we'll realize that we'll be able to put our original families back together again. We are the key. Our struggle is theirs because they feel like somehow they've failed us, which causes us to resent them and one another. And that's when you take stuff for granted. You are an important part of the puzzle man. The foundation. So you gotta keep fighting for your place in this world unapologetically, Jason. Validate yourself. Your family needs you because love is a uncontrollable choice that refuses to have boundaries. You can control the amount you think you should be giving, but bottom line love is love. Being courageous is never fun," Rocwell stated. I shifted my body so that my head was in his lap and sat the glass on the table. I thought for a second about his statement; it really made sense. But the man in me stayed abreast of his emotions.

"Yeah, but being courageous keeps making me lose people. I feel secondary to everyone else. I want to feel real again. Why can't I be selfish, man?" I said trying not to fold my arms to show my defenses were up.

"Because that's not how you're built," he said. I looked up at him and smiled shaking my head.

"I didn't come for a pep talk, Rocwell," I said wanting to change the dynamic of the mood. I took the lead this go round.

"Yo', my fault!" he laughed. "I get on my metaphysical shit when I'm high, B! What'chu come for then?" he smiled looking down at me. He rubbed my eyebrow with his middle finger and finished his glass. I rose up and poured another glass of wine and guzzled it before turning towards him.

"I'm glad you asked me that," I said seductively. I

stood to my feet and stripped. I walked over to the platform and posed in front of the large canvass mimicking the large carving I observed earlier.

"Well, if that doesn't inspire me, I don't know what will." He removed his shirt and walked over to me. He positioned my body the way he wanted to capture it as he walked around me, studying my physique. We smiled at each other as he instructed me to hold my pose. He walked over to the canvass and readied his materials. "This new Jason is something else. Turn your body towards the window and look out towards the city." I did what he asked. "Yup, hence the name Lil' Fatz. Damn shorty, you got ass son. I can't even front. But yo'! Straight up. I get to paint all that, son?" I smiled and gave him a sexy grin while nodding my head. "No doubt!" he chuckled.

Rocwell flicked his paintbrush into the pigment and began to strike the canvass. The sounds of the streets coming in from the open windows mixed with the music playing took my mind to a far off place. I lost track of the time as I stood there being immortalized as the Isley's sang. I casually peeked over at this amazing artist intensely focused on his current project. He seemed to have slowed down his cadence, placing a dab of paint here and there. He looked up and caught my eye.

We stared at one another for a laconic moment as he undid the buckle of his jeans, letting them fall to the floor. He stepped out of them in a lumbering fashion. He shuffled over towards me as my dick began to awaken from its coma. I looked down and noticed he was just as hard. His dick bounced as he made his approach over towards me. He cupped my jaw into his hand tilting my head in a smooth upward motion. I placed my hands on his waist as he leaned in to kiss me. His tongue raced into my mouth as we received one another in lusty passion. There wasn't a tingle or spark or sensation of yearning desire vibrating through my senses, but rather a need to discover if another man's touch could impress my body.

I valued the presence of a dick other than my own to play with. I began to caress and gently stroke it as the breeze coming in from the outside world heightened the moment of this sexual escapade. Rocwell was definitely husband dick. He wasn't too big, and he wasn't too small, and I was glad because it had been a while. He gripped my ass and hoisted me up wrapping my legs around him. He kissed me clumsily with too wet a mouth as we made our way to his bed.

He positioned me on my stomach so that I was facing the painting. He began to lick, eat, and massage my ass. I was glad that we weren't kissing and hoped that the remainder of the experience wouldn't be all bad. The painting he did of me was awesome as I focused on the detail rendered on the large canvass. I studied it more interested in the art than the wet mess he was making between my legs.

In the painting, he caught a three-dimensional view of the windows and me with words of hope, encouragement, and motivations in each window. I was a lone figure in the center of the mural with my arms holding my body and my face looking out at the world evoking questions that greatly outnumber the answers hoped for. It was an awesome piece with colorful exuberance.

I was horribly distracted as I felt his saliva slowly trample over the tiny hairs of my inner thighs. He asked me if I liked that tongue. I chuckled to myself and quickly said no in my mind pretending to not hear what he'd said. He repeated the question and I made a mental note to moan a few ooh's, ahh's, and a yes or two or three to stroke his ego. I rolled my eyes buried my face in my hands, and sighed thinking, *what am I doing?* But I let the situation progress hoping that at least the dick would be good. I was having conflicting thoughts about not doing it. I wasn't enjoying it. So why was I wasting this man's time. "You ready for this dick, Jason?" he asked as he

kissed his way up towards my neck. He was rubbing my body and breathing heavily. I wanted to say no, but maybe this would help me break free. I thought about the old adage, the best way to get over one man is to get under a new one. I realized just how stupid that crap sounds. *What the hell was I doing?!* I screamed in my head.

"Yeah, you got a condom right?" I asked thinking this was going to SUCK! At least he ain't ask me to suck his dick. Then I'd be grossed out. God, I didn't really want to do this. He moved back to the nightstand and opened a drawer. I watched him remove a Trojan packet. I arose from the bed smiling. I took the packet from him, and started kissing on his nipples trying to make myself get into the mood.

"You ready baby?" he said trying to maneuver me back onto my stomach. He glided his body close to me. I looked up at him trying to figure out how to answer the question. "Yo, we can just chill if you want too. I mean as much as I wanna hit, you don't seem like you wanna do this." He pecked my lips and I was relieved he picked up on my vibe.

"Cool, can I use your restroom?" I quickly asked just as the breeze from the window carried the scent from what was now his dried spit on my face up into my nose. I got up and quickly wiped my face.

"Oh yeah, it's to the right. There are some towels in that chest by the sink. I grabbed my clothes.

"Cool, thanks." I said as I hurried to the bathroom to clean up. I was going to take a hoe bath and get up out of there. I noticed he had a clean bathroom and tub, with Dove Body wash, I decided to take a shower. Once the warm water hit my body, a mental image of Gary invaded the privacy of that moment. I felt him in the shower with me as the water hit my face. I finished showering and quickly dried off and got dressed.

I walked out of the bathroom where I found Rocwell in a deep sleep snoring like a baby. I called out his name a couple of times without a response. I found my shoes and put them on before walking over to the painting. I was in awe at how true to life it looked. He did an awesome job capturing not only how I looked during that space in time, but how I felt as well. It spoke to some feelings that I had been avoiding the past few months. Many concerning Darius, whom I hadn't spoken too in quite a while.

I took one last look at Rocwell and smiled shaking my head and left his place as I walked to the train station. A part of me wished I had of driven, but then again, it was pretty cool not having to worry about traffic in the city. The city makes my mind wander and distracts me at the same time so that I'm not totally immersed in me. I climbed the stairs of the platform a couple minutes before the train arrived. The sun was making its way below the horizon coloring the sky a deep fiery orange. When the train arrived, I boarded and found a seat close to the doors. The bold beauty of the orange sky caused me to make a bold statement as well.

I pulled my phone out of my pocket making one more debate on whether or not to call Darius. I pulled up my contacts and found his name, rubbing the face of the phone like it was his. I selected his name with my finger and waited for the call to connect. I put the phone up to my ear trying to control the nervous shakes making an appearance in my arm. I focused on the horizon as the phone rang a few times, then I heard his rich voice...

"You've reached Darius Westbrook. I am unable to speak with you at this time. Feel free to leave a message for a return call. Thanks." I paused briefly after the beep.

Poets and Brushstrokes

"Darius, this is Jason... hey, I wanted to check on you... and wish you a Happy 4th of July... I know it's been... weeks... but please when you get this message let's meet up and talk... okay... I miss you... I... ummm... call me back... please. Alright... bye... " I said hoping that my voicemail would not be in vain. This was the first time that he's not answered my call. I don't think I've ever had to leave him a voicemail. Even if he can't talk he'll pick up to say, "I'll hit you back, Jason," and ask if I'm all right really quick. Why did we have sex, man?

I gripped my phone tightly staring out of the window. Maybe he was tied up with his new life as a father. The baby should have been born by now, and I didn't even think to reach out to him until now. Well, that's not entirely true, I've thought about it on many nights, but I was so cold to him. I meant full well what I said, and I don't take it back, but maybe my delivery could have been a little more user friendly.

The wheels of the train squealed and clamored to a halt as the voice over the intercom announced my stop. I stood up and made my exit walking casually up the block making my way home. I approached the stoplight and pressed the button to cross as my phone rang. My heart jumped as I instinctively pushed the talk button avoiding a glance at the caller ID. In my mind, it could only be one person...

"HELLO!" I said with nervous childlike enthusiasm. "Where you at, bitch? Don't lie either!" A male voice said.

"Hello?" I said in confusion looking at the phone quickly.

"Jason, can you hear me?"

"Hey, hag," I said dryly sucking my teeth. "I'm sorry I was a little distracted."

"By what?" Michael asked.

"Crossing this street I guess," I said a little irritated at the fact that this was not the man I wanted it to be on the other line.

"Boy, you just now learning how to cross the street?" he laughed.

"What do you want hag?" I asked trying not to let my irritation show.

"Damn, what's wrong with you, hoe? You need some dick or something?" Michael asked. I rolled my eyes and couldn't help but laugh thinking about what was supposed to go down about an hour ago.

"No, I'm just thinking and decided to take a train ride to get out of the house," I said making my way across the street.

"Jason, a train ride or a *train ride, shawty?*"

"The Redline, Michael. Shut the hell up trying to be funny," I laughed.

"Since when your bourgeois ass start taking the train? You got a brand new Beamer sittin' at home," Michael asked laughing.

"Michael, really? That's how you gon' do me? And its Bummer. Beamer is the term for their motorcycles," I said shaking my head.

"Well, I'm just saying. You doing new things this

quarter like fighting and buying weapons of mass destruction and shit. I gotta check on you a little more frequently now days," Michael said chuckling.

"Ah kee kee kee kee! I'm doing me!"

"Anyway big booty judy. I was calling to get a head count for the Taste of Chicago tomorrow. You still going, right?"

"Yeah, I'm down. I gotta get some of that Shrimp Primavera they had last time. Oooh! And one of them cupcakes."

"Good. We'll meet at your house. And it's a good thing you got practice on the train today because I was going to suggest that be the mode of transportation," he said laughing again.

"Go to hell, Mike. I am a city boy, you know?" I said

"Jason took the train. I'll be damned. You probably went to go meet some ol' tired nigga, didn't you? Lil' fast ass."

"No, I did not. Thank you very much," I said lying. "Yeah right, I'll get to the bottom of it later."

"There is no tea!" I laughed.

"Yeah right. You ain't just taking the train just to take the train, Jason. The Bible says, he whom lieth today doth dieth tomorrow," that fool said as we both broke out into laugher.

"Shut the hell up making up false doctrine," I said laughing.

"Well, anyway, I gotta date. So I'll see you tomorrow, shawty."

"Bye, boy. I'll call you later," I said hanging up still

laughing. He was right, though. I was trying to do something out of the norm to get both Gary and Darius out of my system. I doubt it worked.

I placed the phone in my pocket and continued my journey home. Dusk had finally arrived as the streetlights in my neighborhood came on with a flickering buzz. I debated on either walking the dog or just letting him run around out back to do his business. The air was a little heavy causing my skin to become clammy to the touch. I was six or seven houses away from home, when I noticed a large truck that I didn't recognize parked in my driveway. I smiled and picked up the pace anticipating a surprise visit from Darius.

When I got closer, I noticed the interior light come on as the driver side door opened. I reached into my pocket to pull out my house keys. The door closed, and fear crept up my spine...

Knitting My Thoughts

I was back in the Chi chillin' with the family for the 4th of July weekend. This was something I hadn't been able to do in quite a long time. Dad and I barbequed the meat and MiMi and my sister Lauren made the sides. Lauren invited her fiancé Russell over and MIMi invited her dear friend Sherman Wilkes as well, who came up from Charlotte, North Carolina, to visit her. She told me this was the gentleman she wanted Jason and I to meet, and I understood why when Lauren and her dude left. It was just the four of us winding down for the evening listening to the sounds of nature one evening at the family Lake House.

The two of them hit it off when my grandfather sold a car to him back in the day. It was an old pink Cadillac that MiMi said she refused to drive because she told my grandfather she wanted it in sky blue. He felt it more appropriate to buy it in pink, a color she absolutely hated.

Mimi said on her birthday when he blindfolded her and took her out back she knew the Cadillac of her dreams would be sitting pretty in the driveway. She said she even bought a brand new blue party dress to match and set off the white leather seats for her pictures. But when Gramps took the blindfold off and yelled surprise she couldn't hide her disappointment. She made him sleep on the couch until the car of her specifications arrived. Mr. Wilkes was the first one to respond to the ad Gramps put in the paper and fell in love with the car.

MiMi said she knew he was "funny" when he got out of the taxi wearing penny loafers. MiMi said, back in the day in Chicago, only the funny men wore those types of shoes. Mr. Wilkes confirmed her suspicions to be true when she asked what kind of man wants to be seen driving a pink Cadillac, and he responded, "Only a grand diva like myself, darling! Whom else?"

Mr. Wilkes was in his 70's and had been medically retired from the Navy due to a serious shrapnel injury. He started out enlisted and became an officer during a time when black men could only be cooks or infantrymen if they joined the military. He was a well-manicured, tall fair skinned kat, who had aged pretty well. The brother was neatly dressed, complete with a bow tie, and a brand new pair of penny loafers on his feet. He actually had a shiny new penny in each one. He didn't mind letting his feminine side lead the way. He had us in stitches telling us stories from his hay day. I sat back in amazement flipping through his old photo album while listening to his final story of the evening...

"See, back in those days darling you were expected to be a little more conservative. I used to call it being petite. Not, like you little young boys of today. I personally didn't care who knew. I really didn't have to say nothing. Shoot, the way I swishy walked told my whole story baby. And even wrote some people a check, even though I never worked at no bank." Mr. Wilkes said placing his hand on his hip and throwing his shoulder. MiMi and me burst into laughter. "They knew I was a sissy when I got drafted; I didn't have to say a thing," Mr. Wilkes said.

"What was that like? Being drafted and all? Could you refuse?" I asked in wonder. If this man could be brave enough to be his complete self during a time when men were truly men, then I had to hear more.

"Why yes you could refuse, darling, and you'd be hauled off to jail. I'm too pretty to be passed around a cell," he laughed. "But I was a little ol' country boy from Hattiesburg, Mississippi, come from a family of sharecroppers. I wanted to make a better way for myself, so I made the trip up North to Chicago to see what I could do about that. I worked at this Secret Nightclub for the boys who liked boys, and my number got called."

"So you more or less volunteered willingly?" I asked. I loved hearing old military stories. It was on point to see the differences and the similarities through the generations of servicemen.

"Well, I knew the danger. I was young and around that time, it was just what you did for the war effort, black or white. I really just wanted the opportunity to buy a new pair of shoes. I never knew what that was like. The motivation hit me when I saw the little poster of the little white boy in his little tight cracker jack uniform, making that cute little muscle," he sighed with delight. "I said sign me up next to him dah'lin! I had them little white nurses on the floor dying, just queenin'. That's gay for coonin'," he said waving his limp wrist in the air. "I honestly didn't know where I was going to end up, especially since colored men were still experiments used in desegregating the Navy ranks. Eleanor Roosevelt was instrumental in making sure during old President Roosevelt's run in office that we were given a fair chance to do the jobs the good ol' boys trained for, instead of being mess men and stewards onboard the carriers and frigates. When you get a chance young man, do a little research of your black Naval history and look up... umm let's see the... uh... yes... the USS Mason. It used to be called the Sea Cloud, darling. Them were some amazing brothas you need to know about, sailor."

"Yes, sir, I will definitely do that," I said.

"Is it safe to say that you read young man?" Mr. Wilkes asked with a serious look on his face. "Yes, sir, I do," I chuckled.

"Good. You might be able to find a book about it. The USCGC Sea Cloud commanded by an old salt named Captain Skinner. He was a white commanding officer in charge of a ship full of sea worthy strong black men with something to prove. They called it an experiment to see if we could cut the mustard, so to speak. But that was a little before my time," he said clearing his throat and smiling.

"Tell him about your friend Reginald," MiMi said laughing. Mr. Wilkes slapped her knee before he broke out into laughter with her. I laughed sitting on the edge of my seat wondering what was so funny. Dad smiled puffing on his cigar lounging in a chair shaking his head at the two of them. He was reading some medical magazine. I glanced over at him and he gave me a wink.

"I was just getting to that part. Be patient. Now, let's see...my little friend, Regina...that's what we called him," he said glancing over at MiMi who was all smiles. "He came down with me because both of our numbers were called. We worked at the same club serving drinks and cigarettes to them white boys who partied there. So we get down to the MEPS station swishy walking past all those beautiful black men and white men and we sign in and wait to see the doctor. Regina had this big leather satchel draped across his little rail thin body. I looked and said, 'Regina, why do you have this purse slung over your shoulder up in here?' He looks at me and says, 'They don't let just anybody in, so I gots me a idea.' I says, 'So what's your big idea?' We're sitting down at this point whispering to one another," Mr. Wilkes said letting out a hearty laugh and squeal. MiMi, burst into tears as she laughed right along with him. "I get called up to the desk, so the nurse could take me in the back for my weight and measurement. So Regina didn't get to tell me his big plan, just yet. Darling! Lord, Jesus! But when I returned...and saw that old bird." Mr. Wilkes took a pause to laugh again. "Regina is sitting in the same chair with his legs crossed, shirt sleeves rolled up above the bicep and he had put on this fabulous blond wig that he was brushing like it was his real hair straight out the root."

"Mr. Wilkes, you are pulling my leg sir. I don't

believe you," I said laughing. I looked over at MiMi who was dabbing her eyes with a handkerchief and laughing.

"Darling, if I'm lying I'm flying. I laughed and sat next to my new little blond hair brown eyed friend and says, is you crazy, they either gon' do one of two things with your ass. Lock it up, or beat it up. Sometimes, you just have to butch it up, I says. Oh, but he didn't care. Now keep in mind this is 1950 during the Korean War era. Baby, he says he gon' tell them he can't go because he was, you know, funny. And he did his little dainty hand like this," Mr. Wilkes stuck his hand out and waved it left to right from the wrist. "I says boy they are not going to buy that. Back then the Don't Ask Don't Tell policy was unspoken. And quiet as it's kept, you could get arrested for being gay if they wanted to be nasty, especially with him putting that pretty little blond wig on top if his head. Now he thought his little plan was a guarantee, but what we didn't know was as long as you were healthy as an ox and wasn't mental, Uncle Sam was going to make you complete that draft."

"Did he have to go?" I asked.

"I'm building up to that answer, darling. Now, we sitting in the lobby, and this fool gets called to the back to see the doctor, and then I go see a doctor too. I think I got finished before he did, so he comes back, and we sit next to one another again and he pulls out a great big ball of yarn and needles and starts knitting a set of booties. I was tickled pink, and the other men in the room were giving us dirty looks at this point, but Regina still didn't care, he had a point to prove. Now he told me he went in there and put on a grand sissified production." Mr. Wilkes closed his eyes, placed his hands on his hips, and straightened his back to place emphasis on this part of the story. "He says, Shermie, I was hitting on the doctor, you know, just putting on real bad, tootse," he laughed. "One of them nurses came out and says if I call your name line up against this far wall to my left. Regina said, oooh, you know if they call your name to stand to the left side that means you going home. I had heard this to be true. So he crosses his little fingers. His was the first name to be called because of his last name, and I was last, of course. When she told us congratulations you made the cut, Regina says but I'm on the left wall! What do you mean, 'Congratulations; this wall is the go home wall, right?' The nurse looks at him and says, 'That's the right side wall. This is your wall. The war wall.' Regina fell limp, dropped to his knees, and fainted. His little pink yarn ball unraveled all the way down the hallway to the last thread, dah'lin." Mr. Wilkes said as we all burst into laughter. "They had up and changed walls on us. That sissy was so beside himself, but we made the best of it."

"That is too funny. I would have died if I had of witnessed that during MEPS IN-processing." I said

"Oh darling, we performed, do you hear me? Now I have plenty more stories where that one came from, but I must go and rest these little old dainty bones of mine," Mr. Wilkes said grabbing his cane. MiMi stood up to assist him out of his chair. "Will you be here in the mernin'? I'm going to cook a great big country breakfast before we head on down to the church house."

"Yes, sir, I will. Lauren and Russell are coming back as well."

"Oh good, well, I will see you all in the mernin'! Goodnight handsome," he said batting his eyes at me and rendering a hand salute.

"You just take your old funny self-upstairs now. Don't be getting fresh with my grandson," MiMi said walking up to kiss me on the cheek. Mr. Wilkes held the door open for her.

"Goodnight, lovie," she said before directing her attention to Dad. "Good night son."

"Good night, Momma. Mr. Wilkes," he said waving his hand. MiMi walked in through the door and Mr. Wilkes followed.

"Don't get mad at me because the diva is back in town. I know young Darius is gon' watch me swishy walk away. Plus, I'm making him a special breakfast in the mernin'," he said making sure I heard him as the two of them broke out into laughter.

"Sherman! You so old that cane makes that walk shuffly now," MiMi cackled.

"Now darling, that isn't even a word. I should have asked if you read books?" He said making MiMi laugh. "And I may be old, but I can still pull them baby!" he said popping his fingers before laughing. "We gon' get you one of them deacons tomorrow at the good ol' church house, yes indeed," Mr. Wilkes said.

"Ohhh, you know I ain't studying none of them old dried up buzzards Sherman," MiMi laughed as the two of them slowly made their way upstairs.

I leaned back in my chair and got comfortable resting my eyes for a brief second or two.

"What's on your mind son?" Dad asked with a warm smile on his face. I could tell he had wanted to ask me that question all day.

"Nothing much, Dad. Just thinking about Mr. Wilkes among other things? It was nice to take my mind off of my troubles this weekend," I said looking over at him and smiling.

"How you holding up? You ready to talk about it?" Dad asked with caution.

"Umm, not tonight, Dad. I'll be okay," I said placing my hands behind my head.

"Well, if you want to talk about it, I'm here for you, son," Dad said with a reassuring smile.

"Thanks, Dad, I know." I said staring out at a boat speeding across the lake. A flash of lightening quickly highlighted it as the wind began to wrestle with the leaves. The sounds of the waves rolling onto the shore were soothing.

"Have you heard from your friend Jason?" Dad asked. I forgot that I talk about Jason from time to time with my dad. I know my dad knows about me, but I don't know if I'm ready to tell him that side of me that actually loves a man.

"No, I still haven't heard back from him, Dad," I said not wanting to talk about him either. I didn't want to be cold and I hoped he got the hint.

"Well, keep trying. I'm sure you two will be friends again soon," Dad smiled. He put his cigar out and motioned his way off of the lounge chair.

"Yes sir. I will," I said trying to muster up a smile. "Alright, I'll give you a little space. I'm going to get some sleep. Goodnight son. I love you," he said gripping my shoulder and making his way into the house.

"I love you too, Dad," I said smiling. "Okay, don't stay up too long."

"I'm gonna try not to. I just want to enjoy some quiet time and fresh air. Good night," I said watching him enter the house.

Once the screen door closed behind him, I reached up and pulled the chain for the light on the ceiling fan. I lay back down on the lounge chair and got comfortable. I didn't want to think about anything. Man, I was tired of thinking. All I wanted to do was just clear my head and drift off to sleep. I let my mind wander and realized I hadn't checked my phone all day. I reached into my pocket and saw that I had several text messages and a voicemail. Most of the text messages were from a couple of females asking what I was up too, or how they were thinking about me, a few messages were from individuals asking how my 4th was or just checking on my overall state of mind.

When I hit talk to check the voicemail, I was

shocked to hear Jason's voice. My heart started beating fast as shit and my stomach fluttered and I started smiling. I could not believe he thought of me on my favorite holiday. I calmed myself down and listened to his voice several more times noticing something different every time I replayed it...

Darius, this is Jason... hey, I wanted to check on you... and wish you a Happy 4th of July... I know it's been... weeks... but please when you get this message let's meet up and talk... okay... I miss you... I... ummm... call me back... please. Alright... bye...

Shit, I missed him too. I checked the time, and thought about driving down to his house for a surprise visit, but opted not to. I wanted to call, but opted against that as well. I listened to the voicemail a few more times before I saved it and slid the phone onto the table next to me. I was tripping on how, Jason, well, let's just say he changed the beat of my heart.

Mr. Wilkes told me you should judge your partner for their increased potential of being that future and not by where they are in the present tense. He said your responsibility will increase towards one another as a joy more so than a duty. He said work is what you're assigned to do, but duty is what you are committed to doing. I guess the work was letting Jason know I am and always will be there for him no matter what, and my duty towards him was and is to reinforce what he means to me and show him that. I've had plenty of time to prepare and practice because patience makes perfect timing to ensure we'd both love and appreciate one another the way we should. That's what I want us to have so the duty in love will be second nature.

The time I spent with Mr. Wilkes this weekend really opened my eyes to a side of myself that I have glossed over dozens of times because I feared it. I ain't saying I'm a queenie dude inside. I just like men. Damn that's funny to me. But when Mr. Wilkes was telling his story tonight, that shit really hit home because my whole little facade hit the deck and unraveled just like that ball of yarn.

What I learned is if you fall victim to fear, you forget yourself. Shit, fear has a voice so there is no silence. It's just you, versus fear, which is you because it's in your mind. This some shit Jason would be able to help me talk out. But tonight, I need to be selfish for just a little while longer. I need to clear my head and think about absolutely not a got-damn thing. I'll holler at him tomorrow after church with the family...

One Man's Trash One Man's Treasure

I stopped dead in my tracks caught up by all of the anxiety rushing in taking over my state of mind. I stood frozen like if I stood there long enough, I wouldn't be seen. I ran through a checklist in my mind because I didn't have a weapon on me and I wasn't close enough to the front door to enter my own home safely. I went through a quick scene size up calculating an escape route. A cold sheet of fear slowly sliced its way through every ounce of my flesh. He looked the same as I remember him looking just a few short months ago as he called my name out with a slight smile on his face as if I were supposed to be happy to see him. I took a deep breath and built up the courage to walk up to the foot of the stairs of my front porch without saying a word.

I backed my way upstairs as he inched closer towards me. He eased his way to the foot of the stairs as I reached into my pocket to grab my keys. I tried to control the trembling of my limbs. Not wanting a moment of weakness to distract me. I backed up against the door and our eyes locked as I looked down at him. The slight smile he had on his face disappeared into a blank look of uncertainty.

"Jason!" he said as if I wasn't paying attention. I flinched and dropped my keys startled by the urgency in his tone. I reached for the screen door handle and bent down to retrieve my keys wondering what was going to happen next. When I stood back up, he was less than an arm's length away from me. I still had a grip on the screen door handle, prying the door from the doorjamb, feeling a need to place some form of barrier between the two of us. He gripped my arm and called out my name in a low forceful tone. I suddenly felt sick to my stomach with a flashback of the night that shook the very core of my being exploding play by play through my mind.

I didn't want him to touch me. He kept saying my name trying to get me to respond to him. I could only see a monster standing before me that fit the description of the male image in my head dragging me up the stairs as I made an effort to fight my way through the drug induced stupor he placed me under. The way he was saying my name in that very instance linked up to what I heard that night. Batman was barking and scratching at the door and in my head I could hear the muffled sounds of his cries for me. I was done being the victim in any situation. I took a deep breath and faced my fear.

"What the hell are you doing over here, Gary?" I said finally snatching my hand away from his firm grip. I nudged him away from me to regain control over my personal space. I was still a little nervous, but I needed to square up to him like a dude. I remembered I had a Swiss army pocketknife on my key ring. I stood there flipping the blade open and gripping it in my hand ready to retaliate with a good old school Detroit ass whooping.

"Jason, I just want to talk, you can put the blade

away. Okay?" Gary said. He put his hands up surrendering and had that same slight smile on his face again. "Can we go inside and have a..."

"No, we can't go inside, you can sit on the bottom step and we can talk right here. Like why are you even here dude? What do you want bruh?"

"Damn, okay, it's like that. I'm *dude* and *bruh* now? What the fuck happened to baby? What happened to us, Jason?" he asked with a puzzled look on his face.

"Are your serious right now, Gary? Are we really going to play charades tonight? YOU! You happened to us? Are you honestly going to stand here and play this innocent 'I didn't do shit' role tonight?" I said trying to control my temper and volume. I closed the screen door and stepped closer to him still holding the knife tightly in my hand.

"Jason, can you put the blade away? I'm not here to fight," he smirked.

"Gary, can you get down on the bottom step. I'm not here to play," I said not moving a muscle. I was still nervous but determined to be in control of my scene.

"Alright, I'm moving, okay. I'm moving babes," he said with a chuckle as he maneuvered down the stairs and took a seat. I folded my arms and leaned up against the house. I still had the knife open with no intention of putting it away. "Are you going to put the blade up?" he asked as I sucked my teeth.

"Bruh, what the hell do you want? Why are you over here bothering me?" I asked very irritated at this point.

"Baby, I..." he said before I interrupted him. "It's Jason, bruh!" I stated plainly.

"Jason, damn, listen to me! I'm sorry for fucking up, but when I saw ol' boy creepin' out of here that night, I lost it. I don't know what came over me, and I just..."

"Decided to take what you thought belonged to you, right? Let me tell you something, Gary. It took a long time for me to get comfortable in my own dick!" I said glaring down on him. "And I'll be damned if I let you come around here any longer being the fantasy you were to me. You were trying to change me into what you wanted me to be...that is until you discovered I'm not a coward that you can bully around like Desjardin! How long were you raw dickin' that fool while you were with me? Cause that tape wasn't just that one time," I stood there waiting for his response. His expression changed dramatically as if I hit the topic of nondisclosure right on the head.

"What the fuck you saying Jay?" he said twisting his face up stalling for time.

"Do I need to spell it out for you? I mean, Come clean, dude! It's over, I'm not stupid. Call it... ummm bottoms intuition," I said tossing my hands in the air coupled with sheer sarcasm. He hated me calling him anything outside of his God given name or some variation of the term baby. I knew I was pissing him off.

"Like that..." he snickered in a huff. He rubbed his nose three times with his thumb, and bit his bottom lip. I knew I had him then because that's his, *this nigga got my ass face.* "What the fuck... the fuck you want me to say?" he said swallowing and looking down the street.

"I want you to say how long you and Nestle Crunch was fucking?! Start there, hell!" I said gritting my teeth wanting him to get on with it.

"Nestle Crunch...?" he asked in annoyed bewilderment.

"Yes! Nestle Crunch, aka Desjardin the razor bump champ. Now how long were you fucking Nestle?" I asked even more annoyed.

"At that point," he paused referring to his little sex tape before continuing, "like three months." He may as well of gut punched me. Oh wait, he did.

"Are you kidding me? Three months? Gary, why would you... you know what... I got it, no need in asking dumb questions. Are we done here? Do I even need to hear why?" I asked feeling hurt all over again as if his infidelity had just happened. I was more stunned than anything. I suspected two or three times, maybe but not three months.

"Both of ya'll turn me on a'ight! You because you stand up to me and say no. You give me a reason to chase. And him because he backs down and tells me yes. I guess he got tired of me and left. I let that toxic shit skip over into our shit, and for that I apologize. I really do. You forced me to step my game up because you bring out the best in me. And to be honest, Jason, that scared me because I worry everyday if I can do that one thing you need me to do above all else. And that's be the man you see in me," he said looking back up at me. I couldn't really read the look in his eyes because it was unfamiliar to me. "Then I see ol' boy who ass I beat in the club mobbing up out this mu'fucka like he just got the business?! Got me thinking, well shit! I can't even stick my finger in the booty! Just so you know, I found the slips in our crib from the post office of you mailing this nigga shit for years like he your man. Fucked me up, babes!"

"Gary... I... how you know we even did anything?" I asked as if I weren't guilty. I still had my hand wrapped tightly around the knife as I carefully watched his every move.

"Stop it, Jason. Don't do that," he said closing his eyes and shaking his head no. "You can tell me. I just want to hear it from you. You were in your fucking draws the night I showed up at your door, babes. Come on, man," he said opening his eyes again.

"Why does it even matter, Gary?"

"Because that's where your heart's been. You took that chance to have it away from me, but I never took mine back. Even after I fucked up. And you gon' stand up here and tell me you ain't let ol' boy fuck?" he said looking up at me as he stood to his feet. "That was real fucked up, Jason. Was that shit good? I mean, we even now, right?"

"Let's not talk about what's jacked up, liar," I said trying to process everything with this new piece of evidence Gary revealed tonight. How is he reversing this on me? Me sending a few care packages isn't sex.

"Admit it to me! Did you let that nigga fuck?" Gary

asked glaring at me with anger brewing in his eyes.

"And what if I did, Gary, then what?" I was kind of afraid to tell him as flashbacks of the night he raped me slowly poured out of my memory bank. My breathing became a little shallow, but I was able to hold my composure. He was just another fear I needed to face.

"How long you known this nigga? The dates on them receipts show a real familiar timeframe. Cause you ain't meet him that night I boxed that fool. I know you, Jason! You don't let no muthafucka's touch all over that ass but me. Who the fuck is this nigga?" he demanded. His gaze was piercing as his jaws tightened.

"He's a friend I've had since before you and I met, Gary. He's one of my shipmates," I said finally telling him just a piece of what Darius was to me.

"So you fuckin' your friends instead of your man? Shit, er'body ain't able, you know?" he stated with pure disdain.

"At least he's not an ex," I fired back.

"Answer me, Jason! It's real simple babes," he stated in all of his cocky arrogance.

"Yeah! Yes! I did! Yes! I LOVED it too! Now what?" I said standing just as confident in my response.

"Was that the only time?" he asked. He sucked his teeth as I took a deep breath.

"Yes. The only time," I said with a shaky tone. He looked at me like he was searching for something in my expression. He finally responded with the side eye.

"You fuckin' lying to me, man, and you know it."
"Gary, I'm not, it was just that one time, unlike

you!" I said wondering why I was pleading with him.

"I thought you were special," he stated coldly. He bit his bottom lip and shook his head at me with what appeared to be disappointment.

"Did I miss something?" I chuckled.

"Apparently so, Jason," he said walking away from the porch. I had never heard him say my name quite like he said it in that moment. It was like being... stabbed. This, it, us, we... felt over. In that moment, he disconnected our cord. I jumped down the stairs after him and followed him to the front of his truck blocking his path.

"Wait a minute. You cheat on me, for months with your ex, violate me, and come over here and talk in riddles. What the hell does that mean?" I said demanding an answer.

"You mentally checked out of the chance of you and I so you could finally fuck ol' boy. Me? Oh, I was a placeholder. You... I don't know. It's going to be hard to get you outta my system, babes, but hey, at the end of the day, it's going to be your loss. I thought you were different, but that's my fault for putting you up on a pedestal the way I did. Wit'cha insensitive ass! Why wouldn't you discuss that shit with me from jump? That's fucked up! But the part that's even more fucked up is you tried to fight me off of you that night too. Calling that nigga's name out with my dick up inside you?! That's why I forced a comparison fuck on you. I was ya' man!" he said grabbing a hand full of my booty.

One Man's Trash One Man's Treasure

"I'm the only one supposed to soak them walls up! You know he can't curve your spine like a cashew and beat that shit up like I can. He can't make you go to work sit in your chair a certain way thinking of me still carving up this phat ass of yours," he said as he let go of my booty. "Be lucky me not murda yah lil' ass that night, slut boy cause I wanted too. Wha'chu was thinkin', fucking a weak ass nigga like that when yah gotta rude boy to take on deck?!" He gripped my arm very tightly, puffed his chest up, and moved in close to my ear. "You're trash to me now, we clear," he said in a hushed tone. He threw my arm back at me and wiped his hand on his jeans as he hocked up a loogie and spit on the ground between he and I. He then stepped around me. I felt like the wind had been kicked out of my sails. I kind of understood the full extent of his anger to say the hurtful things he had said to me.

There was so much I could have said, but at this point I think it would have fallen upon deaf ears. The circulation returned to the section of my arm he grabbed. I watched him get into the truck, back out of the driveway and slowly roll down the block. I didn't know where to go from that point but inside of the house. I was trying to figure out what had just happened. Did he really just say what he just said to me? In that moment, I felt the lower portion of the pocketknife dig its way into my sweaty palm. I'm sure it would have been so easy to jab him in the neck when he called me trash, but then there goes my quality of life. I chuckled to myself thinking, *Damn! This Negro called me trash.* I then burst into a big ball of laughter as I casually walked up the porch steps and into the house. Wow! Trash, though? Okay, he's never left me speechless like this before.

I walked inside the house locked up, set the alarm, and walked towards the living room semi intrigued, yet still amused by Gary. I wanted to feel like everything he said was complete crap, but those were his feelings, and I had to respect that. I guess I couldn't give him all of me because of the feelings I had for Darius in the part of my heart reserved for him. Even Michael picked up on it when he said I was frigid towards Gary sometimes. I didn't realize it. This was a weird mix of everything in my head.

I plopped down on the couch landing on my back. Batman started playing with my hand on the floor as I rubbed and pet him. My body felt as if I were drifting along the surface of a pond. I let my mind wander just thinking about life in general. It's so funny how life can change from minute to minute. I didn't realize that moments are timeless. And with all of the many moments I've had, I wish that I could know for sure if I had done one detail differently, would my remaining moments have come about differently. I mean say for instance if I maybe would have went with Shawn to use the bathroom that night at Club 708 during Atlanta Pride, would I not have met Gary? Or what if I would have never touched Darius's hand in the gym that day? What would have happened? Would I be in love with only Gary? Are we ever really ready to become who we dream about being? And how do we become those individuals if we never know the details that will affect us later in life as a result of our moments?

I ask God this question all the time. Why do I as a black man first have to live like a human padlock? Running towards a combination comprised of ages 18, 21, 30. Every black man on Earth has this etched into his psyche. It's a combination which unlocks his given destiny. We are taught to make it to these three specific ages in life and choose the direction that will make you someone to aspire to be. But if you're gay and go in that same direction it's a waste of a man. And if you make it past 30 you obviously did something right. Some of us figure 30 is a long way off and think they got so much time, so they're like whatever. Then there are those like me, who works to acquire all these things to show to others this is what the good black man looks like. We miss out on pleasing our own selves by doing this, not becoming the black man we want to be. Look at all these DL dudes divorcing their wives at 45 coming up in the punk palace dressed like Run DMC. They're supposed to be teaching my little young butt something. But I digress...

The crazy part is I never got a chance to miss Gary the way I missed Darius. Me missing Gary during our break up was more or less me missing the companionship because the reasons for the break up were such crap, that it diminished the reasons I said I fell in love with him in the first place. Gary wasn't a filler as he stated in his tirade. He was the closet version of

Darius I could have. All relationships seem to have a lot of hidden issues you don't notice until you're in the middle of them.

I drifted further into my thoughts questioning my faith and trying to put the pieces of this puzzle together. I began to do the one thing I hadn't done in a long time. Pray. I started and got everything out that I was feeling before dozing off to sleep. I remember feeling lighter as if I had shed the weight of the world off of my back. In this dream I was walking, but moving at the speed of light. Everything looked beyond 3D and crystal clear. There was brightness all around me. I then heard,

"You asked ME if you were wrong for being you? Remember?"

"Yes. I remember," I said stopping to look around.

"What was my answer?"

"I don't know."

"What does your experience teach you?"

"I think sometimes, if I may be honest, yes. But then I keep on living and I can't turn off how or why I am the way I am. So it's no! Because all I know is me. I'm the only person I truly know, but I'm still trying to defend my masculinity. Why am I good enough for You and myself but not good enough for them? I've never had a problem with my sexuality. They do. I don't even have a problem with them hating me for being gay. I just want to be Jason. Allow me that freedom," I said.

"You are a child of them, but not like them. I don't give you a choice in what shell I merge you with. You are

made from MY understanding. I told you to keep living."

"Yes. But those like me have been holding on for so long, and it just feels like we rely on You for so much, and it makes me ask, why? Because it's like we're forced to create these fabulous grand lives and still get treated as second-class citizens. We over achieve to show we are just as great if not better than them. I don't know," I said.

"Man understands love. Man gets love. Man can see love. Man acts out of love. And that's where you come in. To teach unconditional love. You are something man does not know. True Love. Pure Love. Each of your stories is a testament to that. Dwell in me and I will dwell in you."

Suddenly I felt myself crying. Crying up all the guilt, shame, hurt, and all the pain, I felt. Everything that I was holding on too that made me even question wanting to live. I cried up everything telling me that I was less than a person, that I was a mistake. I cried up the hurtful second daughter reference, the word faggot being used towards me by my own mother, being called trash by Gary, and everything I could think of and I forgave them and the world. I don't understand it, but I have to live in it.

I don't hate Gary I guess I just really wanted to get back at him, but some of what he said was true. This was a vulnerable side that I had never seen from him, and it made me realize my part in this. I decided to take a really long hot shower. My muscles were all relaxed and I didn't feel on edge, finally. I shut the water off and dried my body. I stepped out of the bathroom slipped on a pair of underwear and a fitted tank top. I wanted to watch a little television, so I headed towards the living room and heard the sound of a car parking in front of my house. Batman started growling, and I instructed him to be quiet. I adjusted my glasses and looked through the peephole. When I noticed who was walking up onto the porch, I opened the door ready to forgive and forget.

As soon as our eyes locked, we snapped into one another like magnets kissing, groping, and making our way into the house closing the door behind us. He buried his face in my neck kissing me with those beautiful lips I missed so much and inhaling the hushed pheromones of the fragrance I was wearing.

"What you doing with that on? You don't wear cologne," my late night visitor asked. He was still holding me tightly.

"I sprayed it because it smells like everything I remember you are to me," I said with a nervous pulse thrashing my heart. I had let go and completely gave all of my heart to him.

"You did everything right, you know that. I guess we know what being a rebound feel like. We could have both been real. I was wrong, though. I'm sorry," he said as he kissed me with ravenous fervor.

The rainwater mixed with the sweet warm taste of his lips was delicious, just as I remembered. I removed his damp shirt as he kicked off his shoes. He kissed my chest before scooping me up into his arms, taking me up the stairs. He bent me over the bed and kissed his way from the nape of my neck down to the small of my back. I felt a tug on my pajama bottoms and underwear as they were slid from my body in slow unison. He then burrowed his face between my cheeks and tongued my hole. I gripped the pillow, and thrust my pelvis back and forth as the moist pierce of his darting tongue penetrated my entrance.

He gripped and palmed each cheek, spreading them to gain further deeper access. I reached into the nightstand and grabbed the bottle of lube, and handed it to him. He wet my hole with many fluid strokes of his middle finger, driving me crazy. I was so ready for him to stop teasing me that I took matters into my own hands. I got off the bed, and motioned for him to lie on his back. I lubed his dick, and gently rolled a condom onto him. I straddled him, slowly taking every inch. He let out a deep happy groan once I had all of him inside of me. I could feel it pulsate and throb against the tightness of my walls. I began to ride him drawing him deeper inside of my body, increasing the pace as he gripped my ass and began meeting my downward motion with a strong upward thrust. His rigid love muscle was just what I needed to tame the vicious attitude stirring inside me.

The two of us locked eyes, and gave one another the occasional kiss. We found a nice comfortable rhythm and I began to jack my dick, still looking him in his eyes intensely. There were no words exchanged, rather our lustful moans mixed with chocolate and caramel flesh drumming out the beat of passionate sex as the rain poured heavily from the sky. The heat from our bodies intensified dampening us two. I continued to beat my dick until I felt my body tighten with euphoria releasing my juices onto his sculpted chest. I continued to ride him, taking it like a champ until my baby came. He pulled me close to him and clenched my body once he reached his climax. I wrapped my arms around his neck resting my head next to his, licking and kissing his neck still lost in the amazement of making love.

Our breathing came to a relaxed pace as our bodies took rest in the afterglow. I don't know what made me revisit the sexual tension between us just like the first time we did it. All I remember is how he felt that first time and how safe I felt in his arms. I remembered being in his arms and him kissing and biting my neck that first time. I remembered exactly what clinging to him as if he were the umbilical to my cord felt like all over again. He told me I turned him from a boy to a man and that scared him. He held me tight and dozed off. If only for a moment I knew everything was all right with the world again. It was hard to make believe I didn't miss him. Hell, if only for tonight...

She Just Clung to Me

I could really stand to choke this bitch out right now. I really could. Fuck me for making love to this bitch! But when she said we bout to have a child, I believed her. Forgetting everything selfish about me. I put me on hold because she finally said we. I felt like God was handing me exactly what I asked for, but she killed the dream and my baby girl, I wanted to name her Anita after MiMi. I planned to ramp things up for retirement as a Captain in the Navy for my little baby girl, so what the fuck am I supposed to do now when it seemed like she was ready to finally live this dream with me? My two girls wouldn't have wanted for shit! I had it! Even proudly doing my part protecting the country so that stupid bitches like her can have the right to choose and do stupid shit like this! I just gotta know right now who wins in this situation?

At least my little girl waited on her daddy. At least that's what I choose to believe. I got to hold her. I got a chance to experience what they say love feels like for real. I was now determined not to walk away from it ever again. And if I weren't so in my feelings right now, maybe I could appreciate and get used to someone giving it back. I've been feeling like not giving a damn about anything no more. This was supposed to be the day I was to get the call that would change my life forever. My little baby girl, all shiny and new with her mother's blood and mine was here. I got there just in time to stop her from crying. I touched her lil' pie face wiping her tears with my thumb.

She opened her eyes wide and stared at me looking curious. Her little hand gripped my shirt tight like she was pulling me closer to her. Like she wanted to tell me something. I stayed still as possible holdin' her for a good eight or nine-minutes, man, until I literally felt her tiny grip get weaker and weaker. She took this deep quiet gulp of air and let go of her...life. I watched those same big doe eyes vanish as her eyelids slowly crawled to a close. I held her delicate body close to my chest man hoping the esprit of fatherhood would remind her that Daddy was here for his lil' mama. I wanted her to wake up for a little while longer. I cried which was something new to me. Mom's funeral was the last time I did that. I could feel her body become a limp mass. All I could do was just hold her. I didn't know what to think because she did nothing wrong but everything right in the short lapse of time she'd been here.

I was so mad at God. I didn't know what to do, man. I did everything I could! I prayed; I honored her mother. I went well out of my way to make special accommodations for Cindy. I was ready to be more than just somebody's fuckin' daddy! I was going to be a Father. I was going to be a hero to my baby girl! It was taken from me and I don't understand why some people get the blessings you know deep down in your heart you'd treasure so much more than they ever would. It's subjective, yet we can't question that, right? Just like I couldn't understand how Cindy didn't give a damn about the beautiful girl we made! And I just have to accept it?!

So I just wrapped my baby girl up in my arms, man, and rocked her keeping her as close as I could to my chest in the corner of the room. The staff at the hospital gave me all the time I needed. Because I dared them muthafuckas to make me let her go. This broad gave our baby, my baby girl severe swelling of the brain with her abuse towards her in the womb. And even though the funeral was a breeze, the 4th of July this year was a different story. My favorite holiday was now dark. This was the day two doctors confirmed would be my baby girl's birth date. Today, I didn't have shit to pop a firecracker over. It was the saddest day so far in life as I relived the memories of her in my sleep...

"Lovie, what are you still doing out here? Come in out of this rain," MiMi instructed gently waking me up. I blinked several times taking in a lung full of the moist air. The thunder was barely audible as the rain fell at a steady pace.

"I guess the sound of the rain made me doze off, MiMi," I said yawning and stretching. MiMi wrapped herself tight in her housecoat and sat down next to me. I moved over making room for her to sit comfortably. She grabbed my hand then smiled.

"I know this day was hard for you, lovie. And it's okay to feel whatever way it is you're feeling right now," I turned away from her and sighed rubbing my face.

"MiMi, this is something I want I to forget," I said

looking out into the distance.

"The heart is a filter, lovie. Not the mind. It holds onto everything whether you like it or not. It forces you to appreciate what matters most even when you don't understand why you have too," Mimi said gripping my hand.

"What I don't understand is why I can't question why God let me just hold her for a few minutes, then poof, she gon'! What was the point, huh? I'm just supposed to accept this as it came. It's bad enough I lost my mom before I really got to know who she was, and now I don't even get to feed or change my first born. What kind of God would do that to a person?" I said pissed off.

"Look at me, Darius," she said waiting for me to turn my head. "Do you know who you are? Can you describe yourself?"

"Yes, MiMi, what are you... I don't know if I understand the question," I said wishing I had just gone up to bed. But MiMi always had a way of using her wisdom to unlock the secrets life leaves behind in your footprints.

"You sure don't act like it. Why do you deny who you are, lovie? Let's start there," she stated. I took a moment to think.

"I don't, MiMi. I know who I am, and I am okay with that," I said.

"See, you can't even say it out loud. Or at least loud enough for you to hear," MiMi said, kissing my ear before letting my hand go. I scratched my head, trying to figure out what she was talking about.

"MiMi, no disrespect, but you're giving me a headache," I said taking a deep breath and looking her in the eyes.

"Lovie, you got the world fooled but not God. You strut around here trying to be a carbon copy of your dad. My son. And there is nothing wrong with wanting to be like your father, but you have to live the life God gave you. If you don't wake up, you are going to miss out on the life you think you don't have the courage to lead. That precious little baby, God rest her soul, was not meant to be yours. And the reason I say that is because you were more in love with the idea of what she represented more so than you were in love with her." She pursed her lips and looked out into the distance before continuing. "I know it hurts to hear this, but her spirit knew that. Just because you make a baby don't make you a man. A man who is honest in his own walk makes a man, Darius. And that type of man figures out his own worth. Now, I'm not saying you can't or won't be a father, but what could you have possibly taught her about life, when you won't even live your own?"

"I never thought about it like that, MiMi," I said leaning my head against the back of the chair.

"Sure, you would have done right by her, but at what cost if it's for the wrong reasons. You've got to first learn and accept who you are before you can show someone else the gift they are to the world. You can't steal or borrow anyone else's shadow. It's unique to only them, and stealing from the gift God granted them comes with a price that you may not be too thrilled with while you're living on this Earth. Now you're grown and what you do with that bit of wisdom is on you. You can't be your father and Darius at the same time. You can take and use the same principles he's instilled in you in your own life, but you can't be him, lovie. Is this making any sense?" MiMi asked. What she said hit home and really struck a nerve with me. Hell no, I didn't like it, but I understood why my baby girl couldn't stay with me. I forced her existence.

"Actually, MiMi, it makes perfect sense and I hear what you're saying. I...man...I get it. It just hurts so much, these feelings that I have for men and women. I was really hoping that she would change all of that because I would have someone else's happiness to think about. I thought it would be nice to not have time to think about my own reality. She would have been my scapegoat," I said feeling the grief escape. She gently gripped my head pulling me into her bosom. I wrapped my arms around her and gave her a hug. I felt so much welling up inside.

"Let it go, lovie. It's all right. She was an angel and I'm sorry she couldn't stay with you a little while longer, but that little girl's purpose in your world was a means of encouragement. And that's something you can't fall in love with. You are made to fall in love with the honest to goodness promise because those aren't meant to be broken. She'll always be a part of who you are and she lives right here," MiMi said rubbing my chest. "Now that you know what love is, channel it towards yourself, so that when the time comes for you to claim what God has for you, it won't be lost," she said.

I closed my eyes and thought back to the night I held Jason throughout the night after the fight I had with his ex. I found comfort in knowing that my daughter was a Seraphim assigned to watch over me. It was time to not only right the wrongs I made towards myself but also to those I cared about.

"Thanks for being here, MiMi," I said as we let one another go. I showed her my teeth and she laughed, slapped my knee and kissed me.

"Anytime. I love you so much, I just want you to live your best life because you only get one shot at this thing," she kissed my cheek again and stood up. "Now I don't know about you, but I'm going to bed, again," she cackled.

"I have a phone call to make, MiMi," I smiled. I used my shirt to dry my face.

"Okay, lovie, I'll see you after while," she smiled and walked into the house quietly closing the door behind her.

I punched in the code to unlock my phone. I opened a picture of Cindy when she was three months pregnant. She had the baby bump showing and cupped it with both hands. There was a great big ol' smile on her face with her pretty white teeth showing. She was looking down at her belly and she looked like she was happy if you asked me. It was the only picture she'd sent me while she was pregnant no matter how many times I asked for more. Her mind and heart seemed to be in the right place in this picture, though. This picture got me through some tough nights during my deployment in Iraq. It gave me hope that maybe she really wanted to start a family with me. It turns out she didn't. She took her resentment out on an innocent life the more her body changed because having children was not in her plans. I still can't for the life of me understand how a woman could not embrace motherhood, but I guess if it's not in you, then it's just not in you. I can admit I forced it on her. I was being very selfish, but damn,

she didn't have to... kill...

I closed my eyes and lay back against the chair. I looked back down at the phone and closed the picture. It had been a few months since I had seen or heard from her. We parted ways quick and quiet when we saw each other at the funeral. I went into my contact list and dialed her number. It rang a few times and I could feel myself getting anxious hoping that she'd answer the phone. I almost bitched out until I heard the sound of loud music in the background followed by laughter.

"Hello!" Cindy yelled over the background noise. "Cindy! What's up, girl?"

"Helloooo!" she said sounding irritated as she yelled over the noise.

"Cindy! Can you hear me?" I said a little louder so she could hear me.

She Just Clung to Me

"Who is this?! Wait I can't hear you, hol'on!" she said sucking her teeth. She yelled out to someone in the background that she'd be right back. The noise in the background gradually faded in my ear as she yelled into the phone again.

"Now who is this?" she said in annoyance. "Cindy, it's Darius. How are you?"

"Oh. Hey," she said like I had just ruined her night. I heard her huff as she adjusted the phone. She was probably picking at her nails.

"Yo' I won't be long, I promise. I just wanted to see how you doing?" I said trying to get her to warm up to me just a little.

"I'm fine, Darius, now what do you want? I'm hosting an event," she said coldly. "This will just be a second girl! Mmm hmm, you know I'm not leaving girl. Tell Trey to pop the Moet..." she laughed talking to someone in the background. I was starting to just hang up on this hoe, but I needed to get what I wanted to say off of my chest.

"Cindy!" I yelled attempting to get her attention. "What boy? You called my phone, okay! What?" she said.

"Just two things and I'll let you go, alright?!" "Mmm hmm. Whaaaaat?" she said.

"First, how have you been doing? Are you okay?" I asked out of genuine concern.

"I'm good, is that all?" she stated.

"Okay, look I just wanted to apologize for everything I put you through and..." I said before she

267

cut me off.

"Apologize?" she laughed, *"Apologize? For what?"* she said sucking her teeth.

"Look, I'm sorry for getting you pregnant and forcing my selfish demands on you. I have to apologize to you for all that you went through, and the part I played in traipsing in and out of your life. I was selfish as shit, and I know it may not be now, but I hope that someday you can forgive me," I said feeling a release. There was silence on the other line and a delay in response. "Cindy?"

"Look, I ain't getting back with you if that's why you called. And don't call my phone after midnight like this because I'm not giving you none of this good-good, okay?" She said very coldly.

"Cindy, seriously? That's not why I called you okay. I'm trying to be a man about this and... " I began before she cut me off again.

"Darius! Fuck you, and fuck your tired apology. How 'bout that! You've got a lot of nerve calling my phone with this weak game you be runnin'. It's not going to work this time because I know all about your nasty ass. Ungh huh! I know!" she said.

"Cindy, I'm not trying to run game on you sweetheart?!" I said wondering where this was going.

"I know all about your lil' nasty ass secret double life. I can't believe I was dumb enough to let you touch me. I ain't want to carry no faggot's baby, but the money you broke me off helped me get some really expensive parting gifts... " she said as I interrupted her this time.

"Hold up! Ain't no need for you to get out of pocket, so watch your damn mouth, and where you get all of this shit from?" I said wondering how she knew what she thought she knew. I could give a damn about some little bit of money.

"No, you hold on! I know all about your gay ass! Your business is all up and down the streets of Chicago! I got gay friends that frequent them clubs you sneak off too when you visit home. So do yourself a favor, stay the fuck away from me, or I'm going to have my new man and my cousins to fire your life. You stay the fuck off my phone. You and your stupid ass apology and your dead half a faggot ass baby can kiss my ass! Right is right and wrong is wrong, and you ain't right!"

"Yeah, I forgive you too, cheap bitch! Ol' cheddar bay biscuit eatin' ass," I said shaking my head at the cat being let out of the bag.

"Don't call this number no more wit'cho dick suckin' ass. You probably do it better than me anyway. I have a red carpet soirée to go look fabulous in," she stated. Her rant was followed by the call being disconnected.

I looked at the phone in disbelief - maybe even with a little anger. I can't believe she just snapped off and cussed me out like that. I can't say that I really blame her though. In my head, I saw that going much differently, but maybe I deserved it. Shit! MiMi did say you have to suffer the consequences of your deception sooner or later. This trick even sent the picture that one of her faggoty ass friends sent to her of me in a club of dudes. I couldn't do nothing but laugh. I took a deep breath and let the shit roll off my back. I felt better for at least apologizing, and since she knows my secret, well, damn. I thought about calling Jason, hoping he'd want to talk, but I decided to just chill for a minute, then take it on upstairs and get some sleep. Tomorrow was a new day...

So Ya'll Go Together

I woke up late in the morning to the sounds of Batman barking and tapping his paws down the stairs towards the sounds of my friends. Their noise replaced the peaceful silence with a rather loud and always animated conversation. I jumped up and remembered I was supposed to be going to the Taste of Chicago with them this afternoon, but we were going to hit up some of the shops in Boystown first, which is why they were here so early. It was just past eleven. I jumped up rubbed my face and put on a pair of sweats, making my way downstairs just in time to hear my name being yelled by Preston as Shawn came out of my kitchen scolding Michael...

"I hope that when you do have a kid that he be the cuuuuutest little petite big booty bottom the world eeeeever did see, and that when he goes to black gay pride, gets poked by eeeevry top imaginable... bitch!" Shawn screeched.

"My baby gon' be straight, not that fuck shit you talm'bout, shawty," Michael said in his true Georgia drawl before cracking up.

"Really, ya'll breaking and entering now?" I said as Preston walked out of the kitchen with a bottle of water, two of my granola bars, and a honey bun. Shawn and Michael were seated on the couch. Shawn was flipping through the channels on the TV and Michael was on the phone. I hugged Preston.

So Ya'll Go Together

"Hey sweetie! It looks like someone had a late night creep. Look at you Mr. Disheveled," Preston chuckled as we made our way into the living room. He tugged the elastic waistband on my sweatpants. "Oh my, no draws." I laughed and swatted his hand away.

"Bitch, we knew your shady ass wasn't going to be ready," Shawn said. He had finally started talking to me again but was still making little quick jabs about me being shady because of our fight a few months back.

"Right, chop! Let's hit it big booty! They finally got a sale at Bad Boyz. I need y'all to help me pick out some jeans," Michael said breaking away from making his phone call long enough to give me a quick hug.

"Yes, Jason, you have thirty minutes. We have got to get Mikey out of these hood boy jeans," Preston chimed in as he sat on the couch and placed his water bottle on a coaster.

"Ay! Respect a Top. Bottom!" Michael scoffed pointing at Preston. Preston gave him a side eye sneer.

"Okay, so anyway, it's not going to take me long to get ready, I'm sorry, I had a long day yesterday," I mused. This was about to turn into a real dilemma, I thought to myself. I couldn't think of a solution fast enough with all of their energy intoxicating the room.

"Jason, you got some shoe cleaner? I scuffed the hell outta of my shoe tripping up the stairs," Shawn asked. I looked down at his shoe.

"Yeah, I got something that will take care of that. I'll bring it down to you," I answered quickly. Batman jumped up between his legs and he picked him up and started playing with him. "Let me let him outside real quick. Come on Batty Boy so you can go pee," I said snapping my fingers as he trotted behind me. I slid the screen door open and let him outside.

"Jason, go get ready, and bring me the cleaning stuff shady, so we can get up outta here now. I got the dog," Shawn said as Michael snapped his fingers and gave me a look. He was still entertaining whoever was on his phone.

"Okay, hag, I'll be right back," I said. Just as I started to make my way down the hall to run upstairs, all eyes were fixed on Gary as he caught and embraced me before he spoke to everyone in the room. They were all shocked as Gary grabbed my chin and kissed my lips passionately with a lot of tongue. I was in a cold sweat and kind of embarrassed.

"Hold on, lem'me call you right back," Michael said abruptly hanging up the phone. He had a weird smile pasted on his face. I rolled my eyes and ushered Gary down the hall. We exchanged pleasantries and he told me he couldn't expect me to continue to put up with his bullshit and he also apologized for stringing Batman up in the bathroom that night then made his exit. I closed the door, and chuckled from embarrassment as I took the walk of shame back into the living room to face the judgments of my friends.

"Biiiitch! No wonder you're half naked without any sexy colorful low-cut briefs adorning your derriere. GQ says that's the underwear of choice this season for the bottoms by the way," Preston cheesed, glancing over at

Michael who smiled and shook his head. "Keep that in mind when you go down on some of the trashy bottoms you mess with Mike." Hearing Preston use the word trashy made me relive what Gary said about me the night before.

"Who could wear draws with the bottom of that pudding cup being scraped last night? I know he treated that ass like trash last night! Oooooh, bitch! Yes, yes, yessss! Make-up sex is the beeeest," Shawn said reaching up to give me a high five. Michael laughed for a quick second and shook his head.

"Really, Shawn?" I smirked looking at him snapping back into reality.

"Oh bitch give me those five digits, don't leave me hangin', whore! You back with ya' man? Was the makeup sex good gay and trashy? Hmm?!" Shawn quipped as I reluctantly slapped his hand against mine. I wanted to banish anyone from using the word trash and its derivatives in my presence. I felt like there was a memo that went out surrounding that word that I somehow missed.

"So what, Jason? Ya'll go together or whatever?" Preston said sitting on the edge of his seat with a huge smile on his face. Ever since his trip with his job to New York's fashion week, he had been trying to say things that sounded like New York or whatever.

"No...it's nothing like that...he just, you know stopped by for a visit. Ain't no tea there," I said wishing that my business wasn't on blast just yet because I still needed to sort out who the hell we were to one another these days.

"Ohhhh! It's not like that says the free baller. Then what is it like? Was it good, bitch?" Shawn asked as Preston rested his elbows on his knees.

"Yeah! Get to the sinning part! You ain't getting off that easy ho!" Michael said as Shawn and Preston laughed. I just smiled politely.

"I mean we lightly messed around," I lied. I got up to go and let the dog in.

"Ah, bitch! That wasn't no lightly messin' type of morning after kiss. Ya'll was fuckin' last night," Michael said clapping his hands together sounding as if he was getting pissed off.

"And he should know, so sit yo' ass down and pour each of us a glass of this good sweet gay tea," Shawn said.

"Cause that man is too damn phyne to turn down, Jason!" Preston said standing up to slap Shawn a high five. They both broke out into laughter. I closed the door after Batman ran into the house.

"Okay, shiiiiid! I wish you would lie about this one," Shawn said grabbing my arm pulling me back onto the couch between he and Michael.

"Okay, we... did it," I said looking up at the ceiling. "YES! Come through, Gary!" Shawn said putting me in a headlock and giving me a noogie to the dome. "Bitch! I know you got your life last night! Make up sex is the best! Just ask Andre."

"Ya'll know I don't discuss what me and Gary do," I replied.

"Yeah, yeah, yeah! So what does this mean because you aren't the casual sex type of gentlemen," Preston asked. I thought about my episode with Darius. How true of a statement is that now?

"Well, it doesn't mean anything really. Well... I mean it does, but it just happened, and... Look, Gary thinks just because he was the first piece of dick I had, he should be the only one I have," I said trying to sound hard in front of my friends before Michael interrupted.

"If you're a couple, fuck yeah," Michael said. "Right, but with Gary, there's a catch. See he

wants to do his dirt on the side and keep me under glass at the same time. And that's all I'm going to say about that. It was just good familiar sex, okay guys?" I said trying to make my point clear. To be honest, I really didn't even have a point. I just didn't want to talk about this right now.

"Don't even try it, Jason! You didn't tell them, did you?" Michael said giving me the stop bullshitting face.

"Michael, don't do this right, now. Uh uh, don't do that. Okay? I mean, he came over last night feeling vulnerable and in need of a familiar touch, okay? And we were both feeling that way and we ended up getting' it in. It's a lot going on in both of our worlds right now, and we just needed some company and..." I said as Michael chimed in.

"You needed some dick!" he chuckled. "I didn't think you had it in you, but you always surprise me, shawty," he finished, shaking his head.

"Oop! Don't get kicked out, Mikey!" Shawn said

dying laughing.

"Shut the hell up!" I said sucking my teeth at Shawn.

"Just remember choose your dicks wisely 'cause Poz is the new Neg. Ain't nothing out here but AIDS. Men like him sicken me. You need to lea' his punk ass alone, shawty," Michael warned in full big brother mode.

"You know the hell what?" I said chuckling and shaking my head. I needed to walk away from this. "AIDS ain't the only thing you gotta worry about. Let me go and get ready, so we can get downtown. Dang, I hate when ya'll hoes catch me like this!" I said standing up from the couch to make my way upstairs.

"Wait, bitch, what is this little exchange of words about? Michael, what's going on?" Shawn said yanking the back of my sweats down exposing my booty. I pulled them back and pushed him into the back of the couch.

"You gon' tell them Jason, or should I? Cause either way it goes, I'm gon' wind up hurting' that motherfucka," Michael said.

"Let's just drop it yo'! Please! I'm still dealing with it. But he has a part of me that I can't explain and I don't know where it's going to lead but what I do know is..." I said before Michael interrupted me.

"His jaw gon' be real loose after I get through fuckin' his shit up for what he did to my lil' bro," Michael said in a calm voice looking me deep in the eyes. I felt a little creeped out all of a sudden.

So Ya'll Go Together

"Michael, please let it go. I'm not the little boy you met five years ago. I can handle myself. I'm alright, okay?" I said giving him as much of a smile as I could muster.

"Jason. What is going on? What happened, bitch? We're your friends you can tell us," Shawn said giving me a really concerned look. He glanced at Preston who was nodding his head.

"You guys," I said holding on to my dignity by not crying. I looked up at the ceiling, then back at each of them. "Listen, I don't want the world to see me like that again. I'm fine," I said feigning a smile. Truth is... I didn't know how I felt. But I knew I wanted to be fine. This all just happened and sitting here parsing sentences was not going to help me come up with an answer today.

"Fine, I'll drop it for now. But when you ready. You let me know," he said as I got up and walked up the stairs. He and the others disbursed into conversation as Shawn and Preston tried to find out what we were hinting at.

I rushed upstairs to straighten up my bed and get my scene together so that I could spend the day with the fellas as planned. I still hadn't heard from Darius, and for the first time in a long time I don't think I cared. However, that may be how I was feeling today. I damn sure wasn't expecting Gary to show up at my door last night because deep down the whole world knew who I wanted it to be. But when he did, it was as if we picked up where we left off when things were good between us. It was a chance for a fresh start.

It was more than just comfort sex with a familiar stranger. I let Gary touch me again like nothing ever happened, like he didn't change me. But if I'm trash to him, what rank can I ever hold in his eyes again if he doesn't view me with the same value as he did before? I will always love Gary and I will defend him and be there for him until the day I die because the bond we have has a mind of its own. I think about how crazy that sounds because it's as if I'm justifying his misuse of me both physically and mentally. I don't want him to be viewed as a monster. He's only human and he still has a place in my heart no matter what is said and done. I forgave him.

I quietly watched my friends clown and joke with one another extremely happy that they were a part of my world. They were the one constant in my life just like night and day even though my inner personal life was a mess right now with my parents and this deranged love triangle I was caught in.

I tried my best to appear normal laughing at one of Shawn's animated stories when the train came to a stop at Belmont. We all got up to exit the train and make our way through the busy streets towards Boystown. I just so happened to see a dark skin guy with the same build and stature of Darius walk onto the train with a baby draped in pink sleeping soundly in his arms. I did a double take to make sure my eyes weren't deceiving me. I took a good gander observing that it wasn't Darius. Again I wondered where we'd fit into each other's lives now that he was a father. I basically pushed him back into the arms of his girlfriend or whatever the hell she was to him, and maybe that was a mistake. But growing up in a two- parent home, I know the importance of having two parents as opposed to one. The selfish part of me didn't want to accept his reality, but the logical part of me understood the plight he'd chosen to take.

I stood there on the platform staring at the gentleman and his baby unbeknownst to him as the doors closed and the train made its departure. I was transported back in time to the night he came to my barracks room to tell me something that had been on his mind, he said, in his down to Earth Chicago drawl, *"like forever my dude."* I smiled thinking about what he meant to me then. And come to think of it, the scariest part for me was not the fact that he was going off to fight an unknown war. Oh nah, that would be much to like easy. The scary part for me was, the fact that I was going to miss him...

I reached for my cell phone and realized I had left it at the house. It's funny how things work sometimes when you feel a need to succumb to human vulnerability. The things you hope for, the things you change, the things you deal with, and the things you expect turn out completely different than the picture perfect imagery the heart convinces the mind it can have. There is a constant tug of war going on between the two as I embrace my specifics.

I wasn't quite sure what was next on my timeline. I

just decided to deal with the now and let the chips fall where they may. I then let out a pleasurable exhale summoned by the moment I relaxed enough to understand that love doesn't always look the way you picture it. And just like that I was whisked away by Michael who wrapped his arms around my shoulders kissing my cheek asking me, "Ya'ight, shawty?". We walked down the stairs to street level as I replied; "Yeah, I thought I saw a familiar face." I might be a little dramatic right now, but Darius may now become a ghost from my past, haunting me leaving only questions. What if all of what he poured into those three words he finally spoke was real? What if all he said was true? What if it wasn't Gary who cheated first? Rather me all along...?

To the Color Orange

Today was the first day I purposely didn't go and visit him. I've always seemed to have had him at my disposal, and I wanted to know what it would feel like not to respond to that slick pull he has on me. My days as a little boy playing a game of hide and seek is probably close to the game I play with Jason. Shit but I don't have a place to hide and nowhere to run.

I almost lost my shit during my second tour in Iraq. I was just about to wrap up a conversation with him when the alarm sounded. As a first responder, I had to rush my goodbye and respond to the call. I dug my boots into the sand sprinting my way to the Quarter Deck. When I got to the Battalion Aid Station, they told us we were responding to a downed Osprey navigating a standard off-load. We grabbed medical supplies, food rations, and water and joined a convoy headed towards the crash site to retrieve our troops. I had been there for a while, and some things were just standard procedure, but this felt different.

I had been on several of these emergency response missions, but that night for some reason the air even smelled different. Usually, you got a few bursts of fine sand in your face from the hot breeze looking for something to pummel. There was this creepy feeling I had that was irking the shit out of me. I'm usually on charge ready to take care of business, but my head was on swivel while we were speeding along in the armored

To the Color Orange

Hummvee. I made sure my Kevlar and my sidearm were secure. I remember sweating more than usual and holding my breath for seconds at a time to calm down. I had my eyes closed and opened them when the sound of what I can only describe as millions of screeching eagles pierced through the left rear passenger door straight through the passenger side front. An intense brownish orange light glowed as the Humvee made an aerial somersault on my side of the vehicle.

I watched two men disintegrate into nothing as the Humvee pitched sharply to the right, and then smacked the road bouncing into a ditch. I helped the driver egress so we could begin treating his injuries. He couldn't hold on. I watched three men die that morning and no one knows the sacrifice we make wearing this uniform with the quote unquote integrity you are supposed to wear it with. Just like that, three of my Marines, gone. I love this country just the same as anyone else, but when I thought about the three men who died in front of me, who were all white males, with their own motivating story to get them back home alive, I couldn't help but see the freedom they had to talk about that one special person they missed and couldn't wait to get back to. Only then would they know they are safe. I'd have to lie and talk about one of these chicks I dicked down knowing full well that Jason was on my damn mind.

I hope one day this shit don't matter. I made up in my mind the night I was in Jason's barracks room before I deployed that I was fighting to keep this country safe for him to use that big heart of his to teach the world what the innocence of love can do to a knucklehead like me. He was right about using it loosely. We blame everything on love, including heartbreak, but it wasn't love that did the wrongdoing.

He was my motivational story and I'm sitting here feeling sorry for myself missing out on knowing the man he is. I decided to go for a run when the smell of bacon made my senses stand at attention. I put on my work out gear and made my way downstairs to the kitchen. Mr. Wilkes was happy to see me judging by the flirtatious way he said good morning to me. We had an interesting conversation with me asking a roundabout question without mentioning Jason's name...

"Young man, you've got to learn to ask the right questions and not the right wants. This is what you need to understand. Naw, I want you to do this darling, you gon' do it?" He smiled nodding his head yes.

"Yes, Mr. Wilkes," I said smiling and shaking my head. I swiped a slice of the tender thick cut bacon he was frying. He added six more pieces to the plate and turned the stove off.

"Wonderful. Now we are going to do a little exercise I just know is going to stretch your faith.

"Okay?" He smiled motioning for me to stand up. He turned me towards the large bay window in this kitchen nook. He opened the curtains wide and said, "It's going to happen out there." It looked as if he was pointing at the intersection on the other side of the bridge.

"Oh you want to go jogging? With me? What, for old time's sake old man?" I said chuckling.

"Little boy, please don't let this cunty thing fool you. I may be nobody's spring chicken, but there is still some summer left in this old bird!" He said rolling his eyes and twisting his wrist dismissively. His polished red medical alert bracelet dangled like an expensive piece of jewelry.

"I apologize, Mr. Wilkes. I was just joking, sir, my bad," I said apologetically flashing him my winning smile. I threw a couple of fake jabs his way. He looked at me trying not to smile. He rushed over beside me.

"Mmm hmph! Close your eyes and square up then relax your shoulders. Now like I was saying, it's going to happen out there in the world, what you want, by calling it out. But it's going to start here," he said tapping my temple with his finger. "And connect here," he then tapped my chest.

"Okay, now what?" I asked thinking this was silly, but what could it hurt.

"Shhhhh! Just take some deep breaths and relax yourself. This is just a quick example of asking the right question. Meditate on one thing you want to know the answer to. And remember an answer is simply the want from the question. Put that one thing in the forefront of your mind and if you could have it today, that one thing you just couldn't live without. That one person that makes life make sense to you. How would you ask for it? If that's all you had to do to get it today. Guaranteed. Now open your eyes?" He said.

To the Color Orange

I looked out into the distance. The sun was glowing a beautiful orange making the trees in the background look golden even though I know they were green, the reflection from the lake was sparkling adding to the beauty in the background. It was as if I were staring into the eyes of... Jason. He's going to be okay. I have to keep reminding him because that's my duty to keep him comforted as opposed to safe because he doesn't believe in safe anymore. But he still hopes that he can. I noticed Mr. Wilkes in my peripheral. I started to turn my head and caught a glimpse of a tear in his eye. He ordered me to keep facing forward.

"Today... I finally asked my question, today. It's a burrrrning question dah'lin! And I finally got up the gall to ask it, and I'm okay with the answer. Charles Willy Wray really did love me. Ah hah! Hot dog!" he said clearing his throat, and clapping his hands together with one loud slap. "Baby I think we need to sit down on this. I got me a story to tell. You ready, young blood?" he asked with a schoolboy grin plastered on his matured face.

"I'm ready?" I said waiting for another one of his well-told blasts from the past.

"Charles Willy Wray had my poor little heart in chains for years. And though he never said it, I always felt he loved me. You know, he would show it in his subtle romantic ways, but he was much to macho to say it to another man. Oh, but he showed it in ways that kept me by his side yet still wondering if I was missing something better. Baby, sometimes a person hearing the words I love you can steer their life onto a whole different pathway. You can't be a child at play with love. You keeping up, dah'lin?" he asked folding his arms and looking at me.

"Yes sir! I am," I laughed. "You can't tell?"

"You never can be too sure with you young men now days. Now whom are we talking about?" He seriously asked.

"Charles Willy Wray," I smiled. I felt like a little kid again, but only he wasn't Granddad.

"And he did what?" Mr. Wilkes asked. "Loved you," I said.

"That's right, but he never said it and I did everything I could to get that man's attention and let him know that I was who he was supposed to be with, and he ups and plays house with some old gal after he got her pregnant. Hmph," he kept looking out of the large window. He snickered before continuing. "I remember I was stationed overseas and I bought my first pair of genuine leather shoes with a hard sole bottom. That was taboo for a man to wear hard bottom soles back then. In the States at least 'cause them Euro boys was sharp as a little ol' shiny tack. But anyhow baby, them shoes were bad! They were this deep tan color with this orange appearance buried somewhere deep in that shine," he dabbed a tear with his thumb and looked over at me. "So, I just bought the shoes and click clacked all the way out the store and up the street and through the base. I click clacked, click clacked, click clacked up the stairs and through the hall," he laughed and covered his mouth. "Some of the boys were playing cards and drinking beer and Bourbon. They all stopped when they heard the click clack of my shoes. Usually, when you heard that sound, it was a woman coming up to visit or bring a message to one of us colored boys," he smiled and let out a quick laugh. "So this tall skinny tough guy they nicknamed Sticks, says, "Oh it's just that sissy ass Wilkes. I thought it was a female the way them shoes sound." To which I replied, "Oh Sticks, baby, if you don't have butter tonight, margarine will do. I promise you won't be the only one doing the bending." Mr. Wilkes burst into laughter with me and looked back out at the lake. "My grandmother would say I was smelling my own piss, but hot damn, it finally got Mr. Undercover Willy's attention. Hmph, baby I was a dandelion facing a lawnmower," he said disappearing to his place there in the past for a brief second or two.

"I'm guessing a fight broke out?" I asked fascinated with his boldness in those days. He sighed, snapping out of his daydream and continued.

"Well, my knight in dark shining armor came to my little ol' rescue and grabbed Sticks before his ol' ugly self could get up and deck me. I'm sorry, let me be nice and say he was tender eyed," Mr. Wilkes, said chuckling looking at me crossing his eyes and making me laugh before continuing. "He shook his peanut head with that perfect squared jaw of his motioning for him to let it go. The muscles in his jaw line twitched a little with a flicker of a smile. He had this impressed look on his face. He took a lonnnnng drag on his cigarette; winked and said, '*See you in formation, Wilkes.*' And that was the last time I ever had to worry about the boys ragging on the doll. He had them pressing my uniform and shining my boots before long. But that night we had a little tryst on a blanket he laid out for us in this old abandoned cottage not too far from the base. It was a little spot he said was just for us two. He was an Aquarius and he said that's where he would go when he needed space from everything and everyone. We developed a little secret romance shortly after that, and he always made sure I never went without even when he decided to tell me what I thought would be, 'I love you.' He took me to this little spot out on the beach and laid the blanket his grandma quilted out for us. He said, 'Sherms.' That was his pet name for me, especially when he was getting mushy and romantic," he said glancing over at me. "He says, 'Sherms, I want you in my life always. Wherever I go you gotta be there and we gotta make this, what we got here work, but I have to marry that woman I got pregnant and I need you to be okay with us the way we are, but this way you know the details of the situation. I'm asking you to face it with me.' I couldn't believe he asked me to accept and just deal with his unethical proposition. I was crushed, but with a straight face I told him I wanted him to do whatever made him happy and I was okay with it as long as I was a part of that happiness. I couldn't believe I made a commitment to this secret love affair we had for years. I was a kept man, but he couldn't be kept by me no matter how much I pleaded. I helped raise that man's child when his alcoholic wife would..." he said taking a moment of silence.

"You alright, Mr. Wilkes?" I asked reaching over to rub his shoulder. This story made me wonder if this is how Jason feels waiting on me to come around?

"Oh yes, I'm fine," he said looking away and dabbing his eye. "He would always be there with me for Thanksgiving. But this one particular year, he promised me he would be staying the night with me through Christmas because the wife and kid would be gone down south for a while. Well, let's just say he never made it that Holiday season. I set and cleared the table with the Turkey and all the trimmings for four whole days devastated that he hadn't showed up either day. But if he did, I wanted him to see what the love of his life prepared for him. Even if by that last day, that Turkey was dry from being reheated so much. But I think I learned that I was waiting on somebody to do what I wanted them to do, instead of looking at the possibilities out front. Who knows what I could have experienced by not waiting on him. Sometimes I wish I had of taken that trip to Hawaii that year, instead. But I used that money to buy the food and make the house he bought me look really special. I even spelled out the words do you love me in rose pedals on the bed. Sometimes I love you can be spoken a tad bit late. And at that point, it's not enough to hold on to what you thought you'd have."

To the Color Orange

"So what happened? What was his excuse he gave for not showing up? He went with her, didn't he?" I said waiting for the obvious answer.

"Willy, developed an aggressive form of Alzheimer's. Wheeew, it came on strong. He left me in charge of his estate. And guess who didn't help me with a got-damned thang dah'lin'? I guess for appearance sake in those days she'd be a better fit to be there for something like that. But she abandoned his silly old self. She didn't want anything to do with him all of a sudden and she quickly filed for divorce. And it was me who loved this man so much; watch him turn into a hollow shell rotten with guilt for not allowing himself to be Willy." He paused again and dabbed his eyes. "He told me that during one of his good days. That was the last time I ever saw the Willy I remembered speak. He gave me five more minutes of just plain ol' Willy bear. I just figured out what he truly meant. But I didn't ask the right questions. That beautiful sunrise we just witnessed reminded me of that and remembering those shoes reminds me of him. And he loved me."

"I'm sorry to hear about your loss, Mr. Wilkes," I knew those words couldn't ease the pain he must have felt.

"Oh, it's alright. He left me everything; he was a smart man, after all," he smiled. "Every time I hear 'Footsteps in the Dark', by them Isley boys, I get a reminder of my life with him, though. And I've always wondered how different my life would have been if I would have led it instead of him. What if I'da neva asked myself, what's the sense in going elsewhere?" We sat in silence looking out of the window. "Mind sharing dah'lin?"

"I asked for Jason today. They say a wise man learns from a fool's mistake. Today is going to be the day I restore his hope in love and make him feel safe again..." I got up from the table and took off for my morning jog. "I'll talk with you later, Mr. Wilkes."

I just knew and felt it in my soul that Jason and I were going to wake up today and stop trying to be what they think we ought to be. We were going to be what we need one another to be. I wanted him to be the world I deserved.

I was half a mile into my run when I zoned out and thought back to the night I came to Jason's barracks room to tell him the words I had been so afraid to tell him. Telling my dad, I love him and the men in my family the same is easy. We're family, we are supposed to love one another. At least that is what I was taught. But telling another *man* I love you is something I never thought I could do. Shit, but when I heard him say it that night we sexed, I didn't know what to do...

Everything's Crossing My Mind

I was asked what would I tell my seven-year-old self. I know for sure I didn't have a well thought out answer. I more than likely said something like, gay ain't nothing new under the sun. I actually hope I didn't say that. Who the hell says that to a seven-year- old?

It's like, as an adult you forget the importance of ignorance and arrogance. That is the beauty of a child. A kid is stubborn enough to believe they can do whatever they set out to do. They are ignorant enough not to know how it will happen, but arrogant enough to know they can do it. All they need is a little support even when they are misunderstood. But as we grow, we forget what that feels like. We forget how to slow down that race to the age of sixty-two.

If that same person asked me what I would tell my seven-year-old self and knowing how precocious I was back then, I'd sit his butt down right in front of me. Face to face. And I know he's smart and he'd be paying attention 'cause he's me. So I'd say to him, camels can go six months without water. Support is like water. Sometimes you have to go a while without it, and that's okay. I'd pause for effect, and I'd continue by telling him to start forgiving himself for thinking he is less than the man he will become. I'd tell him be stubborn in who he is because there are people counting on him to turn the world he sees in his imagination into realization. That's what I would tell my main man as my daddy calls me. I'd want him to embrace the freedom I know he can have. And I'd I have to tell him to be the free spirit he was born to be. I'd let him know he has the strength to go through the rawness of what it means to be someone like him. This faggot they despise. I'd tell him he's going to redefine what that means.

Out of all the people I know, and all the people I've met and established some type of rapport with, Darius was the only one I've had the longest relationship with. And what I mean by that is a long- standing fixture holding me up when I need to ask for help, but don't. He just picks up on it and corrects what's wrong. And what do I do? I bark on him and spit in his face when he finally feels comfortable enough to be completely vulnerable with me. All I ever wanted to be was his safe haven instead of a drafty house with a shut door. I don't know what the hell is wrong with me? Maybe I could have made it work because I never exposed my vulnerable side to him outside of my pain and struggle.

So what, I guess we're even or some junk. I just don't want it to be over, this thing we have. I don't want any of it to be over. I've got to be man enough to fix this. I repel when I feel a need to be alone, but I'm meant to bridge the gaps. Understand I live and love and bruise and bleed just like the rest of society, so why can't I get my respect as a black man, and I'm not asking for a pass because I'm no better than the next man. Hell Gary reminded me of that. And that's why I shouldn't leave.

But just like that same man, I often ask God

answers to questions from my past to be prepared for the next lesson. Because my past has been rocky for so long, it gets harder and harder to believe that the road further up my timeline will smooth out. Out of all the things I want, it just seems easier to let my dreams die rather than fight. But I'm determined to prove a point.

Like the time I wanted to tell Mama that this was who I was and that I needed someone who I trusted to talk with me about this. I wanted to feel okay and reassured about these urges I had stirring up. I walked up to her one day and sat down next to her as she was watching a talk show. She was on the phone with one of my aunts. One of the black guests was obviously gay, and she started laughing and loudly declared that I bet not ever come home like that. And though she made it seem like she was joking with my aunt, I took it as if she knew why I had sat there and that I'd better straighten myself out.

Since life can be based off of perception, I developed a fear initially of talking to her about anything other than surface issues. For all these years I let her take my voice when I was in her presence. I didn't want her to find out that I was hiding this from her in the pages of a small notebook, either. I wanted to face her and say, "Mama, I know you know, but I'm still your son." But I had a choice and I lied to her face. I wasn't having sex, but I was gay. I lied about it to survive.

Again, I heard the voices of two women having a conversation. I kept trying to listen to what was going on outside of myself. The feeling in my body slowly started to come back as I tried to wake up and join the voices conversing within close proximity to me. One of the voices belonged to my mother and the other belonged to a female I didn't recognize. They were engaged in a deep conversation and I caught the tail end of it...

"The thing is that he never disappointed me per say. But because of who he is to this world, I had to tell him that so he can keep his skin tough and become the man he needs to become..." Mama said.

"Hmmmm," the other woman mused.

"If that even makes sense. Shoot, I don't know... I just need my child to wake up," Mama said as both women let the cool silence of the hospital strangle their interaction and sporadic laughter.

The laughter faded as all of a sudden I felt the firm grip of Gary's hand constricting my left arm as the large picture on the wall in the living room came crashing down on the hard wood floor shattering the glass as I reached up for anything to grab. I felt my airway being cut off for what seemed like an eternity. I could taste something salty being transferred onto my tongue by Gary, forcing me to swallow as he jammed his tongue further in and out of my mouth while applying all of his weight onto me. He started to unbuckle his pants as I wiggled us both off of the couch with all of the strength I could build. I needed to get out of the house. I could hear my dog barking in the background as I built momentum to stand up.

Everything's Crossing My Mind

I felt myself losing my balance as Gary yanked me down by the pockets of my jeans. He gripped me close to his body and grunted in my ear, *Oh you want to take this upstairs.* I head butted him and pried myself from his grip this time making it to the stairs in time to be grabbed and thrown up against the wall. I felt three solid punches to the ribs and two to the face. He put some more pills into his mouth and began to kiss me violently swirling his tongue in and out of my mouth forcing me to swallow the transfer of pills.

I remember slipping into my happy place, I wanted to survive, but I had to go through what I went through for a reason, right? I just went into my own head because that is the one place I can escape the real dangers of this world. It's the one place I feel safe even though I don't believe in safety anymore. I thought of Darius and pictured it was us making love and I pictured him touching me and making me feel good, and making me feel loved, but instead I got the rough tainted touch of Gary pissed at me for not being interested. I felt a firm grip on my left arm and a small quick stab to the ribs waking me up out of my sleep...

I jerked my arm back. Once I got my focus and noticed I was in my bedroom I looked over to the left side of the bed and noticed Darius there by my side welcoming me back from my nightmare with that awesome smile of his.

"What the hell are you doing back here?" I asked reaching up to rub my head. The dream I just had pissed me off all over again, and made me think about some decisions I needed to make.

"Jaw's, it's a long story baby boy. Are you okay?" Darius asked.

"Yeah, I guess I will be. How did you get up in here?" I asked looking at his smile fade. He turned his head towards the door.

"Aye Mike! He's up now bro!" Darius yelled as I heard someone coming up the stairs. He rushes up to the doorway and peeked inside.

"We go to the same church. And he begged me to let him in, but I didn't want to just leave while you were sleep, so y'all two work this shit out. Because this is the longest relationship you've had with anybody. Git'cha man, bitch! Lucky for him I got some trade in the city waiting face down ass up in prison socks I gotta man handle. Nah thas'sa fantasy come true, shawty!" Michael said without giving me a chance to answer before he was headed down the stairs. "I'll holla!"

"Bye, Mike!" I yelled. I just snickered, shook my head, and directed my attention towards Darius. "Well, what's up? How are you? And how's the baby?" I asked trying to appear happy for him.

"There is no baby," he stated with sadness in his eyes that I now understood. Life seemed to present a challenge that wasn't on his terms. And me knowing Darius the way I do, if he isn't in control, he's not dealing with this too well. Not to mention, it is one thing to want to change the world. It's quite another to change for the world. He held my gaze as I softened up a little to find the right words to comfort him.

"Please come here," I said pulling him into the bed with me. He climbed in and laid his head on my chest. I rubbed his head and started tracing my finger gently around his ear. The weight of his body felt so good. "I know how much the baby meant to you. You have the fullest extent of my understanding and sentiment baby." He encircled my torso tightly in his arms. The most pleasant pulse of energy sent soul stirring warmth through my entire body. "I love you too, Darius. I just feel like, I love you is the most serious statement you can tell someone. I wanted to really know I meant it. I guess it took me what, almost six years to say it?" I snickered.

"That's why I love you. You know just how to handle me, you know that?" he asked making me smile. He relaxed in a way I have never felt him relax while holding him before. I continued to rub his head with the kindest touch. I closed my eyes and enjoyed him being there.

"Darius, I want to apologize for letting the anger I was feeling speak for me. It was unfair to treat you the way I did, and for being so callous towards your baby and her mother. I was disrespectful and out of line," I said glad I could finally release that into the open. Even if he couldn't forgive me, I had to say it so that I could be truthful with him and forgive myself.

"Thank you, but her crazy momma didn't want her. She was the cause of...my baby girl's death. But it made me realize the person I should have been investing more of me into. It made me realize that I took the most important person in my world for granted. I should have told you sooner, but at least I told you. Ain't gon' be no half stepping if you down," he said moving his head to look me in the eyes.

"We'll talk," I said not really ready to have that conversation quite this minute because I knew what I had to do would be harder for him now than me.

"Yeah," he said putting his head back down.

"You are going to be an awesome father, Darius. You're going to get your chance," I said truly believing it.

"I know. And you will too, Jason," he smiled.

"I don't know about all that. I don't have the patience and from what I see with how even family can treat one another, I don't know if I could subject a child to that," I said wondering what it would be like contrary to what I was saying. It's one of those things I go back and forth with in my mind with the rest of the thoughts I keep to myself.

"Don't let your experiences from your upbringing determine the type of father you'll be. You got more patience in people than you even realize. Shiiiiid! With all the shit I've seen and heard about you going through. I know what Jason is capable of. Dude, I learned it's much easier to find a person than to stay with one. My goal is to grow old with you and figure this…" Darius paused. I tried to complete his sentence.

"Gaaaaay thiiiiiing out?" I laughed.

"Don't make me say it out loud yet, Jason. You heard me get close," he laughed burying his head in my lap.

"I hear what you're saying," I responded, trying not to blush.

"You ready to do what we should have done a long time ago?" I held my breath and repeated what I had just heard him say in my head. If I started this with him, I knew I'd have to fully commit. That weird second piece of the advice my dad gave me before I left for boot camp came to mind.

"Darius before I answer your question, answer me this?"

"What's up?" he said looking up at me with a somber look.

"This is going to sound kind of weird, but you already know that bout me. I have to ask this for some reason, like right now," I said looking as serious as possible. I didn't know why this impulsive move hit me. But it felt like it would help clear up the rest of the doubt.

"I want to go sky diving, would you be cool with me doing something like that? Would you join me?" I asked holding his gaze.

"Hell, naw, I ain't joining you. But yo', I'll be on the ground watching yo' ass come down. What's that randomness all about? Jason, stop stalling and get serious. You with me or not," he said dismissing what I had asked. Just like that my dad's advice finally made sense. He was basically telling me beware of those who will watch you fall for their personal gain. I learned that dramatic things happen in relationships when new becomes normal, and that makes me hold on to the dream to have a love with no conditions as it was intended to be. I was just about to give him my honest answer when I heard the front door downstairs fly open followed by a slam.

I figured maybe it was Michael running back in because he forgot something. Batman started barking uncontrollably as I heard the sound of those familiar heavy footsteps drumming up the stairs. Darius rose up and I was freaked out for a second when I saw who was standing in the doorway with his hands in his pockets.

"I'ma fuck you up! So you couldn't give me a day before you bring this nigga back up in your bed? I came over here to apologize and get us right and this is what I come back too?" Gary said glaring at the two of us. He had on a tank top and some basketball shorts looking like he was ready to play ball, beat guts, or beat asses. Thoughts of my dream came rushing to the forefront of my mind.

"Gary, it's not what you think. I'm telling you," I said trying to start reasoning with him.

"Yeah right! So what? Last night ain't mean shit, huh?" Gary said as I tried to figure out how to diffuse this time bomb.

"Gary, last night was awesome. I don't take what we shared for granted, okay?" I said getting out of the bed and standing directly in his face. He looked past me and straight at Darius.

"Jason, this ain't right! You ain't giving me a fair chance to be your man. You don't belong to this kat,

Jason!" Gary said. He was beyond upset and he was doing his best to control the anger trying to spill over. "Gary, I know. I know, babes. Yo' we can talk about this... we can talk about us, okay. You can ask me all of the questions left in your head, okay? Just don't do anything out of anger, okay?" I pleaded with him. He didn't seem to be paying attention to me because he was glaring at Darius like this was the WWF.

"I don't share, nigga, so I'ma need you to gather your shit and head East tlll your hat floats," Gary sneered. He didn't budge from the doorway.

"I ain't going nowhere, dawg, and Jason is way outta your league for you to think you got a claim," Darius said walking up behind me. "Nah, I got this Jay." Gary was still standing there cool as a cucumber with a look of a man on a mission aggressively scowled across his face.

"Am I invisible?" I said looking up at Gary. Darius put his hands on my shoulders and gave them a squeeze. Gary moved his eyes fixing them on the appearance of another man's hands on my naked shoulders. He snickered and rubbed his thumb across his nose quickly. I felt myself hit the floor from the result of him pushing me out of the way. He then punched Darius in the mouth before pulling a gun from his back. It appeared to be the gun I had recently purchased for my own protection.

"You should stick to your ax, Fire Marshal Bill. You're holding it all wrong, homie. Leave the firearms to us military men," Darius said looking ready to pounce.

"I just changed your view of how this is goin' to play out, yardie!" He said glaring at Darius. "I'm not tryin' to give ya'll a happy ending today," Gary warned and glanced at me. He nodded his head as I bit my tongue while stammering to say something.

Out of nowhere, Darius jumped up reaching for Gary's wrist to get the pistol away from him. I jumped in to assist him as we wrestled him to the floor. The sound of a three shots firing exploded in my ear as I scrambled to figure out where the bullets had landed. I felt the spatter of something wet on my face. I searched the room swiftly to see who was left standing as the gun spun towards the corner of the room. It rested against the wall and smoke swirled its way from the shiny barrel.

The full weight of one of the other two men in the room pinned me down. Realizing whom it was, sent me into a panic as I felt blood but no pain. I remember hearing "Shit! Jason!" But I didn't know whose voice screamed my name. I began to replay the scene in my head remembering how the silence around me fell right as the sound of my loud gasp met the first dense thud of the gun as the large weapon made contact with the hard wood floor. Time stood still replacing love with violence... poetically.